Waltzing With

Lady Luck

Clark Snow

Black Rose Writing

www.blackrosewriting.com

ISBN: 978-1-61296-141-5

PUBLISHED BY BLACK ROSE WRITING

www.blackrosewriting.com

Printed in the United States of America

Waltzing With Lady Luck is printed in Aparajita

This book is dedicated firstly to the love of my life, Galen V., whose perpetual optimism has always kept me moving forward and secondly to my son Travis, who is my hero.

ACKNOWLEDGMENTS

Many thanks to the following people who helped me create this yarn. First off I thank my editor, Gerald Harrington, for his steadfast support and positive criticism, always reminding me that less is usually better. Joel Sohn must be thanked for giving me the lowdown on manganese nodules and what some of them contain at their core. He also reminded me that, at 500 fathoms of depth in our oceans, the water pressure is close to 1350 pounds per square inch. Ouch. I thank Tony Parascandolo for giving me my first job on a fishing boat. Sheri Massa must be thanked for asking that Carol-Jean Paya's personality be detailed further. Raoul Moore, Deb Wiley, Jeff Kaelin, Kathleen O'Donnell, Lucien Forbes, Peter Tirpaeck and Sandy Browne all must be thanked for taking the time to read chapters as the story evolved and to encourage me to continue writing. Lastly I need to thank a few who are no longer with us but are none the less, definitely a part of this story—Carol Watchmaker, Sarah Snow, Philip Simonds, Billy Crossen and Julio Notarangelo—may they all RIP and maybe get a laugh out of this book while they are doing it.

Waltzing With

Lady Luck

"Irreverence is, in itself, just another form of reverence."

PRELUDE

It was a wonder that such a face could hold life, but for her eyes. They sparkled like the sun off of breezy water. They laughed and spoke of innocent fun. Her eyes made the man grin and step closer. Just as suddenly he had to step back as he noticed their depth.

The Havasupai woman behind the counter looked, at once, impossibly ancient and radiantly young. Her face was a microcosm of the canyon that her curio shop abutted. They both had been carved out and shaped by wind, water and grit, heat, cold and time—baked then frozen, frozen colder, then baked yet again.

The man gave a shiver and looked away to her hair which hung down her chest in a pair of long, gray braids. Nestled in, hanging from her ears were two curious objects. This first glimpse had him puzzled. Was it obsidian, jet or maybe black coral of some sort? The shape was also odd. They were triangular yet asymmetrical; more like fat, exaggerated comas. He stepped forward again to get a better look. The woman's smile grew wider. The fine, jagged edge of the outer curvature stopped his breath and brought it home. They were teeth, shark teeth, to be exact, very large and very old. Before he could turn the thought into words she said, "Yes, I found them in the canyon."

CHAPTER ONE

VICTOR JANES was having a bad time of it lately. These last few weeks he was often contemplative, unsure of what to think, what to say, or what to do. He felt unsteady on his feet. He looked over his shoulders often. He was flummoxed. At this moment he was asking himself a question that came up with maddening redundancy. "What in hell's name have I created here?"

He stood alone in the pilothouse of his new, state-of-the-art, factory trawler. They'd arrived in New Bedford a month earlier, having left the shipyard in Louisiana after a lengthy re-build process which, all things considered, had gone quite well.

His most current dilemma was anticlimactic at best and purely anti-social at the root of it all. He couldn't find a crew to man the boat. It appeared as if most everyone in town was either jealous of this endeavor of his or thought he was absolutely crazy for even trying it. "What sort of a *maluco na cabesa* would dump all that money, effort and time into an untried, unproven, *estimated* fishery? "He's nuts, plain nuts," they'd said.

This boat, on the other hand, was a gem. Victor was proud of what he had created with the help of Teddy and the shipyard crew down south. Completing the vessel had taken much more time than he had anticipated, but it was done, and the outcome was a testament to the shipyards' outstanding abilities and Teddy's talents as an engineer.

The trip up from the Gulf with his father-in-law, young George, and Teddy had been exhilarating. They'd gotten into a nasty nor'easter just south of Hatteras that Victor figured was going to have them eating the same breakfast twice before it was all done and over. He knew the wind was coming but NOAA Weather Radio was only calling for twenty to thirty knots with gusts up to thirty-five. Before he could even think about turning tail and heading into Charleston or Wilmington it was blowing a good, steady fifty with sixty-five knot gusts. They'd have to ride this one out. The trawler was taking the eighteen foot seas about ten degrees off of the starboard bow, and taking them well. At 130 feet in length-over-all this boat would not be considered a large vessel but she was taking this blow like a rainy day mallard in the damn duck pond. Teddy was hanging onto the consol rail as he stood next to Victor at the wheel. He was grinning ear to ear. "Well shee-it, Cap. I'm tinkin' we done alright wit dis boat. She almos' seem to be likin' dis washin' machine we in."

As they came abeam of Frying Pan Shoal the wind veered coming almost due east and increasing by another ten to fifteen knots. Victor came to starboard to meet the wind and throttled back a touch. To be expected, she was pitching but the side-to-side roll wasn't too bad, maybe 15 degrees each side of zero on the inclinometer. They had put together one outstanding sea-boat.

^

Victor had found her way up Bayou Vista one day when it was rainy, windy, raw, and just plain rotten for a February afternoon on the Atchafalaya Basin. His broker, Teddy Thibodaux, felt much the same. "Mista Janes, les' head fo de barn. Ain no good weda fo' beast or man. Les git!"

They'd come around a bend in the road when Victor spotted her through the trees on the opposite bank of the bayou. It looked like she'd been out of the water for quite some time. Even the rust on her side looked dried up and dead. "Teddy," Victor started, "get me across the creek to that boat over there, would you please?" Teddy gave his best derisive snort and said, "Man, dat ting just a bucket a rust; not wort yo time…"

Victor cajoled, humored and asked again. When they got there Victor was out of the truck before Teddy had come to a full stop. "She looks good," Victor yelled. The rust and disuse wasn't what he was seeing. She had good lines, a high bow and a decent-sized third level wheel-house with an aft control station overlooking the deck. This was a small OSV or

9

oil support vessel and an interesting prospect.

As Teddy got out of the truck Victor scampered up a rickety ladder on the port side leading to the deck. Teddy gave an exasperated shrug and followed after his client.

They spent almost three hours on her that first day going from the wheel-house to the bilges, from the stem to the stern. Teddy had to get back into the truck at one point to fetch more batteries for the flashlights. On his return he found Victor in the rudder-room cursing a blue streak, pressing his balled up shirt to his forehead. Teddy raised an eyebrow and Vic answered, "Didn't duck low enough. Hit the water-tight combing coming through. Gonna have to paint that bitch bright yellow before we're done with this project."

Teddy rolled his eyes and replied, "Mista Janes, y'all ain' serious 'bout buyin dis ting, huh? I'd have a beer, tink real hard on it, me. Hell, I'd have a six-pack an keep tinkin till I got it right! Dis boat sat here las five years I can 'member. She a pile a rust an a bucket o' bolts, is all. Be cheaper to build new from da keel up."

Teddy knew that this was not necessarily the complete truth but he felt he had to rant in principal because he saw no great broker's fee evolving from the sale of this vessel, if, in fact, it was for sale at all.

"Well, come aw! Les git you to da clinic, git yo haid examined; Lord knows it need it, you wantin to buy dis, dis *mauvais bateau!* My gawd, y'all's bleedin!"

This last word was pronounced with as much scorn as he felt he could get away with without angering his new client that he'd learned was actually from Canada, specifically an island called Newfoundland. It sounded as if the guy had moved south to the States some eight or nine years previous. Wherever he was from, Teddy knew the guy had a good eye and a fair point.

The rust was superficial and the boat, without a full survey, appeared to be sound. First Teddy would have to find out who owned it and ask them if they were even interested in selling. If so he'd have to get her surveyed, agree on a price and find a shipyard to get her worked on. He figured he might be able to turn a buck here after all...

...Which is exactly what happened, though Victor Janes had the man working hard for it.

There wasn't much Teddy could get by this guy. Maybe that's why he actually liked Victor. The man definitely *knew* boats and certainly, the fact that Teddy's Cajun ancestors had also migrated south from Canada (although Massachusetts could not, by any stretch, be considered "south") helped sway his opinion. Plus the fact that they spoke French, in part of Canada anyway, definitely went in Victor's favor.

Come to find out, one of Teddy's first wive's second cousin's owned the boat in question. And, yes, said cousin would be very willing to sell, provided the price was agreeable.

"My, my", Teddy mused. "Bidness went so much betta when you dealt wit family!"

Mr. Thibodeaux now figured he had hooked a fat one. Sooner rather than later he'd be wondering about who exactly had hooked who.

∧

Victor purchased the boat in early March and had her towed into the shipyard the next week. He'd expected to be fishing within nine months. His optimism and naiveté were running hand in hand.

Over the next ten months Victor, Teddy, and the yard-crew worked steadily to bring the shell of a boat into her own. She would be the largest factory trawler that the east coast had seen built in close to sixteen years. (The factory trawler Seafreeze Atlantic was commissioned in 1966 and financed, in part, by the federal government in an effort to stimulate the fishing industry. She began fishing in 1968 but was tied up shortly thereafter, in part due to the fact that U.S. fishermen had no desire at all to become factory workers).

Victor was a stickler for detail. The main tenet of any decent mariner is, "hope for the best but always prepare for the worst." Although he had written a substantial business plan, Victor was unprepared for the add-ons and change orders that had come up, almost on a daily basis. It was fortunate that Victor had deep pockets.

A few weeks after the boat had been hauled out of the water Vic and Teddy made an interesting discovery. They were below-decks removing all of the fuel, lube oil, and potable water tank inspection plates. Victor was working on a horizontal plate amidships about where the factory was to begin. He called Teddy over and pointed into the tank.

"Pour quoi pensez-vous ce reservoir?" asked Victor.

Teddy stuck his head into the tank, sniffed, detected no fuel oil vapors, asked for a flashlight, and looked again. This tank was only about four feet in depth on the centerline from the bilge up to the deck plates, about forty feet long, and ran the full breadth, port to starboard, of the boat. What had Victor stymied was the placement and number of the baffles in the tank.

Most any commercial work-boat has below-deck tanks that hold either fuel oil (diesel), potable water for human consumption and coolant, lube oil for the engines, or hydraulic oil for the machinery. Any liquid tank running side to side, such as the one Teddy and Victor were looking at, must be baffled to prevent the liquid from moving freely from one side of the tank to the other with the roll of the boat. An un-baffled tank created the danger of capsizing the vessel if the tank contents are able to shift unimpeded as the boat rolled from side to side. This tank had lots of baffles, but they were spaced oddly.

Teddy pulled back from the tank and grinned. He loved it when he got one-up on Victor Janes who said, *"OK. Arete tons sourire. Qu'est-ce que c'est?"*

"Is a flume tank, Victor. You know, man. You fill dis tank bout tree quata or so full wid wata, deese baffles keep de wata from movin too fast or too slow. Wone stop de roll of da boat but will damp it down, you fill dis tank just right"

Victor thought about it a bit then asked, "So, you think we should leave it as is?"

"I would, me. You done' like it, fill it full when da hold's empty then pump it all out when you fill up dat big hold wid deese fancy s'rimp a yo's!"

So Victor took Teddy's advice and left the flume tank in. It did improve the stability of the boat but some months later Victor would receive an interesting surprise related to this tank.

…And so it went; lots of minor structural problems but, between the two of them, nothing insurmountable. When Teddy thought back he couldn't put a date or time on it but somewhere along the line he'd come onto the project full-time.

"My, my, my, and I din even feel dat hook set!"

CHAPTER TWO

LORETTA JANES KNEW that her youngest-born son was of a different ilk as soon as he went from the womb out into the world. Victor did not hold his eyes tight-shut against the intense light or scream out his displeasure at this abrupt, cold transition of birthing. Victor came out with his eyes wide open. Before the doctor could swat him on the bum this baby took a deep breath and expelled it impatiently. He gazed up at his mother's eyes, smiled, took her all in and then looked around the room, stopping at the television set mounted on the wall.

His tiny forehead wrinkled in concentration as he stared at this apparatus that was droning on about Ice Age fossils. After a few moments he turned his attention again towards his mother who smiled back at him and said, "It's O.K. Victor Janes. Here. Better have a drink before the rest of the family comes 'round. Lord knows, we'll be hard-pressed to find a moment to ourselves once they all getta holda ye."

Loretta knew it from the get-go. This little bundle was going to be a watcher. A watcher and, therefore, a traveler. As he grew he went through all of the normal progressions but his speech, although fine and fluent, was something that had to be coaxed out of the child. It seemed as if, at an early age, he'd silently elected to hold his tongue except when absolutely needed. This trait was, as most personal traits go, both a blessing and a bane to the owner. Victor Janes would be a man of few words but of many, many thoughts.

^

The Grand Banks in the northwest Atlantic Ocean off of the coast of Newfoundland have been fished specifically for codfish for over a thousand years. One of the first peoples to discover the wealth of these waters was the Basques that inhabit a portion of the western Pyrenees Mountains between present-day France and Spain. And, back in the early days, they knew how to keep a good thing to themselves. For close to nine centuries this group of close-knit people sailed for the banks across the Atlantic, fished the cod, salted and packed the catch in their holds then headed back to Europe.

Some of these fishermen went a step further and set up stations on Newfoundland and on the Gaspe Peninsula further to the southwest where they would salt and also dry their catches during the warm months. For hundreds of years they would return home with nobody the wiser as to where all these, large, beautiful fish came from.

Cod fishing on 'The Rock' had gone through many cycles over the last one-hundred years alone; from boom to bust and back again. 'Fishery Management' was not even close to a viable concept in the early 1900's in Canada or just about anywhere else globally for that matter. If the fish were there you caught them; if they weren't you raised turnips and milked the cows or did something else until they were there again. This all started to change in the early 1960s, but it would still be many years before workable management plans came into focus.

The pressure on the cod fishery in Newfoundland would be somewhat alleviated in the 1980's when the Japanese started to go further afield to sate their growing appetite for many 'underutilized' species that most other cultures left out of their food pyramids. Newfoundland fishermen were happy to help and harvest species other than cod, though they wouldn't have placed many of the Japanese delicacies on their own tables. Yet, in all fairness, how could a Newfy fisherman scoff at sea cukecumbers, monkfish livers or sea urchins, and then go home to a meal of cod tongues and scruntchins or flipper pie?

Growing into a teenager during the 1970's on the island of Newfoundland was a bright, exuberant time for Victor Janes. The drugs and angst of that era hadn't yet taken hold in the village of Hollyrood, which sat at the southern head of Conception Bay. If he wasn't in school he was fishing, or working at the plant packing and freezing capelin, squid or herring, most of which was used as bait by the cod and crab fishermen.

There was a palpable, genetic, socio-economic, stew flowing within young Janes' blood. His instincts were definitely intact and very dynamic. His four brothers fished while his three sisters worked at the processing plant in Hollyrood that was managed by their father Stanley who had fished for twenty-three years himself until a compound fracture put him on the beach for good. Most of the men and a fair number of the women on both sides of the family had fished for a living for five generations. Nobody had bothered to count exactly how many they numbered through the years; it was just part of the natural order of things.

Victor was the newest, the youngest. He learned it all from them and then some. His mother Loretta (nee Hilliard) was the one that stayed home, grew and canned the vegetables, tended the cow, chickens and geese, and planned for that inevitable day when the fish would go away again. She knew the men didn't care much to think about this likely-hood but she preferred to have her hope served up with a side of reality.

At 5'6" Victor wouldn't be considered an imposing figure initially until the observer noted that his shoulders would have better fit a man who was about nine inches taller. His strength, combined with a gymnast's agility, made him a natural on the deck of a boat. He loved being on the water. His sanguine persona was matched only by his voracious desire to learn and experience life to the fullest of his own capabilities. He wanted that oyster and hoped it was chock-full of pearls.

One summer when Victor was 17 his uncle Bud Hilliard returned home to Hollyrood from the States for a visit. Bud was Loretta's younger brother who had lived in New Bedford, Massachusetts for the past fifteen years, being drawn there by new fishing grounds and U.S. dollars.

Victor sat through the night into the early morning watching the Screech bottle go around, semi-listening to all the stories he'd heard many times before as the family gathering grew more animated. Bud started talking about his life in the States. Victor perked up and paid more attention. This was interesting, something new.

"...by god, one trip we had farty-two taosand pound in tree days fishin! Averged niney cent a pound for da cod, eighty-five for da yellow-tail an a buck-five for da lemon sole! A dam buck five! I got a check fer almos tirt-teen huneret dollars! An on top a dat, ba'ay, I got two-huneret fifty cash for da lobster sold on da side, separate, which dey call "shack". Tree days out, I'm tellin ya!"

Bud went on to explain that New Bedford, Massachusetts was the whale-oil capitol of the world back in the 1800's. Currently the city was populated by a large Portuguese community with a smaller Norwegian population that lived across the bridge next door in Fairhaven. Most everybody was involved in the fishing industry in one way or another.

People were friendly, all and all, and Bud never had a problem finding a boat that needed a good twine-man, he being one of the best. Mending the tears in large trawls was something of an art-form. Having at least one person on board that could do this quickly and keep the symmetrical shape in the trawl was an important facet of ensuring that a boat completed a successful trip. When you were twenty-four to forty-eight hours out of port you couldn't just run in to pick up a new net when the ones on board were shredded after going over some hard bottom in forty fathoms of water.

Bud went on to say that the weather was also more forgiving down south. The summers were longer and it really didn't get too snotty till December and then it started to turn warm again as early as March. (He had conveniently omitted the mention of hurricane season.)

"And no icebergs, by god, nary a one!"

∧

Victor had a bag packed a week after his uncle left and headed back down south but it took the teenager another three months of mental tug-a-war before he figured out that he really meant to use it.

"It's OK, Victor. We seen yer bag 'neath the bed months ago," Loretta said, "we just figured you had to be the one to decide if you really wanted to use it. So go ahead, use it. Ye can always come home, dearie."

17

Victor had no problem hitching a ride on the Trans-Canadian Highway towards Port au Basques on the southwestern tip of the island where he intended to catch a ferry over to Nova Scotia. While stopped in Black Duck he met a fisherman from Quebec that said he was leaving for Gaspe with his boat and crew in the morning. He could get Victor to the mainland for free. Off they went and thirty-six hours later Victor found himself in the province of Quebec for the first time. From Gaspe he wandered out to Percé, where he met a group of college kids that were up on the peninsula for a long week-end. Three days later they headed back to Montreal and Vic went with them. They'd stopped in Quebec City for lunch. Victor wanted to explore this beautiful town further so he stayed and didn't leave for three months.

While sitting at a sidewalk café Victor was waited on by a lovely Quebecois gal by the name of Josie Pineault. They tried to converse but Vic's French was non-existent and Josie's English accent was so thick that it made Victor grin, then laugh. They kept trying long after Josie got off work and before the night turned to morning Victor found himself at the girl's apartment.

Victor learned a good bit of the French language, among other things, over the next months. He also learned to be a pretty good waiter working along-side Josie in the café. They laughed a lot, enjoying each-other's company during the warm, long summer days on the St. Lawrence but in September they both felt the need for a change.

From Quebec City Victor tagged a ride down to Halifax where he stayed for only one day, having an urge to keep moving. After crossing the border at Calais he hitched down Route 1, not stopping until he came to Portland, where he stayed for six months working on a gillnetter fishing for cod, pollock and haddock. Portland made him home-sick because the city reminded him of St. John's. Both cities ran along the water-front against a long hill up behind the harbor. Also, it was what Victor called "bite-ass cold" during those winter months.

One day in the coffee shop he over-heard a trucker say that he was headed down to New Bedford. Victor asked for a lift and five hours later he was knocking on his uncle's door. Bud Hilliard was happy to see his young nephew. They talked about Victor's trip down and Bud asked him about his plans. "Well, I guess I'll fish if I can find a boat that'll take me on. I might stay here awhile".

"Fret not about that me ba'ay. Findin' you a boat should be no problem," Uncle Bud assured his nephew.

Bud took him around the docks the next day, put in a few good words for him, and three days later Victor was steaming out of the hurricane barrier on an eastern rigged (pilothouse aft) dragger headed for George's Banks.

Victor found a second home in New Bedford. His skills in navigation, marlinespike seamanship, net building, and repair were quickly recognized to the point that boat owners and captains were asking him to come and work for them. Inside of seven months Victor had his own rented apartment in the south end of town, a pick-up truck and a somewhat girlfriend. He was bird-dogging this girl whenever he was onshore but she was a trifle stand-offish, which made Victor's pursuit all the more intense.

One late spring day in-between trips Vic was sitting in the Cap Log having a beer and a sandwich when a very large man came up and poked him on the shoulder.

"Youse name's Victa?" asked the behemoth.

"Well… ah, yes sir, it is", said Vic, as he choked on some pastrami and rye. "What…can I do for you?" All the while Victor was thinking, trying to figure out how he'd wronged this guy that stood at least six feet seven inches tall and was just plain *huge* all around.

The beast extended a ham-hock hand and said, "Name's Edmund DaSilva. Youse been chasin' after my daughter, Fabulia. Hadda find out for myself what yer all about…"

Victor had placed his hand into the extended vise-grip as Captain DaSilva slowly settled onto the bar-stool next to Victor.

"I'm told youse's from up Newfoundland. Whatsa matta, no fish up they'a dese days?" Edmund asked as he slowly released Victor's compressed hand.

With an inward gasp of breath Victor stuttered, "Well ah...yes ah... we... still have fish back home but...ah, well hell...I've always heard good things about New Bedford so I figured..."

"Hey, Joey. Give us a couple more beas hea," ordered Da Silva who let out a gusty breath of his own, while at the same time appearing to go into a state of deep contemplation looking at Victor, who was beginning to perspire. As the beers arrived Edmund swept one up, tipped it back to his mouth, drained half of it, returned the bottle gently to the bar and turned back towards Victor. "So first, tell me now, 'Mista Victa from Newfoundland', are you Cat-Lick?"

"Well a... we have a town called Cat's Tongue..."

"No, no. Are you *Cath-o-lic* as in the religion, as in God, as in the Father, the Son and the Holy-Ghost-Catlick..."

As if he had finally found the bottom with his feet while treading water for way too long, Victor said, "Why, yes. Yes, my family's been Catholic for five generations! More, probably, much more! Yeah, we've been Catholic since Day One!"

Edmund DaSilva grinned and said "Well, thank Christ for that. At least I'll have *something* positive to report back to Rose about this 'Victor Janes' we been hearin' about... Victor this, Victor that...Victor Victor Victor."

So began a friendship that was as unlikely as it was destined to be. Edmund DaSilva was a first generation immigrant, old-school Portuguese, very religious, family-means-all, and very conservative. He drank alcohol, mostly his own home-made wine, but he drank it sparingly. Edmund never got beyond a fourth grade education back in the Azores yet he demanded that all of his children, of which there were six, graduate from high-school, at the least. The Captain held on to an anchor that was firmly embedded in the past while he slowly fed out the anchor's chain into the future.

The other side of this coin was Victor. He was young and a trifle immature. He felt that religion was much too convoluted. Victor drank a fair bit and didn't care much about where any of it was made. He was proud to say he was a Newfoundlander, but he didn't dwell on it. He had graduated from high-school with an A-minus average and couldn't have cared less. He lived minute to minute while Edmund always tried to think at least three moves ahead in this Game of Life. The glue between them, aside from fish, was Fabulia. She was Edmund's joy, his favorite, and she was Victor's crystal into the future. He just didn't quite know it yet.

After a dozen beers between them, Victor figured that this man wasn't going to turn him into pulp for the time being and Edmund deduced that this kid had a lot of sea-sense and quite a bit of talent for someone his age.

"Now Victor, listen to me, please. My new boat's just about finished down Alabama. She's ninety-two foot long, got a Caterpillar 399 for a main engine rated at about 1000 horsepower connected to a big wheel in a Kort nozzle. I got two net reels on the stern 'an a big-ass hold. I'll give you a full crew-share plus fifty bucks a day as twine-man. What do you say? I need you to work for me so's I can keep an eye on you, so's Fabulia can be thinkin' 'bout something else besides *Victor!*"

So Victor signed on with Edmund that day and brought the "*Sagrada Familia*" back to New Bedford a month later. After rolling the nets onto the reels, putting fifty tons of ice into the hold, and taking on grub they steamed back out of the hurricane barrier heading for George's Bank. They were a five man crew including Edmund and Victor, Inacio, the engineer, and two deckhands, one of which was Edmund's youngest son George. This would be his first trip out at seventeen years old.

On her first trip out the *Sagrada* returned to New Bedford six days later with a banner trip of 68,000 pounds of cod, haddock, yellowtail flounder, hake, lemon sole, and blackback flounder. Victor got a check for $2,800 and change plus $300.00 for his twine-man daily rate. Some trips there-after were better, some were worse, but Edmund worked them hard that first year. He had a large note with the bank to pay off.

Victor enjoyed socking away all the dough he was making but he didn't have much time to spend with Fabulia. When they got in from a trip the crew'd unload the boat, scrub down the hold and then Victor would head for the Pier Tavern for a beer. He could expect to have two, maybe three days on shore before they went out again. Victor would call Fabulia from the bar, not being able to wait till he got home.

"Hello?"

"Hi Fabi. It's me, Victor."

"Hiya Vic. You sound drunk or tired... or both."

"No, no.. I mean I am tired but I've only had one beer."

"Only one, huh?"

"Yeah, only one. I want to see you tonight."

"Victor, if you're so tired that one beer makes you sound like you've had ten then maybe you should go home to bed. Last time I came over right after you got in you fell asleep on me, so to speak, in fifteen minutes. I've got tomorrow off. I'll see you in the morning."

"Ah, but, no no..."

"Victor, go to bed. I'll see you tomorrow."

"But...no...Fabi..."

Click...

Edmund heard this conversation from the living room. He grinned and snickered, at which point Rose looked up from her knitting and asked him, "Are you laughing for your own amusement or are you going to share it, Eddie?"

Edmund didn't say a word, he just put a finger to his lips. He knew what time Vic got off the boat; he knew Victor'd been at the bar for about ten minutes and he knew he loved it when he heard Fabulia giving Victor a hard time.

^

Spring bloomed and slid into summer. Edmund had the boat hauled out of the water to re-work the propeller, paint the hull below the waterline, and replace zincs. Victor worked up on the dock, building a couple of new nets and refurbishing the old ones. This break in the offshore routine also gave him much more time to spend with Fabulia. They had lunch together every day, went to the movies at night, or just enjoyed the night air down on the waterfront.

Victor was totally taken by Fabulia DaSilva and for good reason. Here was a young woman who was not only physically gorgeous but had a personality and temperament that could have turned Ghengis Khan into a fawning adolescent. Though Fabi was petite in stature she tended to fill up a room upon entry. She had a full head of long, satiny, black hair that fell over her shoulders in waves that reflected the full spectrum of the rainbow when the light hit it just so. Her naturally white teeth, light coffee skin and honey-colored eyes tended to stop people, men and women alike, in their tracks. She was not aware of any of this. If she had ever stopped to think about it she would have reasoned that vanity took up way too much time to be bothered with.

Victor took a Saturday off so that he and Fabi could drive over to Newport, Rhode Island and poke around. Vic had an ulterior motive in mind for this little trip but he would find it difficult to pull off.

"Victor, what's your deal today? You're all nerved up and sort of preoccupied. Your palms are all sweaty. *Yuck*," said Fabulia.

Vic was very preoccupied. He was searching for the 'right time' and making himself a nervous wreck in the meantime. The shops were not suitable and the lunch crowd was much too loud. They wandered the streets through the afternoon, stopping in one store where Victor bought Fabi a beautiful silk scarf that complemented those luscious, full lips that added to Victor's nervous state. Sweaty palms indeed.

Dinnertime rolled around and they found themselves cozied-up in a little restaurant on lower Thames St. Victor started to relax. Yeah, this was the ticket. He could get the job done properly in this place. But five minutes after ordering drinks two of Fabulia's old high-school chums walked in and were seated at a two-top right next to Fabi and Vic. His prospects went from good to glum. Fabulia yacked with the girls and Victor watched the street-scene go by. Finally, with dinner and coffee over, they all said their good-byes. Victor and Fabulia headed back up Thames Street.

Fabulia said, "Wow, what a wonderful night, and that meal, I've gotta tell my mom about that monkfish recipe…what's up, Vic? You were kind of quiet during supper."

"Oh, nothing. Kinda hard to get a word in edge-wise between you, Donna and Marie." He didn't mean for it to come out as a whine, but it did.

"Come on, Victor, give it up. You're sounding a trifle infantile and it does not suit you. So, I'll ask you again, what's going on? Why are you acting so strange today?"

"Well, I just wanted today to be different from how it's turned out so far. Today was sort of pre-conceived in my mind. I realize that it usually never works out the way you want it to when you do that, but I had it in my mind anyway. Sorry for being a baby…"

They stopped in front of St. Spyridon church, both sitting down on the front steps.

"It's OK Victor, no apology needed but tell me- why the preconception about today? I mean we're doing great, aren't we? I love you. What more for now, huh?"

"Wha… well, what more…?" Victor jumped up, sputtering, waving his arms. "Oh, hell Fabulia what's more is I just wanted to ask you to marry me in some kind of a, well, some kind of a romantic setting, that's what's more. I just couldn't find the right place or time or…oh, hell…"

Fabulia then leapt up, gasping with her hands in front of her mouth. She let out a yelp that could have been classified anywhere between unbridled ecstasy and pure pain. She fell to the sidewalk, started kicking her legs and laughing.

"Oh, Victor…" before she could get any further two men bounded across the street and grabbed Victor. "Alright, asshole, what did you do to her?" one of them demanded while the other guy knelt by Fabulia. "Are you alright, Miss? What did this guy do to you?"

"C'mon guys. Knock it off! You don't understand…"

"Yeah, sure buddy. Tell it to the cops", said the guy still holding Victor, as a cruiser pulled up alongside the four of them. By the time the policemen got out of the car Fabulia was laughing uncontrollably. The guy holding Victor relaxed his grip and all five men gawked at Fabi who was curled up in a fetal ball, going red, blue, red in the flashing cruiser lights. As her laughter subsided she said, "Oh Victor, you really know how to knock a girl off her feet. You blind-sided me with that one. Yes, of course I'll marry you."

After much explaining and many apologies by Fabulia the cops decided that all was well. Victor's obvious embarrassment was cause for some needling as they departed. "Way to go, Don Juan. Next time pick a darker street and wait till 3a.m.!"

So the heroine, the dragon and the two knights were left standing awkwardly on the sidewalk. One knight said, "I guess maybe we should buy you guys a drink," which, all concerned agreed, was an excellent idea. Off they all went, laughing and recounting the circumstance of their chance meeting. Thank God you don't have to walk too far to find a bar in Newport, Rhode Island.

^

Carol-Jean Paya turned off of the pavement onto the hard-pack road that led to her double-wide trailer some two miles on. She stopped the truck and cut off the engine after crossing over the cattle-guard. The view facing west was, as usual, spectacular. The sun still had ten minutes or so to go before it set. Carol-Jean, as usual, had to stop and take in the scene in front of her. Just to the left the light bounced and reverberated off of twin buttes and made them appear to be dancing together. The heat coming off of the mesa and badlands shimmered. The earth undulated before her eyes and she laughed to herself, "I do so wonder what an ocean would look like in this light... Probably much the same but a different color...maybe a nice turquoise blue? Ah, well, maybe there's time for me to see that yet." Smiling still, she started the truck and headed home.

CHAPTER THREE

LIFE ROLLED ON for Victor and Fabulia. They managed to stay married and very much in love some eight years after that night in Newport, which was a feat not the majority percentage of married couples could lay claim to in those increasingly trying and complex times.

Fabulia gave birth to three babies. First came Rosa who was not only named after Fabi's mother but was, in many ways, just like her Gramma— a very serious girl. Next came Loretta, named after Victor's mother. This little gem was quite the opposite of her sister in-that she loved to sing, laugh, and caper around the house making sure she missed nothing. Little Eddie was the youngest, named for the patriarch himself, who was now taking every other trip off from the boat, letting Victor take the reins. All of Edmund's sons except for George, who worked aboard the *Sagrada Familia*, had opted for different careers.

Everyone in this circle was comfortable if not a bit complacent. Life had a rhythm, small changes came slowly so that everyone had lots of adjustment space. They all knew that this was probably the exact time when one would want to post a guard, stand up, take stock of one's surroundings and pay attention, but who in their right mind wanted to be constantly looking over their shoulders? The years rolled on.

∧

Victor was not a habitual gambler; in fact the only reason that he participated sporadically in the lottery was because the numbers were so large that they were almost unfathomable. He didn't have a set of numbers that he always played, and he didn't play every drawing. He played whenever the pot caught his eye and he always got 'quick-pick' numbers spit out by the machine at the convenience store. He often forgot that he had the tickets, sometimes holding them in his wallet, not bothering to have them checked for months.

One afternoon Victor stopped in at the Pier for a beer after Inacio, Georgie, and he had finished changing the oil in the main engine aboard the *Sagrada*. He was grubby, sweaty, and tired but he figured he'd have one brew then head home. He ordered a beer for himself and a fresh round for the guys at the end of the bar. He pulled a twenty from out of his wallet, noticed the lottery ticket which he also pulled out, and gave to Armando the bartender.

He got one swig of beer down before the lottery machine started playing "You're In the Money." The whole bar went quiet. Everyone looked at Armando who had a quizzical, almost beatific look on his face. He did one more double-take at the ticket and the machine then yelled, "Victor, you fuck! It's been you all this time, you asshole. You won it, you fuck. This drawing was months ago; one of the largest pots in the history of the goddamn game! Where the hell you been?"

The whole bar went crazy. Before Victor could even put his beer back on the bar he was swarmed by people slapping him on the back, punching him, kissing him, and generally enjoying the hype of the moment. In no time he had ten beers and assorted shots lined up in front of him then someone yelled, "Hey, why are we buyin' him beers? Should be the other way around, huh? In fact, Victor oughta' just buy the whole goddamn bar from Armando."

The bar erupted in more hysterical laughter. Inside of an hour the word had spread and the place was swamped, jammed up like a back-stage party at a Rolling Stones concert. Victor mumbled under his breath, *"Lottery groupies...yikes."*

Two hours later Fabulia pulled up in front of the bar after receiving an anonymous, semi-coherent phone call at home.

"Gidown to dabah, quick. Vics in dashit!"

She walked in on a scene that would have made Salvador Dali drool. The bar was jam-packed at 7:30 on a Monday evening.There were two girls dancing on a four-top to the mega-decibel sound of Jimi Hendrix's

"Purple Haze" pumping out of the juke-box. An old friend of her father's was passed out on the floor under the table that the girls were dancing on.

The bar was about six to eight people deep along its' full length. Everyone seemed to be grinning ghoulishly. One group was howling in unison like a pack of wolves. In a back corner of the bar there appeared to be a doubles wrestling match going on with four men, one guy each on his partner's shoulders; grappling to knock each other down or hold each other up? The top guys were already shirtless.

Fabulia glanced over in the opposite corner and looked away quickly. She knew what those two were doing. She glanced back towards the bar and saw Armando waving and pointing frantically. There sat Victor surrounded by a passel of partiers. The bar was awash in bottles and glasses, some empty, some half-full. The place smelled like a giant Scorpion Bowl.

The steam must have been boiling out of Fabi's ears because a four-foot swath opened for her as she locomoted up to the bar towards her husband. "Vic...VICTOR... Victor....look at me. What the hell is this all about? Victor... look... at... me."

Victor managed to turn his head while it also bounced and bobbed. He should have been mounted in the back window of a low-rider.

"Fabi-baby," he slurred, "...we won."

"Don't you 'wee-one' me," she barked, "I want to know why you are totally trashed." She sent eye-daggers out at the people behind Victor, hoping maybe *someone* might be coherent enough to give her an answer. They all just grinned like a pack of idiots.

"I...I'm telling you Fa... Fabi, wewon...we...won," Victor mumbled, raising his voice as he struggled to annunciate each word.

With the help of Armando she managed to get Victor out of the bar and into her old Ford. Before she got behind the wheel Armando said, "Good Luck." It didn't sound like he really meant it.

Getting the Big Winner into the house was interesting. Getting him into bed was no problem. She just gave him a little push and down he went, face first. She managed to get his boots, socks, and pants off, but left the rest. As an after-thought she went into his pant pockets and found a wadded up ball of bills, small change, a bloodied band-aid, pocket lint, and a small, crumpled up, frayed piece of yellow paper.

"Hey. Victor. What should I do with this ticket?"

"Put it in the bottom of the bucket that you're going to bring me."

"What do you want a bucket for ?"

"Don't want me pukin' all over the bed, do ya?" came the muffled reply.

She started to laugh at the absurdity of it all. A stupid, little piece of grungy, oil-stained paper, worth millions. Peanuts into gold. Modern-day alchemy. Now life might get interesting, she thought, as she continued to softly laugh. These thoughts and more tumbled through her head but they all siphoned down to one simple wish.

"I hope this damned piece of paper doesn't turn my husband into someone I don't really want to know."

Λ

Fabulia was right, life started to get interesting, but a month after they went to the lottery office and cashed in the ticket the hubbub and hoopty-doo died down, leaving Victor and Fabi to figure out what was next. The people close to the family left them alone. Everyone else had plenty of questions and advice such as,

"So, watcha gonna do, Vic? No more boats, I hope. If I had that kinda dough I swear I'd move to Montana. Fuck the Atlantic *and* the Pacific... Fuck'em all... I swear, I wouldn't even *drink* water ever again."

Or

"Now, Mr. Janes, I know you are a good-hearted young man and *I know* that you will remember the St. Augustus Orphanage is always in need of donations *and* your prayers."

One day Victor went for a drive in Fabi's car just to do something other than pace around the house and think too much. He stopped at a Volvo dealership in Middletown, Rhode Island. Three hours later he

29

pulled up in front of the house in a brand-new wagon with all the bells and whistles. Victor beeped the funny horn then waited. Fabulia and her mother soon arrived at the front door. In his best John Wayne voice Vic said, "Well, that old car needed an oil change so's I traded her in for ya.' Whatcha think?"

Fabulia looked at her mom and piped, "Oh, look, Ma. Victor has bought me a new Vulva. How nice. But I really wanted one with a pair of those yuppie coffins on the roof." Having said that both women stalked back into the house with Gramma Rose shaking her head, leaving Victor standing outside stewing.

Ten minutes later he skidded the Volvo to a stop in front of the *Sagrada Familia* where he found Edmund in the galley. Without even a 'hello' Vic said, "Hey Eddie, any chance of going out fishing soon? I need to get outta Dodge."

Edmund started to laugh then thought better of it. "Well, sure. Weather looks good through Sunday. We might get almost a week in. Let's call the boys and get some grub onboard. You need to take it or can I come along?"

"No, no Edmund. Could you come along, please? I need to bump a few ideas off of you."

They didn't fish all too hard that trip. Victor and Edmund spent a fair piece of time in the pilot-house talking. "I just don't know whether to shit or go blind, Edmund. I mean, well ah, do I quit working and stay drunk or do I just keep on fishing and pretend that the money doesn't even exist? It feels like everyone has all these different expectations of me."

"You really don't have to do either of those things, Victor," replied Edmund. "Hell, with all that money you could build your own fleet of boats and just stay on the beach managing them."

"Well, yeah. I guess I could but I'm not sure I want to own a slew of boats. I mean, just one boat's enough of a pain in the ass, wouldn't you say?"

"Yeah, well I guess you got a point there but there's gotta be some facet of this crazy business that you could tap into, considering what yer

30

bank account looks like now. Hey, you heard Marty Famagano talking about those shrimp someone found in a crab trap out in deep water over the shelf? Maybe that'd be worth lookin' into," Edmund mused.

"I do remember Marty talking about that. I'll do some checking around but then what the hell am I going to do with the other 99 percent of this money?"

By the time they'd figured it was best to return to New Bedford Victor had a sketchy, something-of-a-plan aligned in his head. Now he needed to pass it all by Fabulia.

^

Victor slam-banged into the house. He found Fabi in the kitchen with young Eddy who had developed an affinity for breaded fish-sticks and banana/tapioca pudding. Victor bent down to kiss their youngest then quickly thought better of it after he saw the kid's smeared face. Some things even a hardened fisherman found repugnant.

"Hey, Vic… How was the trip?" Fabulia asked.

"Oh, the trip was fine. We did OK, caught our limit on Fluke. But Edmund and I had a lot of time to talk. I think I've got an idea about what to do with this money thing. You think Rose would mind taking the kids for a few days so you and I could get away and have some time to ourselves?"

"That won't be a problem at all. Whata ya got in mind?"

"Well we got a new friggin' car, I guess we better use it. How's about a roadtrip? Let's head her north and see where we end up."

The next day they loaded up the new vehicle, dropped off the kids, and hit the road. They did head north and ended up in Portland a few hours later. Victor pulled into what looked like the highest-end hotel off of Commercial St. Fabulia was throwing a fit. "Victor, what are you doing driving in here? This place has got to cost as much as you make in a one-week trip for one lousy night," she scoffed.

"Don't worry," Vic shot back, "I think we can afford it."

At the front desk Victor asked if they had a suite. When he learned that, yes, in fact there were five suites to choose from, Victor said, "Swell. Just give us the one with the biggest Jacuzzi and the best view."

The concierge took them up to the top floor. Victor stepped into the first room and shouted, "Oh, yeah. This looks promising." The suite comprised three rooms with an incredible view to the east looking out over Portland Head to the Atlantic. The bed was the size of a football field, and the Jacuzzi could have hosted the Olympic swim team. They became much like two kids at FAO Schwartz one month before Christmas. It was play-time.

Victor loved it all while Fabulia seemed to be partial to the steam sauna. They ordered room-service with champagne and fish eggs. They ordered more towels with chocolate mousse. They talked not about dollars and cents. In fact, they talked very little about anything of substance that evening, but laughed loudly and often.

The morning dawned with a sun that was as red as a section of ruby grapefruit. Victor and Fabi ventured out into the downtown area spending most of the day exploring. It was late afternoon when Victor suggested that they head back to the hotel, "I guess we've procrastinated long enough," he said, "We gotta talk about what to do with all this friggin money."

Once they were in the hot-tub Victor started in, "Fabi, let me talk here for a while then I need to know what you think of it all. Eddie and I talked a lot this last trip. We talked about me retiring early which seems to be what most people are expecting me to do now that our bank account has all those numbers and commas. I've been mulling that one over for some weeks but don't really think too much of the idea. I mean what the hell would I do? Sit around the house, build a few nets for the guys? More like turn into another rich drunk, is what it would boil down to..." Victor paused, trying to gauge Fabulia's reaction. She didn't say a thing, letting him continue.

"...So where's that leave me? I've gotta' keep fishing but I don't necessarily have to do it in the same old conservative fashion as everyone else. I mean, it's not like I need to be super-careful with the bank-book, you know…" he hesitated then forged ahead.

"Edmund and I talked about these shrimp out in real deep water in the Atlantic, sort of on the edge of the continental shelf. They're called Royal Reds and they might be fishable with the right gear and the right boat. I would need a special net and a whole lot of trawl wire to reach that far down. I'd need a small processing plant onboard with a freezer because these shrimp start to go bad as soon as they hit air. I want to give this a whirl. Hell, I think I could either buy or build a boat down south for under half a million bucks. These shrimp should be worth a bundle, if I can just catch them and get'em into a freezer…"

"…So that's what I want to do. That still leaves us with a large pile in the bank. I was thinking we could set up educational accounts, trusts, whatever you call them, for all of your brothers' and sisters' kids. I'll talk with the crew in Newfoundland. I'd like to do the same for them. That in itself will still leave us with an ungodly sum. I guess we should put some away safe for us for later on but we don't need all of it. Well, I was thinking that maybe you'd be good at setting up some kind of a foundation where you gave away the interest made by this money, sort of like a benefactor or philanthropist. I mean, we don't have to start living large now, do we? OK, I'm talked out. What d'ya think?"

Fabulia launched herself at Victor and said, "I like it all in principal, Vic. So I'd be like some kind of benefactress, huh? Doling out 'alms for the poor', or some such thing?" she asked, as her hands searched beneath the water. "My gut tells me there's more to it than that. This is not going to be a simple deal. Let's keep talking about it. In the meantime I feel like a prune. See ya out in the back forty," She leapt from the tub, grabbed a towel and headed out of the fogbank.

The next day they had breakfast in the suite then decided to hit the road and head home. After many thank-you's and promises to return they pointed the new ride south.

Why is it so much easier and spontaneous for two people to carry on a lengthy discussion while inside an automobile going seventy miles an hour down a four-lane highway? Maybe the rapid movement excites the senses putting the imagination into overdrive. Whatever it was, they talked all the way home with Fabi holding the floor for the majority of the ride.

"Victor, I know why you have to do this shrimp thing and I respect that but I have some misgivings. Once you start looking for this boat you'll be gone from home a lot; not to say you weren't gone much when you were fishing with Dad but now I can see you being away for even longer periods. I want you to promise me that you'll make an effort to find someone you can trust to help you with this enterprise so that you can take time off now and then. I'm not going to totally lose you to a damn boat at this point in our lives."

"No problem, my dear. I'm going to find the best of the best to crew this boat. I should have plenty of time off," Victor promised as Fabulia went on to her next point of consideration.

"Now, this educational trust is a great idea. Our lawyer can handle these family details without a problem, I'm sure. However, I think the foundation idea may be a little trickier. Don't get me wrong—I want to do it but I want to do it properly from the start and that may mean it would be safest if we get some people involved that have experience with this sort of thing. I'm going to start looking around."

When they arrived home they were happy and energized with a joint sense of purpose and anticipation. "Let's give it a whirl, Vic," said Fabulia. "Hell, what's the worst that can happen? If we end up with only ten grand in the bank we'll still be a few hundred ahead of the game!"

CHAPTER FOUR

FROM THE AFT control station in the pilot-house Victor had an unobstructed view out over the deck of this boat that he'd finally named *Gambling Lady*. From the onset Victor wanted to name her Fallen Angel but Rosa DaSilva came close to apoplexy when she heard this and Teddy Thibodaux just laughed and said, "Y'alls axin' for trouble there, Bubba."

After Fabulia reasoned it out with Victor he agreed that he couldn't do that to the family even though he'd meant no inference to the devil when he considered the name; she was just an angel of a boat paid for with mana from heaven.

From this vantage point in the pilothouse he could manually control all of the deck machinery and hydraulics including the net drums, trawl winches, and the various whips and tackles suspended above the deck. Too bad he couldn't control human nature from this vantage point also.

Some of the folks in town were treating him, well, aloofly. He couldn't put a finger on a definitive instance but it was there. It was as if he had a case of some rare, exotic disease or as if he was touched in the head but tolerated none the less. The fact that he and Fabi were just trying to do it right no matter what luck fed them was, apparently, of no interest to some of those that surrounded them.

So far he had only two crewmembers signed up. Thank God there was Teddy onboard as engineer. Victor knew he could count on Teddy through thick or thin. Jazzy Coehlo, a semi-retired, life-long friend of the DaSilvas, was signed on as cook. Jazzy was a kind-hearted bull of a man, one of the strongest men Victor had ever encountered, which was impressive given the fact that the man had just turned 73 years old two months earlier.

But that was it so far and Victor really didn't foresee any changes coming his way at this point in time. This was a very close-knit fishing town. If these guys didn't want to work for you, you were screwed. Besides, this was not Victor's only problem.

One of the many brick walls that Victor ran up against with this project was with the National Marine Fisheries Service. He'd driven up to the main office in Gloucester to fill out all of the paperwork for his fishing permits. Suddenly NMFS didn't want to issue him any permits at all, they said, because, for one, they had no federal guidelines in the Code of Federal Regulations listed for *Pleoticus robustus* (Royal Red Shrimp) and therefore could not set up harvest tonnage parameters on any forth-coming permit.

Also, and more important from a bureaucratic standpoint, they had no control over by-catch allowances while he was fishing for the shrimp. (By-catch refers to the incidental species that may also be caught while fishing for a directed species such as Royal Reds.) Victor got a little heated and some harsh words were traded back and forth. Victor abruptly walked out, leaving the promise that they would hear from his lawyer, whom he called straight away.

After weeks of haggling NMFS relented but the permit stipulated that the *Gambling Lady* was only allowed a five percent general by-catch allotment by volume of gross tonnage per trip and that said vessel had to carry an accredited and approved observer onboard to ensure that the by-catch guidelines were met. In essence they were saying something to the extent of, *"Fine, we must give you this permit because we have no legal grounds to do otherwise but you've got to have some strings attached and these are the best ones we can come up with."*

This also meant that, beyond the five percent allowance, whatever else the *Gambling Lady* caught had to be sent right back over the side, into the water, dead and wasted, which really frosted Victor. But he felt he had to acquiesce. If he tried to fight this any further he'd probably have to stay tied to the dock for months, maybe more. He'd already wasted enough time on what he felt was, "extraneous crap."

^

A few weeks later Victor and Teddy were putting the final touches on the winch hydraulics. Maybe it was the background noise that prevented Teddy or Vic from hearing the guy yelling at them from the dock, but either way, all of a sudden there was a man with coke bottle glasses, and a Brooklyn accent yelling in Vic's ear. "Hey, fella! Got the ear plugs in? I been yelling at you for days," he exclaimed.

He continued on, not waiting for a response. "Where's the captain, the boss, whomever? I need to talk to the guy in charge of this rig, capice? Gotta catch a ferry to the Vineyard and I'm, like, squeezed for time. Got any ideas? Where's he at?"

Victor crawled off of his knees, giving Teddy a sidelong glance, who just smiled a little, shook his head, and shrugged as if to say, "Don't look at me, you're the ringleader here."

"I am the *whomever*," said Vic, "what can I do for you?"

"Oh, oh…OK. *Sorry*. Guess I was expecting scrambled eggs on the hat with admiral's stars or something," the man shouted. "Gideon Bloom," he said in a softer tone as he shot out his hand. They shook and grinned at each other. Gideon continued speaking before Victor could utter a word.

"I've been hearing about your venture down in Wood's Hole. I wrote a graduate paper on Royal Reds about ten years ago. I'm kinda in between jobs right now. I'd like to go out with you…Well, you know what I mean. I wanna' go fishing."

Victor studied Gideon for a moment and mumbled, "Follow me."

Victor led him off of the deck, into the galley where Jazzy was stowing canned goods while the cassette player was booming a Portuguese fado tune. Vic motioned to the companionway stairs. Up they went two levels to the pilot-house. Bloom immediately ran over to the electronics mounted into the consol. "Whoa," he gasped with a big grin, "this is something I've only seen on research vessels. A ScanMar MK—4 sonar. Low and high frequency ranges. Simultaneous dual screen capabilities.

Great for really deep water. You going to wire this into a head-rope transducer?"

Victor scrunched up his face and looked puzzled. He had assumed that this man was a nut-case. This piece of electronics was one of his secret weapons, and, in his eyes, nobody was supposed to have a clue about what this thing was capable of doing or seeing.

As they walked over to the chart table Vic asked, "So, Mr. Bloom. What exactly was your last job? Who'd you hear about us from?"

"As I said, I heard about you down in Wood's Hole where I was employed at the Institute," replied Dr. Bloom.

They ended up talking for a good hour. Dr. Bloom had, until the previous Thursday, worked at Wood's Hole Oceanographic Institute as an invertebrate researcher. His specialty was cephalopods, specifically, squid. He'd done his undergrad work at the University of Rhode Island inclusive of two years at the Fisheries and Marine Technology School. His post-graduate work was split between the University of Maine and Washington University. He'd rounded it all off with his doctoral work at University of California, LaJolla. He'd also run a commercial squid boat out of Monterey. This guy seemed to have as much paper as he did enthusiasm.

As they edged into the present Victor learned that Gideon Bloom had been fired from his position at Wood's Hole due to an argument with his boss; something to do with, "the abhorrent mixing of science and politics." In a fit of unprofessional anger Gideon had suggested that his boss, "go take a flying fuck at a rolling donut." Not missing a beat, the boss had countered that Dr. Bloom could, "now realize his utmost dreams and fantasies by going down to the local Dunkin Donuts and applying for a job there since he was no longer employed at WHOI."

Victor liked him. He wasn't repentant, depressed, or angry about getting canned. In fact, he seemed to be happy about it. As they finished the interview Gideon said, "Holy shit, I feel liberated. No more blatant bureaucratic bullshit for this boy. Let's go fishing!"

Victor hired him on the spot.

As they walked back out onto the fish deck Gideon was saying,

"Yeah, yeah. OK. Great, I'll spend a week on the Vineyard and then be back here for the following Monday. Great. Great. I can't thank you enough. I'm excited… *pumped* actually. See you in a few days." Gideon vaulted off of the boat, already looking towards the ferry dock.

Teddy watched the guy jink up the wharf for a few seconds then asked, "Wha's dat boy's deal? He got bote oars in da wata?"

"Yes, I believe he does," Victor responded, "probably more-so than a lot of folks I know…I hired him."

Teddy laughed. It seemed as if a bonafide *trios cirque d'anneau* was taking shape here.

Victor's next monkey-wrench in the works came from his insurance company. Even though the *Gambling Lady's* gross tonnage fell far below the numbers that mandated a United States Coast Guard licensed crew, the insurance underwriter was demanding that she sail with, at the least, a licensed captain.

Their logic was that, since the vessel would possibly be working well over 200 nautical miles from shore, their request was not unreasonable. Victor could elect to sail without a licensed skipper but his annual premium would then jump 300 percent, starting out at well into six figures per year.

Victor looked into getting the license himself but soon realized that this option would most likely keep him tied to the dock for another six months because he would have to go to school for awhile in order to pass the extensive set of exams. He'd also have to get all of his past sea-time documented and notarized then pass a complete physical examination. This last hurdle was the most worrisome for Vic because he was color-blind. Nobody else knew this except Fabulia and Josie Pineault up in Quebec City.

Victor wasn't anxious to have anyone at the United States Coast Guard office in Boston know about it either—fearing they frowned on people that could not differentiate between red and green, wondering if they could possibly ban him from ever working on boats again. He did not want to put it to the test.

Three days after hiring on Gideon Bloom, Victor was called up to the galley from the engine-room. Once topside he found Jazzy and another man standing next to each other somewhat awkwardly; as if neither one of them quite knew what to make of the other. If Jazzy was a blunt bulldog the other man was a fox terrier, diminutive and sharp. Vic wanted to laugh at the instant simile but he held it in check. "Assume nothing," was Vic's new mantra.

The newcomer stepped forward, gave a slight bow and said, "Good afternoon, sir. My name is Nguyen Van. I saw your vessel from the bridge and felt I had to come and investigate. You see, I have spent the last seven years fishing Alaskan Pollock in the Bering Sea. Most recently I have moved to the eastern seaboard to be with my extended family here in Massachusetts. I would like to know if you may possibly have any positions available."

Victor's first thought was that maybe this guy could work in the factory but he couldn't see him working on deck. He was so slight. "Thanks for stopping by Mr. Van," replied Victor. "If you'll give me a minute I'll get you an application."

Victor'd gotten the boiler-plate applications almost a year ago thinking that he'd be swamped with guys wanting to work for him, but this was the first time he had ever used them.

Nguyen Van took the proffered paper then looked around for a space at the table from which to fill it out. Victor clumsily cleared off a stool and a bit of table area for him, then went searching for a pencil. He hadn't thought that the man would fill it out here. He handed over the pencil and headed back to the engine-room.

Some three hours later Victor came up into the galley ready to head home for the day when he saw the completed application with the pencil placed squarely in the middle of it on the galley table. His first impulse was to leave it there until the morning, but then he decided he'd look it over later that evening.

After tucking in Rose and Lori then checking on Eddie he told Fabulia that he had some office stuff to do. He went into the small den where he sat down and started scanning Mr. Van's application. He stopped and sat up straight when he read that the guy held a United States Coast Guard license rated at 1,600 tons that was also unlimited globally in scope.

He continued to scan the rest of the application until he got to the three references, all of which were listed as Seattle addresses. He looked at his watch then picked up the phone and randomly dialed the last company's telephone number. After asking for the contact name given on the reference he was put on hold for thirty seconds then put through to George McVey.

"Hello, this is George."

"Hi, George. My name's Victor Janes from New Bedford, Massachusetts. I'm calling about a guy that has used you as a reference on a job application. Man's name is Mr. Van…"

"Oh yes. You must mean Mr. Nguyen. I wish he were still working with us. I could have used five of that man. Incredible work ethic."

"Huh. Well that's interesting," said Vic. "What else can you tell me?"

"Have you got a little time?" George asked, "You might find this story of interest."

^

After Saigon had fallen to the communists and the U.S. had departed Vietnam, Nguyen Van's family made a strong effort to tow the party line on a survivalist level. The problem was that there were many professionals within the Nguyen family and, as with many despotic leaders throughout history, Ho Chi Minh felt that his cause would be best served without having anyone of intelligence around that might be able to second-guess his noble initiatives. Van's father was a medical doctor of wide renown within Vietnam and head of the family. When it became apparent that his number was almost up he literally snuck twenty-three family members past the bad guys as they were on their way to grab Dr. Nguyen and take him off to his own, personal blanket-party.

He'd loaded the group into a panel truck and drove to Ca Mau on the

41

southern-most tip of the country where they managed to 'requisition' a naval patrol boat. Their ultimate goal was to reach Bangkok but en route they were attacked by pirates in the Gulf of Thailand. One of Van's aunts, a brother, and two cousins were killed in the ensuing small-arms battle but the Nguyens managed to overpower the pirates, killing all but one of them. They continued on with their journey but the engine in the patrol boat quit on them the next morning. After drifting for eight long days a Malaysian patrol vessel picked them up and delivered the whole clan to the authorities in Kuala Terengganu.

Malaysia was not Dr. Nguyen's first choice for a landing but, at the least, they were somewhat safe for the time being. The whole family was thrown in jail, being labeled as illegal immigrants. A month later the women and children were allowed out as a "humanitarian" gesture which turned out to be the opposite side of a double-edged sword. The newly released members of the family had no food, no shelter, and what funds they had escaped Vietnam with were confiscated upon landfall. They were treated as castaways.

Three weeks later a Christian mission organization took them in. Six weeks after that the release of the remaining Nguyen men was negotiated with the promise that the whole family would be flown out of the country within one month. Hence, Van's father, mother, grandparents and four siblings were sent to Seattle while the remaining uncles, aunts and cousins were flown to Boston.

Nguyen Van entered Garfield High in Seattle that same year as a freshman. He was fourteen years old, and started out with only a rudimentary knowledge of the English language. One year later he was fluent without a hint of an accent. Three years later he graduated with an A average and was third in his class.

His guidance counselor begged him to apply to college, any college. He could have had his pick on a full scholarship. Van politely informed him that he wanted to go to Alaska to fish commercially. A compromise of sorts was reached and Van enrolled in the Fisheries and Marine Technology School at Bellingham Technical College. He graduated two years later and on his 19th birthday he boarded a plane and flew out to Dutch Harbor, Alaska in the middle of the Aleutian Island chain.

After he landed, Van went outside and stepped up to the only cab idling in front of the small terminal.

Through the cold, biting wind Van asked, "Excuse me ma'am. Could you possibly tell me if there is an employment office on the island?"

The woman behind the wheel snorted and said, "Hell, there ain't no office per se but I know where to take you if you're looking for work. Climb in."

Van expected to be taken to a company office or maybe directly to a boat. He had not expected to be dropped off at a barroom.

"Now listen up," yelled the cabbie. "This place ain't no church vestry. You shouldn't have a problem keeping a low profile by the looks of ya... but watch yerself. Here's my card. Give me a call if ya' need to get a room. I'll take ya' to the motel."

Van began to fork over some money.

"No, no. This one's on me. You're gonna need all the help you can garnish out here. Good luck, bub."

With this advice Van exited the cab and headed for the front door of the Rompa Room.

Now, it should be noted that the Rompa Room was most definitely in a class of its own as barrooms go. If there was a Michelin Saloon Guide this place would have had a one-star rating. But it would have been a *big* star. Back in the 1970's with the advent of the second Alaskan gold rush (King Crab) the bar became the focal point of the island. The booze ebbed out and the money flooded in. The only problem was that this alcoholic tidal surge also created animosities, some real, and some imagined.

At one point the owner of the establishment was so tired of replacing the mangled front door that he had a special one made out of sandwiched quarter inch steel complete with an angle-iron frame. It was still there as Van approached, though a bit dented and tarnished from years of nasty weather and man-made abuse.

With his small bag in hand, Nguyen Van approached the bar and took the only remaining stool. The bartender eyed him skeptically then relented and gave him the requested Budweiser, but only after making a show of looking at his driver's license, much to the amusement of the other customers in the immediate area. Van sipped his beer and looked around, thinking that this place was definitely the Employment Office from Hell. The man next to him leaned over and said, "Hey. Sonny. What the fuck are you doin' way out here?"

Van turned to the man and said, "I am here looking for a job. I want to go fishing."

The guy considered this for a moment and then said, "Huh. What kind of fishing do you want to do?"

"Any kind. Any kind at all, just to get started," replied Van.

"Oh, OK. Hm. Hey, Ralphy," he yelled to a man across the barroom, "this here kid's looking for a chance. Think we could use him as a baiter?"

"Baiter, hell," Ralph yelled, "boy's small enough, he'd probably get lost inside the damn pot."

This brought on a chorus of laughter and the full attention of the whole bar onto Van. Suddenly he felt like bait inside a small tank filled with barracudas. One redheaded guy that looked like some kind of Norse Berserker stumbled up from the opposite end of the long bar and headed towards Van, all the while staring at him with an exaggerated scowl.

He stepped in close, sniffed, and said, "Chinese'd be my guess. Don't think the crab up here'bout'd care for Chinese meat. I believe you in the wrong place, *chink*. I think you need to *git*, go make some noodles or something. Go ahead now. Git."

Nguyen Van didn't budge. The drunk went to grab him but before he could get a paw on the kid's coat Van got a firm grip on one of the guy's pinkies. He twisted, spun the man around, then kicked him in the back of the knees. Down he went. Van released him, backed up, and went into a defensive posture saying, "I have no desire to leave. I have not found a job yet. Please do not try to touch me again."

The sodden oaf got up with a look of bewildered rage on his face. He charged. This time Van quickly side-stepped, dropped down, spun, and kicked the feet out from underneath the man, all in one fluid motion. The forward-falling impetus brought the big man's forehead into direct contact with Van's empty bar stool and put the guy out for the count. The bar went silent and motionless, as if a "pause" button had been hit. After ten seconds somebody must have punched "play" because it instantly all started up again as if nothing had transpired.

Two men picked up Red and took him back to the other end of the bar. It was no big deal, just another brief moment of entertainment in the Rompa Room. To nobody in particular Van said, "I am sorry for this but I will not be manhandled."

The man that was sitting next to Van motioned for him to sit back down. "I think I'm the one owes you an apology. I probably started that with my big mouth. Never have learned yet to think before I open it. Can I buy you a beer? Name's Arne Bergeson," he said as he offered his hand.

Van sat back down and learned that Arne and his brother Ralphie were joint owners and operators of a king crab boat by the name of the *Golden Fleece.* Arne motioned Ralph over and said, "We really do need a baiter, Ralphie. How bout we take this kid on at a half-share for the first trip, see how he does?"

So Nguyen Van had his first job on a fishing boat. The scruffy kid from Vietnam felt that he'd been pointed towards Alaska for as long as he could remember. It was sort of like a homecoming even though he'd never been here before. His first trip out on the *Golden Fleece* had him bewildered, scared and ecstatic, all in one emotion.

This was the culmination of the last six years, why he'd done it all, and come up here to the middle of nowhere. He was seasick for the first three days but he quickly learned that if he kept working it wasn't so bad. The Bering Sea was a constant amazement to him with sea conditions so convoluted that, at times, the seas seemed to come at the boat from three different directions. And the color of the water was surreal.

He could squint his eyes and almost believe that he was in the tropics. The water color went from a brilliant turquoise blue to deep emerald green. And the volume of birds around the boat was amazing. The combined din they created was deafening and he quickly learned never to look up. Gull shit could blind you for days with a direct hit. But the three-hour sunsets were spectacular. It was all better than he had ever imagined it could be.

Ralph and Arne Bergeson were both well over 60 years old. What they lacked in youthful stamina they made up for with the combined knowledge of the fishing grounds and the migratory patterns of king crab. They didn't fish as many pots as some of the other boats but they definitely made up for it in overall catch rates.

Van stayed with the Fleece for two seasons. The money was absolutely grand to the point that he was able to send money off to Seattle and Boston for his family on a monthly basis. It was good, but he wanted to put some of the other skills he'd learned at fisheries school to use.

He asked around and soon found a job on a factory trawler fishing for Alaskan pollock which they caught and then transformed in the vessel's factory into surimi, also known as 'crab legs.'

Nguyen worked the deck of the huge vessel but he also had to work in the factory below decks which equated to a demanding 12 hour shift with only 6 hours off per rotation for thirty days straight. This was definitely a young man's game. It paid well but there was no longevity to the job if you remained a deck-hand.

Van needed 1095 days of sea-time to be eligible for a United States Coast Guard license. When he hit 1100 days he got all of his paperwork in order and headed for the United States Coast Guard Regional Exam Center in Seattle. He'd been studying for this test for the past three years. He passed the five day exam in three days and walked out with a license for "Steam or Motor Vessels of Not More Than 1600 Tons, Oceans." Back in Alaska Van went aboard the same factory processor that he was on before but this time he was signed on as second-mate.

George McVey was saying, "…and then last spring one of our factory workers got his finger caught between two frozen production blocks as they were going down the chute into the hold, damn near took his index finger clean off above the nail. Rather than evacuate the guy or break off the trip Nguyen Van sewed this kid's dang finger tip back on in the pilot-house on the chart table! Everyone onboard called him "The Doctor" after that…"

"…We were sorry to see him go but I heard he moved the whole family to the Boston area so they could all be together. I gotta' tell you, Mr. Janes, if Van's looking for work you would be well-advised to call him ASAP. Van won't be sitting around waiting for your call."

It was close to 10p.m. but Victor decided to give Van a try anyway. After six rings someone picked up.

"Xin chao!"

"Yes, ah, hello…is Nguyen Van there please?" asked Vic.

"Xin vui long cho. Doi. Doi."

"Well, ah…"

"Doi! You Stop, Stop."

With this Vic heard a lot of yelling in the background. It sounded like there were quite a few people in that room, wherever it was. After a few seconds Van came on the line. "Hello, this is Nguyen Van. Who is calling, please?"

"Hello Mr. Van. This is Victor Janes calling. I met you today down on my boat."

"Yes Mr. Janes," Van shouted, "How can I help you this evening?"

"Well Mr. Van, around here I'm told I need help in quite a few different capacities but I was calling you to see if you could come back down to the boat sometime tomorrow. I'd like to offer you a job."

"Yes. I see. Could you possibly tell me what this job offering entails?"

"Of course. I would like to talk to you about the mate's position. I talked with George McVey out in Seattle. You come highly recommended".

"Yes, yes. Thank-you. I could be back in New Bedford tomorrow. At what time would you like to see me?"

"I'll be there all day. You can come down anytime."

"Very good. I will plan on being there at 11 o'clock in the morning."

"Well, okay. We'll see you then, Mr. Van. Good night."

"Yes, thank-you again. Good night Mr. Victor."

Victor hung up the receiver then mumbled to himself, "*Sin chow doy*...wonder what that means."

Victor hired Van aboard as "mate" but on paper Nguyen Van was actually going to sail as the captain. This kind of went against the grain with Vic but it placated the insurance company. Now, if he could only shanghai a few more warm bodies, maybe he could finally go fishing.

∧

As she pulled up to the trailer she saw her husband closing up the small barn. Their two horses in the corral nickered, ears up, in hopes of a treat from Carol-Jean. Joe came around the front of the truck and said, "Good evening, my beautiful, young lady. And how was your day with the tourists?"

"Ah, my dear... Still trying to sweet-talk me, all these years past. Well it still works; please don't ever stop. And my day was just fine, thank-you. Not too many disagreeable types and I sold two more sets of earrings. For one fifty each... Now I only have five sets left. I do hope you've been busy?"

"Yes, yes, my darling. I have another spool of silver wire being delivered into town tomorrow. I should have five more sets for you by the end of the week."

Carol-Jean smiled and half-sang, "'You are my sunshine', you old goat. Let's go inside and get some supper going. I'm half famished."

CHAPTER FIVE

ON A RAINY DAY in April, Victor had his skelton-crew assembled in the galley. He was chomping at the bit. The boat was close to being ready. He still needed more crew, specifically people to work the factory, but he figured that if he couldn't find them, he was going to go out anyway. Maybe if they came back in with a few thousand pounds of shrimp people would re-consider and decide that they might want to work for him after all.

Victor laid out the game plan, explaining what needed to be done before they could put out to sea on the maiden voyage. Van and Gideon were assigned the task of getting the nets, doors, and ground gear in readiness for fishing. Teddy and Victor would continue with some glitches in the factory. Before they left the galley for their respective jobs Victor said,

"And boys, don't forget that we need some more crewmembers to make this rig work. We won't be seeing much help locally. I'm going to an employment agency in Providence tomorrow but I'm not hopeful. Bottom line is six more people to work in the factory. If anybody has any ideas please let me know."

The final touches progressed. Teddy and Vic finally got the shrimp grading machine running then they charged the freezer units with ammonia. Gideon and Van were working well together attaching towing wires to ground tackle, winding the trawls onto the two net reels, and doing some last-minute twine work. Jazzy helped out wherever he was asked to, always in perpetual good humor.

The following day three men showed up on the dock. None of them spoke English but, with some hand gestures, it became apparent that they wanted to go to work on the boat. Victor came back aboard with them, looked at his current crew, and asked if anyone onboard spoke Spanish.

Dr. Gideon said he spoke a bit of the language and joined the group.

After fifteen minutes of back and forth interpreting, Victor learned that all three men were Nicaraguan, had experience fishing coastally, and would be willing to primarily work in the factory aboard the *Gambling Lady*. Emilio Santos, Octavio Guzman, and Rafael Chamorro were hired and asked to show up at 0800 hours three days later, prepared to be away for a minimum of two weeks.

Vic watched them climb into a car and drive off of the wharf. He asked himself, "Can this get any crazier? Guess I better learn Spanish next."

^

Victor drove up to the wharf on what was promising to be a beautiful spring day; the first sign of warm weather so far this year. He was in a fine frame of mind. Finally they were going fishing. He could not remember when he had last been away from sight-of- land. As he climbed on to the boat he thought he heard loud, insistent voices emanating from the partially open galley door. Maybe it was Jazzy's music.

As he traversed the deck and got closer he realized that it wasn't music at all. He slowly opened the door the rest of the way. Apparently his current crew and three strangers were onboard and some kind of a heated argument was going on. Gideon was in one corner of the galley with the Nicaraguans. He kept repeating, "Tranquilo, tranquilo, por favor!"

Teddy and Edmund were leaning up against the portside bulkhead. Teddy's whole face was smiling. *"Bonjour, mon capitaine! Comment etes-vous? Le cirque a commence sans vous!"*

Jazzy was banging pots and pans around and swearing profusely in Portuguese. Standing with Nguyen Van was a small woman wearing a black head-scarf. She, Van and two other men were now conversing loudly in Vietnamese. Jazzy saw Vic at that moment and immediately stopped his antics.

"Ah, good morning," Victor yelled, "would anyone, anyone at all, care to tell me what the Christ is going on here?"

Van stepped forward and said, "I am sorry for all this, Victor. I must take full blame. I have brought my aunt and two cousins down to the boat to meet you. They have all performed factory work and were anxious to work for you after I explained your predicament. Unfortunately the question of *rice* came up and this argument between Jazzy and my Auntie Di ensued."

Apparently Van's Auntie Di asked him about the food arrangements aboard, specifically what kind of rice they planned to serve on this vessel. Van passed the query along to Jazzy in English, not thinking anything of it. Jazzy understood none of the words that flowed between Van and the woman but he caught the intonation and felt that he may have a usurper to his domain right in front of him. He quickly grabbed a box of Minute-Rice and a can of beans from a cupboard then went to the fridge and took out a pack of chourico. As he ceremoniously placed each item on the galley table he said, "Here's the rice, here's the beans and this is the char*eese!* This is what's for supper tonight."

Auntie Di knocked over the rice box spilling it all over the deck as she yelled, "Rac, rac." She turned to Van saying, *"Chau, chung toi khong the an nay rac... Dieu nay trau khong biet gao tu sao. Chung toi an tot hon trong tu.* Nephew, we cannot eat this garbage. This water buffalo does not know rice from worms. We ate better in jail."

Nguyen Van said, *"Doi, xin vui long, Di. Chung toi co the sua loy nay. Doi, doi.* Stop, please auntie. We can fix this. Stop."

The stage had been set and everyone was yammering away. When Victor showed up he was instantly upset. It was supposed to be a beautiful day. They were going to go fishing. He hadn't even agreed to hire Van's aunt and cousins, and yet, all of a sudden he had a pile of multi-lingual problems to deal with.

"Ok... *Alright...* Van, get your relatives up to the pilothouse. Gideon, take your gang down to the factory and show them around. Find out if they eat rice in Nicaragua. Teddy and Edmund, stop grinning and find something to do, huh? Jazzy, clean up this goddamn mess so we don't have an accident; somebody might slip and die before I even get this rig out past the hurricane barrier. Everybody, go."

People scattered like roches in a flashlight beam. Victor stood still in the silence, closed his eyes, breathed strongly for a ten count, then headed up the companionway to the pilothouse. For a moment he wished that Fabulia were here to help him sort out this foolishness. His patience was waning.

Van's three relatives were all seated at the small settee on the starboard side of the pilothouse. All of them were looking down at the tabletop. Van was left standing, but before he could continue his apology Victor said, "OK, what's the deal here, Van? I mean, rice is friggin *rice*, isn't it? If we're going to have to fight about rice what the hell's going to happen when something important comes up? I just do not get it. Talk to me, please."

"Captain Janes, I do not mean to counter your suggestion but I must tell you that rice is not just 'rice.' It is not all the same. There are thousands of varieties world-wide. Each culture that uses rice as its' staple has their own distinct preferences. In Vietnam there are eleven different kinds that are cultivated. In some cases two villages side by side will have two dissimilar preferences. Rice can be complicated, Victor."

"Hm…well ah, jeez," Victor digested this then asked, "Well, why don't they bring their own rice? I mean, that would be the easiest solution, right? Maybe we could even get Jazzy to cook it properly."

The four *Nguoi Viet* whispered for a minute, nodded in agreement simultaneously, then looked at Vic and smiled. Van said, "We have agreed that this is a very equitable solution though, I must tell you that my aunt has some small misgivings about Jazzy's cooking skills. She was somewhat insulted by the, ah, donkey penises that he showed her. She says that she has had to eat many unpalatable things in the past in order to survive but penises were not among them." Van suppressed a smile but Victor couldn't hold it back. He burst out laughing.

"Yeah, OK. I get it but let's not tell Jazzy about your aunts' misgivings. And tell her that what Jazzy showed her was a type of

Portuguese sausage called Chorico. She may even want to give it a try.

OK. Now why don't you introduce me to your family here? I guess we'd better have some sort of an interview for form's sake."

So Van presented Nguyen Thi Bian, Nguyen Vinh and Nguyen Dan, all of whom were inducted into the crew of the *Gambling Lady*. Finally, it was time to go fishing.

CHAPTER SIX

THE GRAND CANYON is over 250 miles long, eighteen miles wide, about one mile deep and was created over a 5 million year period. Similarly, there are twenty-four ocean canyons along the eastern seaboard between Cape Hatteras and Canada that delineate the edge of the continental shelf along a portion of the western side of the North Atlantic Ocean. The largest of these is the Hudson Canyon, which starts about seventy nautical miles southeast of New York City at a depth of fifty fathoms and runs another fifty nautical miles out until it falls off the shelf into over 7,000 feet of vertical water.

This canyon starts in the crook of the elbow between New York and New Jersey and is an important spot due to the fact that it is in the direct area where the Gulf Stream makes its' easterly turn towards Canada and then Europe. Gulf Stream springtime offshoot eddies create *upwelling* which brings in much of the needed nutrients that support life in the vertical water column along the continental shelf and inshore of it.

This was one of the reasons why Victor decided to try the area for his first shot at catching Royal Red Shrimp. He had fished here before for squid and whiting with Edmund, and he knew the area was a natural corral for a myriad of different aquatic species; though the deepest that he, or any other fisherman had ever set a net out was in about 100 fathoms or 600 feet of water. Victor was looking at setting the net out in 500 to 600 fathoms which equated to roughly a half-mile of vertical water.

Setting a trawl out in even ten fathoms of water can be a sketchy deal if one doesn't pay close attention. Basically, the boat is towing a huge funnel astern. Water pressure is key in keeping the funnel open. To facilitate this opening there is the forward motion of the boat, a footrope along the bottom edge of the opening that is made up of chain, and a headrope along the top edge of the net that has floats attached to it. The counter-physics of the headrope and footrope are the basic forces – but now the boat has to spread the net horizontally as well so that it is opened to its' fullest capacity.

From the wings or sides of the net, a set of wires lead out to 'doors' that are attached to the actual towing wires, which are run out slowly from the boat. These doors are set at outward angles so that the water pressure from the forward motion of the vessel makes them want to spread horizontally away from each other and thus open the net up. These doors are made of steel and also assist in getting the complete rig to the ocean floor where it will hopefully 'tend bottom,' or stay opened and dredge fish into the trawl as the vessel moves forward.

Running out the towing wires is the toughest part of the whole operation because the two wires are each separate, on their own winch drum. Usually two men, one on each winch, have to set out the wires in unison, careful to keep them paying out evenly. These towing wires have marks spliced into them every ten fathoms or so, to the captain's specifications. These marks aid the winch-men in keeping the trawl symmetrical as they run out wire. It gives them a count to stop at predicated on the depth of water they are fishing in.

This whole process would be much the same as two kids deciding to make a game by tying their kites together with a ten foot piece of string between the two, both kids then running and letting out their respective tethers so that the kites went up evenly and they didn't break the string that attached one kite to the other.

Victor was in somewhat untested territory here. Nobody he knew of had ever tried to put a fishing trawl on the bottom at these depths. He had a few advantages in his favor. Firstly, he had a head-rope transducer connected to a mile and a half of insulated, water-proof cable on a reel that connected to a separate sonar unit in the pilothouse which would tell him if the net was tending bottom and fishing. He hoped that it would also show him what was being swept into the net although even his electronics guy could not guarantee it because the unit had never been tested in this depth of water.

Also, there was a second, high-powered sonar unit with a transducer attached to the hull. This piece of wizardry would tell Vic what kind of bottom he was looking at and give him a good bit of fore-warning if he was going over an area that had potential snags that could rip or even hold the net to the bottom. It could also differentiate warm and cold water eddies that ran in different directions horizontally. At these depths there could be four or five of these eddies from surface to bottom, all running in different directions.

The last ace in the pocket was Victor's winches. He'd debated this expense with Teddy for a long time. Once again Teddy prevailed.

"Hell, man! You got da cabbage, use it, If ya'll go and try to hand-mark all dat wire you *know* we gonna' be off on da measure some by da time we get done. An' ya' also know dat wire gonna stretch after time and use. Me, even if I didn't have the dough, I'd see a great need for dat ting if I was goin to put dat dam net down over a half mile wid over a mile of trawl wire set out in front of it."

So Victor, with much trepidation, bought a computerized, automated trawl winch system from a Japanese company that had just developed it. Said company didn't really want to sell this technology to an American so they gave him an extreme dollar figure. They were quite surprised when Victor said, "Okeedoke, how soon can you install it?"

Victor, Teddy, Edmund, Van, and Gideon were all standing mutely on deck looking out through the net ramp that led down into the water. The net, doors and wire were twisted into an ungodly spider-web mass. Their maiden set of the net had gone off smoothly enough until it entered a Gulf Stream warm water eddy at 800 feet going in the same direction as the net, opposite of the direction of the boat, at about one knot. This put extra strain against the trawl doors and stopped the decent of the net.

Victor saw this happening on the winch meters and the headrope transducer. He compensated by increasing the speed of the wire being paid out. The descent of the net then continued smoothly until it hit another eddy at 2000 feet going in the same direction as the Gambling Lady, but in the opposite direction of the first eddy, and moving at a speed of two to three knots.

This caused the net and doors to collapse and head straight for the bottom. Conversely, the trawl wires, the majority of which were still under the influence of the first eddy, were ballooning upward from the sudden lack of pressure until the net and doors' decent brought everything up short and stopped.

Victor saw this happening on the tension readings of the winch meters and the head-rope transducer, yet it all happened very rapidly. His reaction time was much too slow and late. By the time he'd reversed the winches the net had already been carried by the second current up past the doors and in between both trawl wires *then* had done three 360 degree vertical turns around the trawl wires as the strain came back on everything when Victor started to reverse the whole process.

Van was thinking out loud. "We have gotten one full twist out by turning hard to starboard and counter-spinning it, but I believe the only way we will get the remainder of this tangle out is to get one of the doors up alongside the stern so that we can chain it off and start unshackling it from the rest of the uh...jumble. Then possibly we can chain off the other door and haul the net up on deck..."

The other four men nodded in agreement. Without a word everyone went to work. Vic went to his control station in the pilot-house, Teddy went to grab tools, Gideon went after some chain lengths, while Van and Edmund went to the stern to figure out where to grab the first door.

Some six hours later, with the job completed, they all stumbled into the galley looking for some food and coffee. Gideon had a nasty looking bruise across one forearm received when a slackened wire decided to untwist rapidly. Edmund had a black eye that he'd gotten when a shackle, after much tugging, finally came free.

Jazzy sprang into action and had them all in a somewhat better frame of mind with kale soup and coffee. The remaining crewmembers eyed the tired men furtively, as if this was all some kind of a joke these other guys were playing on them. They were all thinking, "where were these mythical shrimp? Let's stop playing around and make some money here."

Auntie Di moved over next to Van and whispered, *"Lien nguoi dan ong nay biet nhung gi anh ta dang lam gi?* Does this guy really have any idea what he is doing?"

"Toi co lo ngai cua toi bang cach nhin vao mess tren san tau nay. I have my doubts after looking at that mess on the floor of this boat."

Van responded in an equally soft tone, *"Chung toi mot so van de nhode lam viec ra. Xin hay kien nhan, Di.* We have some problems to work out. Please be patient, Aunt."

Victor saw this brief exchange and felt pretty sure that he knew what it was about. "Hey: Gideon and Van—Why don't you explain to your guys that all's well. We'll get the bugs ironed out. Have some patience with us please. Tranquillite. Tranquilo. Please."

With that Victor, Gideon, and Van headed towards the pilothouse to look at the charts in order to find a spot that might possibly have less severe currents.

Auntie Di headed for her quarters. One of the advantages of being the only female on this vessel was that she got her own living space. Aside from the engine and mechanical noises, this was pure bliss. She couldn't remember the last time she had been alone for hours at a time.

Gideon could have been back in some university lecture hall. This was his ballywick and he was into it. "The point where you set out the net the first time was probably the worst place to choose with regard to multi-current convergence. Yes, probably the best spot for catching *Pleoticus robustus* but definitely the worst for deep-water eddies, and we only saw two opposing currents. There were probably two or three more below those. This has mostly to do with that right-hand turn that the Gulf Stream does just to the south of this spot…

…I suggest that we head east to either Block or Atlantis Canyon. The influence of the Gulf Stream will have subsided by the time it passes to the south of those areas."

"Sounds about right, Professor," said Victor. "Do you have a specific spot you think'd be a good shot or shall I cover my eyes and jab at a place on the chart?"

"Oh hell. Jab away, Cap. Your guess is as good as mine on that score. Let's just get a good 50 miles to the east," grinned Gideon.

So east they went to a spot mid-way between the next two canyons. Out went the net, then the doors. Victor had to consciously un-clench his jaw. It was already starting to cramp up on him. Edmund said a little prayer for Vic's sake, hoping for the best; or at least something a little better than the last debacle.

Teddy, Van and Gideon came back into the pilothouse after getting the rig in the water. It was all Victor's now. He asked Van and Gideon to watch the high and low frequencies on the sonar display. The advantage of this dual frequency unit was that the high frequency worked well in shallower water up to 200 fathoms or until it hit a thermocline then it tended to fade and distort. The low frequency needed a longer stretch or distance to work properly and did well from 200 to 1500 fathoms.

After five minutes of paying out wire Gideon said, "We just lost the high frequency at 230 fathoms. It's definitely a thermocline gradient but it looks weak. Where's the head-rope?"

"One hundred ninety fathoms," said Victor, "oh yeah, just passed into it. The tension meter slacked off some but nothing drastic like last time."

The trawl went through two more eddies on the way down but held its' shape. Ten minutes later Victor said, "And...touchdown. *Gambling Lady* has contact in 689 fathoms of water."

The rig was on the bottom and fishing. Victor looked at the clock. Thirty-three minutes from surface to bottom. He let out a long breath then brought the RPMs up on the main engines till his speed registered two and a half knots-over-ground. The head-rope transducer was registering eight feet off of the bottom, and the low frequency sonar was showing a flat ocean floor with no upward spikes to denote possible hang-ups or obstacles. All was well, so far.

"OK guys," Victor barked, "Let's let her fish for a half-hour on this one. Grab a coffee. I'll call ya'll when I'm ready to haul the rig back."

Teddy grinned and said, "What's this '*Y'all*' stuff Vic? Ya'll ain't all nerved up or sumthin' are ya? Startin' to sound way too Cajun, huh?"

Victor waved him off and said, "Any port in a storm, amigo. I would *appreciate* it if you all brought me up a cup of coffee. *C'est possible?"*

Retrieving the net was much less critical than setting it out. Victor had the doors up, hanging off of the stern in twenty minutes with the net on the reel in another five. Gideon threw a strap around the fine mesh cod-end and hooked on one of the overhead whips. Victor hoisted it up as Van tripped the cod-end release. Everything that the net scooped up while trawling along the ocean floor came tumbling out.

There were two large twenty to thirty pound monkfish that were all mouth…a half circle of needle-like teeth going every which-way with a brief body tapering into a plump, ham-like tail. There were four nematodes that looked like giant, prehistoric fleas, and a lot of these round rocks that looked like big, discolored, purplish snowballs. Also, there were these funny pink things that looked like infant ballerina slippers.

Victor let out a whoop, ran over to the pile on deck, grabbed up a few slippers, and yelled to nobody in particular and everyone in the world, "these are them, ladies and gentlemen. These are what all this is about."

The whole crew was on deck. Everyone stepped in closer to get a better view, as if they wouldn't be getting up close and personal with these creatures over the next few months…

Victor was saying, "If we can catch enough of these babies then pack and freeze them properly we will all make a good chunk of change. Gideon and Van- please have your crews get these rocks or whatever they are off into a side-pen. We can put them overboard later. Then open up that deck hatch and get the shrimp and other fish down into the factory pen. Be gentle with those shrimp, we've only got about 200 pounds on deck here but let's make it all count. Everybody else, down to the factory to learn how to grade, pack, and freeze Royal Reds. Let's hustle, folks. I want to get everyone familiar in the factory before we put the net back in the water."

Edmund headed for the pilothouse to keep an eye on the autopilot while Van and Victor were below. Everyone else headed for the factory except for Gideon who grabbed up a shovel and started sorting out the pile. He picked up one of the purplish brown balls, inspected it closely for a few seconds, then threw it hard against the deck. It broke open easily to reveal a somewhat shiny core with a dull black object at the center.

Dr. Bloom just stared for a full minute then said out loud, "Well, hell. This is amazing."

Gideon had only seen one of these before but that one didn't have a shark's tooth embedded in the middle of it. It was a manganese nodule, rare in that they were hard to lay hands on due to their earthly location which was usually in very deep water throughout the oceans of the world.

He picked up a few more of varying size and rapped them on the deck. They all had teeth inside of them. He asked himself, "how do I begin to explain the possibilities and ramifications of these things to Victor?"

Teddy came onto the deck looking for Gideon. "Hey man, yo crew's lookin fo ya'll…whatchoo got hea?" he said, as he looked at what Bloom was holding. "Well look at dis…kinda like a present inside a present, huh? What is it?"

Gideon gave him a brief explanation then said, "Let's keep this low-key for now Teddy, *ok*? I gotta' talk to Victor about these things."

Teddy gave him a look with a question in it then said, "Yeah, no problem, man." They sorted out the remainder of the pile and headed below to the factory.

^

Joe Watahomigie let his horse lead the way. They were deep in the canyon but Dodger knew where they were going. They'd made the same trip together innumerable times over the last eight years but this one could be their last trip here. 'Slim pickings' was the rule now. This site was yielding fewer and fewer teeth. He was thinking he'd have to start prospecting elsewhere, which didn't make him happy. Change always meant more work. "Well, Dodger old boy, at least we have a good day for it. With any luck we'll find ten pieces fast and be home for lunch."

CHAPTER SEVEN

SUPER-HEATED MANGANESE oozes up to the ocean floor through vents or fissures that are pressure point releases much like the steam vent release on an old fashioned pressure cooker. When the pressure builds up to a certain point the weighted vent cap will no longer be able to hold it all in. The cap will rise and the pressure will thus be released. In the case of these particular ocean vents, liquid manganese as well as other minerals is released instead of steam.

After this super-heated, molten ore emerges it starts to cool and seems to search for something with which to adhere to but there's not a whole lot of stationary mass at these depths for the ore to attach itself. Except maybe an old shark tooth still showing some serrations along its' edges after eons on the bottom. The manganese gloms onto the shark tooth. More manganese catches on, and this added surface area is caught by weak currents making the whole mass roll along the ocean floor like a small snowball.

This calcified, metallic mass will keep rolling and collecting until its' weight will let it roll no further. This takes a long time—a million years plus for a centimeter of diameter.

A manganese nodule is not only composed of manganese. It can also hold variable amounts of copper, nickel, and other metals. Nodules occur at any ocean depth, but are most prevalent at depths of between 1,000 to 3,000 fathoms of water. It's at these depths where ocean venting is more pronounced.

It is estimated that there are over 500 billion tons of these nodules scattered throughout the planet's oceans, but it's hard to know exact numbers. More is known about the surface of the moon than the extreme depths of our planet Earth's oceans.

These brownish balls were first discovered in the 1800's but were not given much attention until the 1960's and 70's when a number of mining companies showed interest in them, mainly for their nickel content. By the late 70's an international joint venture was successful in harvesting multi-ton volumes from the eastern equatorial abyssal plain in the Pacific Ocean in depths of around 3000 fathoms. How these "multi-tons" were harvested was secret information but it was estimated that between $3.5 and 4 billion dollars would be needed back then to realize commercial volume harvesting. However, the project was subsequently squashed when a glut of nickel came onto the world market from land-based mines.

In the early 1980's a group of nations joined together and decided that deep-sea mining outside of national jurisdictions should be governed under a "common heritage of mankind," the basic crux of which said that not just anyone could mine for manganese nodules but, if they did, they'd have to share the proceeds and technology with everyone else in the mining consortium— even if they weren't bonafide members of the club just yet.

This veiled initiative was a sub-chapter within the formation of the third United Nations Convention on the Law of The Sea and, more directly, the International Seabed Authority, whose many mandates included keeping a thumb on all deep water mining efforts in international waters. As a result, true to exclusionary club ethics, the ISA signed long term contracts with a number of private and public corporations granting them huge tracts of seabed for the specific purpose of mining manganese nodules. Victor Janes knew about none of this and had never even heard of the International Seabed Authority... yet.

^

The Vietnamese and Nicaraguan crewmembers on the *Gambling Lady* were freaking out in two opposite directions. Emilio, Octavio, and Rafael were all in the galley refusing to work. They were extremely upset and inexplicably frightened. On the other hand Auntie Di, Vinh, and Dan were in the factory working away, all smiles and joy. Sharks were big *may man* or luck in Vietnam but not so in Nicaragua.

The San Juan River runs from Lake Nicaragua down to the Caribbean Sea on the eastern coast of the country. This is where a canal from the Caribbean to the Pacific was originally going to go, but Panama won out. Another story. This river was of no special interest beyond that, except for the fact that an unusual creature called a Bull Shark inhabited it.

Scientists separated *Carcino erectus* from the rest of the family because it could survive, and thrive, in fresh water as well as salt. The Nile has the Crocodile, and the Mississippi has its' Gators, but in the San Juan River and in Lago de Nicaragua there was the Bull Shark.

The beast had a tail so powerful that it could launch itself from a shallow pool up onto the river bank and grab an unsuspecting goat, cow, horse or human in the blink of an eye. It appeared as if these sharks preferred man. The attacks on humans were so prevalent that in the 1800's most any Nicaraguan family could say that they knew someone who was a victim of, or had lost a family member to the Bull Shark.

So Rafael, Octavio, and Emilio were not impressed favorably with all these mud balls that had shark teeth hidden inside of them. This was an omen of the worst kind. They all refused to work— sitting huddled together at the galley table. They wanted to get back shore-side and off this boat as soon as possible.

Auntie Di on the other hand, understood that any tangible, old, natural object from the oceans would hold big power and luck within the Vietnamese community. She intended to cash in on this windfall in the form of shark's teeth. Di, Vinh, and Dan were working away and talking animatedly in the factory. She couldn't wait to get her hands on those rocks and break them all open. But first they had to get the shrimp packaged and frozen properly.

^

When Victor had researched the potential markets for Royal Red shrimp, he'd discovered that Europe was most likely going to be the best venue for these crustaceans. Edmund had contacted family in Lisbon, the upshot being that Victor was put in touch with a Portuguese company that contracted to take the *Gambling Lady*'s complete annual production. This sounded great until Vic saw the packing parameters which stated that the sizing had to be done in thirty gram increments. For this purpose Victor purchased a Micro-Weigh Ten grading machine that could grade 240 shrimp per minute- in *ten* gram increments if need be.

Van and Teddy were in the Factory with the "Vietnam Shift." The product looked good. The grading machine was finally behaving after constant adjustment by Teddy. Van was supervising the cleaning and packaging. The double-contact plate freezers were the next step. After that, the frozen boxes of shrimp were master-packed and sent into the freezer hold.

As this was taking place in the factory Victor and Gideon were having a multi-level conversation in the pilothouse.

"...OK, OK... so now I've got these Mesozoic, petrified, dinosaur turds on deck that are loaded with quasi-exotic minerals *and* shark's teeth. Oh yeah, and we have a few hundred pounds of inconsequential by-product: these beautiful, large, red prawns. Talk to me, Dr. Bloom. I'm about at the end of my friggin' rope with all this added fluff between those balls, shark's teeth, and a crew that believes in two different kinds of voodoo," Victor shouted. "*I just want to catch shrimp.* So the Nicaraguan contingent believes we're all going to die because there is now a curse on this boat... They refuse to work...Holy Shit, Gideon. This is the twentieth friggin' century. They're just teeth, old teeth I'll grant you but, still, just teeth. Can't you coax these guys out of this? I am not going to head in just because three members of my crew are obsessed with horror films and God knows what kind of superstitions."

Gideon drew a deep breath and said, "Victor, listen. First of all everyone has to calm down here. Nobody's going to die from the *Curse of the Fang,* but I don't think it's going to do any good to keep talking to those guys about this. Let's leave them alone and concentrate on the shrimp. Those guys will figure this out on their own and it would be best to let them do just that. Set the net out in a different area, see if we can get away from the nodules. When we get back into New Bedford I'll take a few down to Wood's Hole and see what I can find out about them. In the meantime let's go fishing. I think our Nicaraguan party will come around eventually. Whew. What a crazy day. Can we set out the net soon? I need a damn nap."

"Go take a kink now, man. I'm going to steam for a few hours. See if I can get away from these turds with teeth." It was just an errant, dismissive thought that skittered through Victor's gray matter but down the road, soon, he would find out that getting away from the nodules was infinitely easier said than done.

CHAPTER EIGHT

FABULIA JANES was dealing with what some might call land sharks. She was sitting in the Boston offices of Houlihan, Logan, and Ghilouly, a law firm that the DaSilva's New Bedford lawyer had suggested to Fabulia as a potential firm for use in setting up her non-profit corporation. Mr. Evan Ghilouly was wrapping up his discourse on large sums of money, trusts and NP corporations.

"So you see, my dear, it is just not that easy to bequeath monies in charitable form as it once was not so long ago. One must be ever so vigilant. One cannot just fling the money out there and hope for the best. Rockefeller could, but that was a different era. Why, just the other day a friend of my wife reported that she had made a five figure donation to an organization that she was led to believe watched after stray kittens and disenfranchised dogs. Well, she wrote out the check after a full minute's deliberation to ensure that she felt right about it and that she was, at the least, *trying* to help *something*. She mailed it off and gave the matter not a further thought until the bank telephoned her some three days later..."

"Mr. Ghilouly", Fabulia interjected, "that is all fine and well but, as yet, you have not told me how you are going to help set up my not-for-profit organization. All you have done so far is allude to a "five-figure check" that I am going to have to write you as a "pre-emptive retainer" so that we may then, possibly, get started. Why don't we cut to the chase, sir. What are you going to do for me?"

Ghilouly, Esquire gave a nervous chuckle and tried to start in again, "Well, my dear, firstly of course, our firm would have to do a background check on you and your family and then—"

"Whoa. Hold on there, bub. Are you seriously trying to tell me that, after I give you a check for ten grand you will then feel free to do a figurative strip-search on me and my family? Is that what you are telling me? Something is askew here. Let me suggest that perhaps I have erred. Perhaps I should have done a touch more homework myself before I wasted our time. I believe I should have done a damn *background check* on you, you silly little man. I may be born to first generation immigrants in low-brow New Bedford but I am not a fool. You sir, are a disenfranchised dope. Forget about the dogs."

Fabulia jumped to her feet, gathered her valise and coat, gave Ghilouly a withering, long glare, then headed for the door. The staredown must have worked. The old fellow sat transfixed at his desk, eyes frozen on the door, mouth agape, with little flecks of white gunk glued into the corners of his lips. He had seemingly turned to stone.

Fabi managed to hold it back until she was out of the office and heading down the steps to Newbury St. She burst out in a gut-wrenching guffaw. An older couple was starting up the steps. They did a hasty about-face and hurried up the street a safe distance until they were out of immediate danger from what they perceived as a potentially deranged woman. They both assumed that it must have been bad news from her lawyer.

"A dope, a disenfranchised dope; that was prime," she exclaimed to herself. "Dogs and lawyers. Oh dear, that was fun."

The few people staring at her finally dispersed and she walked into a nearby phonebooth.

"Hi Lucien, it's Fabulia Janes...Yes, I just left their offices... No, the meeting was far from satisfactory... I think I need someone who's a little more down to earth, if you know what I mean... Yes. OK. I don't care if she's a little bit grumpy and gay as long as she makes sense... Yes, you call her first and I'll get a cup of coffee then call you back in fifteen minutes or so."

An hour and a half later Fabulia was sitting in the offices of the Boston Independent Food Bank. Her host, Martha Vanderhorn, the director of the organization, was saying, "Yes, Lucien told me about your unique dilemma. What a problem to have. I *must* commend you and your husband. Most people that experience an instant monetary transformation by way of the lottery either end up at the bottom of a bourbon bottle, broke in a year, or in court forever. It sounds like you may have a handle on it."

Fabulia was feeling a touch uncomfortable. She'd not been ogled like this by too many women. She thought she could actually feel the heat that this lady was exuding. Fabi shrugged it off and continued, "...Don't get me wrong. We've salted away a tidy sum to take care of our respective families, but we realize that if we ever tried to burn through the remainder we'd most likely burn up with it. That's a given. So what do we do with this huge pile of cash? Leave it in the bank to accrue interest so that our kids have even more money to poison themselves with after we kick? Nah, better to see if we can do something useful with it. It seems to me that this whole world is in the toilet. Maybe we can help change that; maybe we can't but we can give a hell of a try."

Martha thought for a bit then asked Fabulia, "Did you have some specific area that you wanted to delve into? Environmental, human or social services, animal rights...?

"No", responded Fabi, "all I really know for certain is that the old saying about the road to hell being paved with good intent is very apt, especially in our case. I think I'd better be very careful. This is definitely new territory for me and my family. We lived on a month-to-month basis before this fell in our laps. We're not well versed in the more intricate workings of the financial world. We need some help." Fabulia abruptly shut her mouth. She wasn't used to talking with strangers like this and she most definitely had a hard time telling someone that she'd just met that she needed help.

Vanderhorn laughed gently, sensing this woman's discomfort. Martha had very dark skin, close cropped gray hair, and she was large. Her eyes usually surprised everyone she met. They were as aquamarine-blue as the waters that surrounded Antigua, the island of her birth.

Her mother was a forth generation native of that island and her father was a Dutch seaman who came for a visit and decided to stay. Martha got a scholarship grant to Boston University and she ended up staying also. She was a person that needed to keep busy. She loved the Windward

Islands but she felt a bit bored down there. It was beautiful and serene, definitely low-key, but she thrived in Boston. It was a great city offering more than enough to keep her active, interested, and engaged year 'round.

"OK, Mrs. Janes. I can tell you what you need to do to start a not-for-profit, but first we have to set up some parameters to aid you in that process. A 501C(3) corporation may not suit your needs. At some point in time I think you will have to give me an idea of the amount of money you intend on utilizing for the corporation. I can almost guarantee that you are going to need a full-time accountant and lawyer. *Please* trust me on this point above all others," Martha stressed.

The two women talked, went to lunch, and talked some more. Martha had food bank business to attend to in the afternoon but they agreed to meet again after 5pm for dinner. Fabulia took a cab to the Boston Museum of Fine Arts. She wandered around, appreciating the paintings, sculptures, and exhibits—but she never stopped dwelling on the 'money thing.' By the time she caught another cab to meet Martha for dinner she was pretty well set on what she was going to pose to her new acquaintance.

They met at a small restaurant in the North End. After they each had a glass of wine in front of them Fabulia said, "Martha, I have had the afternoon to look at some incredible artwork and to consider what you've told me earlier today. I've got a proposal for you. I would like you to consider coming to work with me on this project full-time. I think I need your expertise and experience in this area. I don't have a clue about what kind of money you make now but I'll make this changeover worth your while. Secondly, to help ease the pain of their loss at the food bank I suggest that we make our first endowment to that organization for $100,000…

… Also, it is obvious to me that you love living in Boston. If you are at all interested in this proposal I would consider renting you an apartment in New Bedford so that you could spend three days a week there and four in Boston working out of your place as needed. I considered setting up shop in Boston, but I have kids and family to look after and my husband is going to be offshore quite often in the coming months. Oh, and you asked for a start-up dollar figure for this project..."

Fabulia pushed a piece of paper across the table to Martha Vandehorn...

"I've been wanting to unload that since about 3:30. Shall we order? I'm thinking the Lobster Fra Diavlo sounds about right."

Martha was speechless.

"Do you realize that this sum is on the same level with what Andrew Carnegie started his first endowment corporation with? This is really big money. I've gotta re-think your whole deal now."

After some good food, a touch more wine, and a lot of laughter they agreed to meet during the coming week to edge a little closer towards bringing this whole thought train to some form of reality.

^

It was a slow day at the curio shop. A quick storm cell had barreled through earlier in the morning scattering the tourists. Carol-Jean loved these storms. The thunder bouncing off of the canyon walls accentuated the sound, and the lightning made her think of giant camera flashes. She thought maybe some god up in the sky was taking pictures for his scrapbook.

She dusted and tidied up a bit, then sat down behind the counter and picked up a retail trade magazine. She stopped at an ad that caught her attention. The heading said, "SHARK AFICIANODO EXTRAVAGANZA. Jaws. Fins. Skin. Fossil Teeth. Liver Oil. Great White Videos, and more..." This was interesting to her. She scanned the ad three times and wrote down the dates, address and telephone numbers.

CHAPTER NINE

VICTOR JANES was trying his damnedest not to act smug, but sometimes he couldn't help himself. It now appeared as if the whole town of New Bedford wanted to work on the *Gambling Lady*. It actually sounded as if some people in town expected him to fire the Nicaraguan and Vietnamese portion of the crew so that some "real Americans," as one man put it, could take their places on the boat. But Victor's whole crew was working out really well. They were part of his team. He never considered replacing any of them.

During the second day of their maiden voyage Raphael, Octavio, and Emilio noted that nobody had died, and the boat had not sunk. In fact, it appeared as if everyone else aboard was quite pleased. It was obvious that money was being made here. It wasn't the first time that a superstition had left all concerned feeling somehow cheated. They ended their brief strike and hopped on the band wagon.

It was now mid-August and the *Gambling Lady* had logged five back-to-back trips in roughly three months. Victor could have squeezed in one or two more, but it was imperative that he be present with his freight forwarder to get the first two shipments of the finished product loaded and off to Lisbon. He sent off two ocean-freight freezer containers holding 40,000 lbs. of shrimp in each one.

The fishing had been good. They'd all gotten the routine down as pat as could be. Victor, Van, and Gideon gleaned a little more knowledge each time they set out and hauled back the trawl. They were all learning about streamlining the harvesting and packaging processes.

It soon became clear that Auntie Di was the factory boss. She had a knack for arranging these beautiful shrimp perfectly prior to freezing them. Nobody onboard was surprised or opposed to this development— it seemed natural. Teddy and Di got along like long-lost siblings. When mechanical difficulties arose these two found that they could discuss the problem in French without too much misunderstanding. Fact was, the whole crew could have handled three to four times the volume output, but quality would have then taken a down-turn, and everyone understood that they had to keep the quality up if they wanted to get top dollar.

The only sore spot with Victor were the nodules. He couldn't get away from them. They were present to one degree or another wherever he caught shrimp. When he did lose the nodules he would lose the shrimp also. There was something almost symbiotic between these two items. Far be it from Victor to even try to figure out the reason for this. As long as he saw shrimp he was happy. He didn't really care about the rocks.

Di just smiled to herself and kept working. 'Mum' was definitely the word, as far as she was concerned.

Gideon Bloom kept *his* word and had taken a few of the nodules down to Wood's Hole Oceanographic Institute so that a couple of his academic chums could have a look. The response was fairly ho-hum on the face of it, but it didn't take long for the corporate grapevine to start churning and soon talk of these "turds with teeth" found its' way to a CEO's office in New York, and then into the Department of the Interior in Washington D.C. Thereafter a lot of whispering took place in the hallowed Capitol halls, within five boardrooms around the globe, and then finally, inside of City Hall in New Bedford, Massachusetts.

The problem, if a person did in fact view it as a problem, was a number of specific rare metals had suddenly become widely sought after. Computer technology advancements were leapfrogging at an alarming rate. These nodules not only contained manganese, copper, nickel, and iron, but also held small percentages of precious and semi-precious metals such as cadmium, lithium, cobalt, molybdenum, platinum and gold.

Compounding this 'problem', was the fact that new smelting procedures made separation of these various elements infinitely easier than it had ever been before. Capping it all off, value speculation on the nodules was now running from one dollar per pound to as high as eight dollars per pound. And these nodules were *dense.*

Victor Janes couldn't have cared less. In his eyes they provided no sustenance, he couldn't eat them, therefore they did not warrant his attention. Victor was intent on using all of his hours towards the capture of Royal Reds.

∧

During her first five trips the *Gambling Lady* had only grossed 123,000 pounds at an average price of $5.30 per pound. Victor had a hefty set of expenses each month, but he did not have a bank note, and he wanted to keep everyone happy. He took forty percent off of the top of each trip and paid the crew. Van, Teddy, and Gideon were considered "officers" so they also received a small percentage from the boat's sixty percent net after all expenses were paid. Nobody was complaining so far and the future looked great as their per-trip volume was increasing every time they went out.

∧

During their fourth trip Victor discovered that it was useless to set the net out during darkness when the moon was in the final week of a full moon phase. It seemed as if the shrimp either burrowed deep into the bottom, or rose upwards in the water column well above the height of the head-rope on the trawl. He couldn't catch a one at night until the full moon phase was at least three days past. For this reason they were laying-to one evening during their sixth trip out to Atlantis Canyon, letting the boat drift where it may. It was mirror-calm with not a breath of wind. A slight shroud of fog drifted around them which exaggerated the three dimensional effect of the sodium vapor deck lights.

Everyone but Van and Octavio were either in the galley playing cards or in their racks catching a nap. While they smoked, Van and Octavio conversed sporadically in English and Spanish. It was an interesting exercise that both men enjoyed. Octavio found the English language somewhat odd and contradictory in its idiomatic structure and Van was enjoying the straight-forwardness of Spanish.

Suddenly, Octavio grabbed Van's arm and pointed over the rail. Van gasped and his knees started to give out on him as he let his eyes scan away from the boat. Thousands, no, *tens* of thousands of eyes were all staring at them. They were so thick that he could not discern water between them. It was alien, and eerie, and gave him instant goose-bumps. It took him a good ten seconds to recognize them as squid, all attracted to the deck lights, all hovering around the boat as if they were basking in the sodium vapor glow. Van pulled his eyes away and made a beeline for the galley.

Auntie Di was the first one out on deck. She immediately started yelling orders in Vietnamese, then in French, with a few English "hurry, hurries" mixed in. Within ten minutes Victor, Van, and Gideon had a fine-mesh net attached to a wooden gaff-hook pole. Vinh, Dan, and Emilio took one side while Jazzy, Octavio, and Rafael handled the other. In a ragged unison, they all worked the net into the water then down the side of the boat until they came to the stern and could go no further.

With Di yelling instructions, they closed up the net and started hauling it onboard. Finally the whole mass came over the rail. Everyone scrambled to open up this make-shift trawl. Jazzy was the first one to have a jet of ink hit him square in the face. Di started laughing and pointing at him as they got the net fully opened, then the ink really started to fly. It was pandemonium, everyone laughing and yelling. Nobody was spared. They'd managed to catch about 200 pounds of live squid. Everyone was whooping and hollering. Jazzy scooped up a bucketful and headed for the galley. He had a great recipe for baked squid, stuffed with chourico, of course.

Gideon was saying, "This is great…just so cool. These are *Illex illecebrosus* or summer squid. See how they change color? Those are chromatophores in their skin that expand and contract as the squid get agitated. These cephalopods only have a life-span of about a year and I'd say that they're close to the end of their life cycle. Look… some of them are carrying eggs…"

Di butted in and said, "Hey, teacha. Tomorrow you teach. Now we catch, OK?"

In a blink everyone got back to it without thinking twice. Within fifteen minutes they had their side-trawl modified and back in the water. After the second pass and about 200 more pounds of squid on deck, Auntie Di organized the factory crew down below and they started freezing. Around 4:00 a.m. the squid seemed to lose interest. The deck crew stumbled into the galley to be met by the unmistakable smell of chourico and squid. Di arrived shortly after and announced that they had frozen 305 ten kilo boxes of squid. Everyone was happy except for Gideon.

"Victor, what are we going to do with all this squid?"

"Well, I guess we'll sell them, Gid. They're really good eating and they got a good freeze. Worst comes to worse I guess they could be sold to the Swordfish long-liners for bait..."

"But Vic, you'd better hope the Clam Cops aren't around when we get in. You're forgetting about those fucking by-catch rules they attached to your fishing permit."

"Oh hell, Gideon. It's just a little bit of squid for Christ sake," Vic shouted. "Besides, they haven't boarded us once since the first trip. We'll be fine. You can log every pound of squid in the reports you have to submit to the Feds. I'm not too worried about it."

Gideon shook his head doubtfully and said, "Alrighty then, Vic, I'll do that, but I think you'd do well to pay a little more attention to the small details here. Whether you know it or not, you are a marked man back in town. People like a success story, but they just *adore* an about-face failure follow-up." With that Gideon turned and headed for his bunk, shaking his head as he moved.

Victor was left standing on deck, alone, scratching his brow, wondering, *"What's gotten into him, anyway?"* But in the back of his head the 'pay attention' alarm was pinging. He dismissed it and headed for his own bunk. He also was tired from their long night of squidding.

CHAPTER TEN

FABULIA and Martha were in their new offices in New Bedford poring over statistic sheets for non-profit organizations and endowment foundations within the United States. This was the first time Fabulia had ever used a computer. They had become commercially available about a year or so prior, but nobody in the DaSilva or Janes households had seen fit to buy one until now. Martha Vanderhorn insisted that they start out with two of them for the office. She felt that Fabulia needed to have her own unit to work on so that she could learn at her own pace after Martha got her started on the basics.

"As you can well imagine, this internet thing is going to change the whole damn structure of society," Martha said. "Five years ago we would have been looking through mimeographed paper lists that we would have then had to categorize ourselves by hand. Now all the grunt work is done and collated and we can even access a trends chart, as you can see here."

Fabulia was actually beginning to see an array of factors inherent to this charity business. It was all new, all interesting, and some of it was disconcerting to the point that she began questioning the validity of this endeavor. Her night-time reading was giving her pangs of anxiety.

She was wondering, *"was this the right thing to do?"* Could she, through her foundation, help cure some of the ills of society, and thus create a better world? Or would she actually make a negative impact through her own misguided moral concept of right and wrong? Many of the books she'd read in the last month were full of energized ideals and dreams, but there were also a few that cataloged the misdeeds and misdirection of many a foundation based on intellectual elitist concepts, and ego-driven stubbornness. It appeared as if many foundations started out on sure footing at inception, but veered far off of their primary course after the original founders either stepped aside or died off.

Steel magnate Andrew Carnegie started his first endowment corporation in 1911 under the tenet of educational advancement for the general population of the United States. He believed that knowledge was the basis for invention, and that invention was critical to the growth of industrial America.

Were his motives purely altruistic? Fabulia was skeptical, thinking that, as with many concepts, humans could dream them up but were, in fact, unable to act upon them without throwing *self* into the mix. Carnegie's philanthropy soon melded in with politics which Fabulia saw as inevitable. Indirectly his influence and power grew exponentially. Fabi smiled to herself thinking that, sometimes the easiest way to get what you *really* wanted, was to walk to the back door.

In the early years of the 20th century there seemed to be, according to the media, a contest going on between Andrew Carnegie and John D. Rockefeller. The competition being, which one could give away the most money the fastest. "Newspaper hyperbole," Fabulia thought. Much good was actually created by these two men, no matter how much money they threw out there or what anyone thought of their motives.

These were the early, pristine, years of monetary philanthropy. Carnegie built libraries across the country. Rockefeller concentrated on health and scientific philanthropy. Both men created universities and institutions of learning. This was all good, and fit in well with the growth of the United States— but times were changing.

In the 1930's Henry and Edsel Ford started the Ford Foundation, primarily as a tax shelter. By 1954 its endowments and expenditures far surpassed the Carnegie and Rockefeller Foundations combined output. An era of free money had begun right alongside free love in the 1960's. Second generation Ford Foundation trustees decided that it was time to go *"progressive."*

As a result, a number of activist plans or Community Action Programs were initiated that were subsequently adopted by the federal government. In essence many of these programs were skewed to the point that they were more detrimental to many of the general population that they were set up to benefit. It soon became apparent that moral haut monde and social activism were one and the same *and also* the new rule.

Fabulia voiced her concerns to Martha which brought them into an ongoing debate. Martha felt certain that a large portion of the current socio-economic problems in the U.S. were created by big business and right wing politics. It seemed as if Martha had her own built-in set of fears that she had to blame on *something*.

She was proud to be labeled a left-wing liberal, and she was sure that the only way to combat the total evil take-over of society by *"Polibiz,"* was to be ever vigilant and ensure that the government was never allowed to ignore the needs of those less fortunate in our society.

On the other hand Martha's new friend and business partner was now learning that sitting on the fence was painful. Fabulia never felt politically connected before, but she was realizing that a personal belief structure involved politics whether you wanted to participate or not. She grew up learning that, if she wanted something, she had to go out and get it. If she had to work hard in the interim to achieve her goal, so be it.

Fabulia was now at a point where she saw philanthropy as a savior with a silver spoon. She was worried that many people on the welfare train had given up on trying to find work in order to survive and fulfill any kind of an "American Dream."

"Martha, I'm just saying that I think we have got to be very careful about where we start throwing money. We're both agreed, the shape that this country is in now is pretty wretched, but we differ in our views on the reasons. You feel that more has to be done to support the masses, and I'm just not so sure that's such a great idea. Free money, free *anything* is asking for trouble. 'Hey, gimme a dolla. Cool. OK, now gimme a nutha.' This kind of pandering just perpetuates the moment and does nothing to help anybody in the long-haul."

"Well, jeez Fabulia, I've never thought that trying to help people could be viewed in such a light but I guess I've got to admit that you may have a fair point. So what do you suggest? How do you want to proceed?"

"I'm thinking that we could concentrate on children and the elderly.

I'm not saying that we should totally forget about everyone in between, but, as I see it, if we help just one child start out right that kid may just carry it into his adult years. If we can keep just one kid from taking the low road we've succeeded. As for the elderly, well their options are running out with age and a lot of them have no help from their children or anyone else. Why not support assisted living or adult day-care? I think that if we dug into these two age groups we'd find a pile of areas where we could actually help children get set up for the long-haul...

... When they fall into the latter category maybe they'll be better equipped to deal with their own needs. Maybe they'll have passed along some stronger standards to their children who will then be in a better position to care for their parents when they get older. I just don't know. As Victor would say, maybe I'm just pissing into the wind. I mean I've got high hopes tempered with a lot of misgivings. We can do some good here, but I don't want to end up with egg on my face in the process."

"O.K. Fabulia, I get the jist of it. Listen, I met this woman yesterday at lunch. She works in the district attorney's office in town here. Let me call her. I'll bet that she could give us some ideas. Maybe we could start out right here in New Bedford."

The next day they met with Leslie MacLanahan over lunch. She gave them an ear-full and then some.

"I can give you a list of every organization in Bristol County that could use some financial help. There are probably about 150 of them. You can pick and choose. If you need background on any of them call me. I'd like to get involved with you on this project but I've got to be careful considering where I work. I can't officially give you any legal help, but we can keep meeting for lunch. Don't hesitate to call me. Some of these organizations are definitely better than others. I'll do the weeding for you. And this afternoon I will fax you the particulars on the two women that I can suggest as candidates for your legal and accounting needs."

Rita Montrose was retained as corporate counsel, and Emily Fagundes was hired as in-house accountant. The *Constant Vigil Foundation* made its' second endowment four months later directly to the

80

city of New Bedford under a contract whose main points stated that the monies could only be used towards an after-school day care program for school children in grades one through six. The funding would become available on an annual basis only after *Constant Vigil* reviewed the previous year's books and deemed the spending within the contractual parameters. Lastly it was stipulated that the city must put forth a question in the next electoral cycle asking the tax-payers for matching funding. It was also verbally agreed upon that, if *Constant Vigil* was happy with the first annual report and the taxpayers stepped up to the plate, *CVF* would increase the endowment two-fold so that grades seven through twelve could be wrapped into the program.

Constant Vigil's second endowment went to the Walker Retirement Center. This one involved a three year endowment contract to help with the refurbishment of the existing nursing home structure and the construction of a new assisted-living wing.

CVF's third endowment went off the 'children and elderly' track line but all four of *Constant Vigil's* principals felt that this was a necessary cause especially after Leslie MacLanahan showed them some statistics. The one that hit Fabulia estimated that six percent of all pregnant women in the United States were physically abused. She did some quick math in her head and was surprised to see that her figures coincided with what Leslie MacLanahan was saying.

"Every single day that the county courthouse is open we see, at the least, one case coming through that involves some form of domestic violence against women. Of those cases, every fifth one involves a pregnancy. One a week, fifty-two weeks in the year. Those are just the cases that we've seen coming through the courts, excluding the women who are too scared to step forward...

...In Bristol County alone there are only five privately funded women's shelters and they are all full. Of those five the largest one is the best organized..."

"Can you get us some figures from this organization?" Fabulia interjected, "I want to know how much money they spend and on what.

How many women go through their doors in a year? What are they lacking that they really need? I want to go see the place. I think we all need to go."

Six days later, led by Leslie MacLanahan, Fabulia, Martha, Rita, and Emily arrived at the New Hope Women's Shelter. There was no sign out front and what windows there were had been placed high on the concrete structure and were all firmly barred—not to keep people from getting out, but to keep some from getting in.

The four new-comers all wore dubious expressions which only increased when Leslie rang the bell and a two by six inch slat in the door slid open. She stated her name and their appointment time with the director. After a pause they could all hear a steel bar scraping against the inside of the reinforced door. Locks turned and the door squeaked open on four oversized hinges. A very large, bald, heavily tattooed gentleman greeted and ushered them into the building.

Victor and Gramma Rose were both in the kitchen at the Janes residence when Fabulia arrived home that evening. She didn't say anything at first, just walked over to Victor, wrapped her arms around him and started to cry softly. "You fucking men," she said after a while. Rose drew in a sharp breath but sensed that something serious was going on here so she made no comment on Fabulia's language .

The three kids inched their way into the kitchen cautiously. Eddie started to cry when he saw his mom. She released Victor, snatched up her youngest and said, "It's OK kiddo. Mommy's just had a really bad day of it."

"What is it Mother?" asked young Rosa.

"Well I guess you could say I got an eye-opener this afternoon. A real painful, open wide, eye-opener. I'll be OK and I'll talk with you later about it, but right now I need to decompress a little." With that she handed off Eddie to Lori, went to the fridge, grabbed two beers, and headed for the living room with Victor in tow.

"So what gives Fabi? You look like you've aged five years since I saw you this morning. You look all of eighteen years old this evening." This got a small smile out of Fabi as she flopped onto the couch, took a pull off of her beer and shook her head to clear it, as if she'd just been sucker-punched.

"Remember, a few weeks ago I told you about a women's shelter that we were considering helping out..."

Victor nodded.

"...Well, today the five of us went over there for a visit. It was gruesome. In my wildest imagination I wouldn't have been able to come up with the violent shit that has been doled out to every one of these women and girls in that place. I mean, what sort of sick bastard would hit his fourteen year-old daughter in the face with a clothes iron because she was late getting home with his fucking pizza? And the iron was hot... then he beats the shit out of his pregnant wife when she tries to stop him from hurting their daughter any further? Holy Christ, what a shit-show... and these were just two of the women that place. Now there are 47 of them living inside of a cement box."

After a moment Victor sat down next to Fabulia and gently turned her chin so that she was looking at him.

"Sounds like that was surely a tough one today, Fabi. I think that I, at the least, understand your anger. Any guy that resorts to violence against women, and family to boot, most likely deserves to have his balls rearranged. But listen to me here, please. First off, don't start thinking in terms of 'fucking men.' That's just another overused, dangerous, generalization trap. All men are not pigs and all women are surely not angels. The fact is we're all human and therefore very, very *very* fallible. My personal concept of social progress works around decreasing that fallability. It's kinda why we came up with this plan for the foundation that you are now the boss of."

Fabulia let out a sigh and said, "OK. It *was* a tough one though. Jesus, what a world. I'll figure it out. But, tell me, Victor. Did I really look all of eighteen this morning?"

^

Joe made it home fifteen minutes before his wife rolled to a stop in front of the trailer. As he curried Dodger, Carol-Jean walked over to the corral, gave her horse, Yankee, an apple and asked, "So, how'd you make out today, Joe?"

"Eh, so-so, I guess. I only dug out six good teeth and that took me all day. I think I gotta start looking around for a new site. This one's about tapped out."

"About that, Joe. I was doing some reading today and found an ad for some sort of shark convention, of all things. It advertised shark teeth for sale. Maybe I should go to this thing next spring back east in Boston and see if I could buy the teeth and get you off of your knees and out of the canyon. Out of it for the work part, anyway.

Joe thought a moment then said, "Well, it's an idea, for sure. But you know, if the teeth don't come from the canyon you won't be able to tell the touristas that they do." His eyes glittered and he smiled as he waited for his wife's reply to this.

Carol-Jean lowered her voice as far as it would go and said, "Oh, heck. I'll just say, 'Many ancient teeth have been dug out of this canyon' or some such ominous thing, then I won't be fibbing."

CHAPTER ELEVEN

The fishing had gone from good to exceptional. In the past five months they had stocked close to 800,000 pounds of finished product. Victor hired on a full time port-captain who was in charge of not only ensuring that the frozen product was shipped out to Portugal in a timely fashion, but also made certain that Victor's company was paid likewise. He also was in charge of ordering mechanical parts for the engine-room, paper goods, packaging materials for the factory, and grub for Jazzy. Everything was running smoothly.

The boat was in port due to a wicked nor'easter that had stalled east of Nantucket whipping up winds reaching eighty knots in gusts, creating twenty-five foot seas, raining torrentially, and keeping the whole fleet tied up in the harbor.

It was mid-afternoon and all eight seats at the galley table were taken. Teddy picked up the deck of cards but before he could resume the game the weather deck hatch squeaked open and three wet men entered the galley. They looked at the game in progress then at all of the players around the galley table. The last guy seemed most interested in the pile of shark teeth at the center. After an awkward moment the lead man said, "I am Special Agent Robert Vargas from the National Marine Fisheries Service enforcement division. This is Sergeant Harold Biggs with Massachusetts Fish and Game, and Lieutenant Mierken Yorks with the Massachusetts State Police. We have a warrant to search this vessel. Is the captain onboard?"

Victor'd watched the men grope their way onto the boat from his perch in the aft control station, all the time wondering who this trio was, and what they wanted. He wasn't feeling overly optimistic, arriving in the galley just as Vargas started his introductions.

"Ah, yes sir. My name is Victor Janes. I am the captain and owner.

How can I help you today?"

"Captain Janes, as I stated we have a warrant with us to search this vessel. As a preliminary, I need to go through all of your licensing, paperwork, and logbooks. Would you please take us to your office onboard?"

"Okay then. Why don't we all go up to the pilot-house. I'll show you whatever you need. Jazzy, would you please bring up a pot of coffee and some mugs. I'm sure these gentlemen could use something hot. Dr. Bloom, would you please join us?"

With that Victor abruptly turned and headed up to the pilot-house. As Gideon took up the rear of the parade he motioned to his fellow card players, signaling them to clean up the gambling evidence. Gambling was still illegal in this state as far as he knew.

After three hours in the pilot-house under microscopic scrutiny by Vargas and Biggs, a haggard Victor re-entered the galley but he didn't stop. The whole troupe followed him down the companionway leading to the factory. Victor and Gideon gave them the full tour and they felt somewhat heartened. They were in full compliance with regulations down here, no question about it. Victor was trying to wrap it up when Lt. Yorks bent down and tugged at a small piece of rope extending out from between a water-tight inspection plate and the deck.

"Why is this piece of rope hanging out from this deck-plate? Do you have something in here, Cap? I want this plate opened."

Victor rolled his eyes and almost let loose with a snide remark, but Gideon caught his eye and shook his head. "Ah, well, okeedokee, lieutenant. Let me grab a wrench," Vic mumbled.

Victor removed the plate that accessed the now-dry flume tank. All five men peered into it. Ken Yorks bent down, grabbed the rope and yanked then pulled again, harder. It didn't budge and the lieutenant, very obviously, did not want to kneel on the deck and soil his suit. Gideon grabbed the line, knelt down and pulled. Slowly a burlap sack appeared, much to the delight of Yorks.

Victor muttered, "What the hell?"

All three law enforcement officials looked at him skeptically. Gideon hoisted the bag out of the tank, noting that there was another rope attached to the first bag that led back into the tank. Gideon started pulling again. Some fifteen minutes later the last bag in the chain came out of the tank. There were twenty-three stacked on the deck of the factory, all weighing about fifty pounds each. Vargas, Biggs, and Yorks were all staring at Victor Janes with predatory glee.

Victor stepped forward and said, "I guess I may as well do the honors." In one motion he opened his twine knife and slit the top bag length-wise. A cascade of manganese nodules poured forth. It was Lt. Yorks' turn to be surprised. "What the hell are these things?" He demanded.

Special Agent Vargas crouched down, picked up a nodule, and put it in his coat pocket.

Victor was caught completely off-guard for the third time that day. Gideon looked somewhat guilty. He'd known about these sacks for months as had everyone else on the boat, with the exception of Victor. Victor looked at Gideon with a puzzled face, "Ah, could you field this one, Gideon?" He asked, "I am kinda speechless right now."

Gideon told the law enforcement officers what the manganese nodules were, and where they came from. He broke a few open and showed them the metallic middle core with the shark tooth inside. He tried further to explain that the teeth were the reason that *someone* in the crew was amassing all of these bags.

Kenny Yorks appeared downcast, perhaps because he could see no way that these rocks were a violation of any law that he knew of—but his depression was short-lived.

"Captain Janes," Sergeant Biggs spoke up, "I should have asked you while we were in the wheel-house but it slipped my mind. Let's head back up there, please. I need to see your city permit for off-loading a commercial product across dockage within city limits."

Victor had a vague recollection of this permit being mentioned to him somewhere along the line, but he also seemed to remember someone else telling him that it was of no consequence, that the law pertaining to the permit had not been used actively for twenty years. This permit actually dated back to the eighteen hundreds when the city needed a way to make more money from barrels of whale oil being off-loaded by whalers. He'd certainly never heard of anyone getting pinched for not having one.

"Well, hell Sergeant," Victor started, "I've never even heard of any such permit. I do not have one. I hope it's not an arrestable offense." This last statement was made tongue-in-cheek with a grin, but apparently the state wildlife officer was not in a jocular frame of mind today.

"Mr. Janes, it is, in fact, an arrestable offense that holds a $2000 dollar fine, and/or up to a month in prison for the first time offenders. I am here-by placing you under arrest. Lt. Yorks, please cuff this man."

The Lieutenant had Victor spun around, cuffed, and headed for the companionway within five seconds. Gideon was dumbfounded. He'd never heard of anyone getting busted over this particular permit. As they all climbed the steps to the galley Gideon was rapidly analyzing the last four hours. Before he could get any further they all entered the galley. Jazzy stopped talking to Teddy as Victor entered with Ken Yorks right behind him. Jazzy was puzzled with Victor's posture then he caught the glint of the cuffs. With a roar he sprang across the galley swearing profusely in Portuguese.

Teddy had time to grab Jazzy's right arm and slow down the man's forward momentum but Jazzy's left hand shot out and caught the lieutenant with a glancing punch off of his fore-head.

Gideon grabbed Jazzy's left arm as Di got in between Victor and Jazzy and started pushing him backwards. Everyone was yelling. Portuguese, French, Vietnamese, Spanish. Multi-lingual mayhem. Yorks finally got his pistol out but Bob Vargas yelled, "Put that fucking thing away, you fool. This boat is made of steel. If you fire that the ricochet could come back and kill *you*. Everyone back off and allow us to get Captain Janes up to the dock." Before they got to the entry-way Victor said, "Someone should call Fabulia so she can call our lawyer…please."

With that Victor and the law enforcement officers were out onto the deck. It was dark, pouring rain, and the wind was screeching. The icing on the ugly-cake was the low tide. After a short discussion the law officers determined that Victor would have to be briefly un-cuffed so that he could climb the wharf ladder up to the dock. Kenny Yorks went up first to make sure that the prisoner didn't bolt when he got top-side. They finally all got off the boat and up to the Crown Victoria on the wharf. Captain Janes looked like a very despondent, bedraggled, drowned rat as he was slid into the back seat.

The *Gambling Lady* crew made up the rear of the procession out onto the deck. They all stood there after Victor was gone, gawking at each other, wondering what had just happened. Finally Gideon said, "Alright guys, let's get back inside and dry off. I gotta go make some phone calls. Teddy, please find out from Di where Van is. We better get him back here in case we have to move the boat. Jazzy— get something hot going. I'm starved as I'm sure everyone else is. Let's not all get mired down because of this crap. I'm sure it looks worse than it really is."

This last pronouncement by Dr. Bloom was met with dubious expressions all around. Without Victor where were they all at?

CHAPTER TWELVE

FABULIA was mulling over the concept of fate as she sat at her kitchen table. Specifically, she was wondering if kismet and karma were interchangeable. Were these charges against Victor perpetrated by town's people who took offense to the *Gambling Lady's* ethnic crew? Or maybe it was a result of the well known fact that they were bringing in loads of money? She could easily see it all happening. *"Predestination, my ass,"* she muttered to herself. She'd been so wrapped up in the *Constant Vigil* business that she had ignored all of the signs: the cynical looks, people turning away from her in the supermarket and more. She asked herself, *"…or am I becoming paranoid?"*

She was alone this morning. All three of her children were at school. Victor was hopefully going to be released after seeing the judge sometime today. He'd been in jail all weekend waiting on the guy. Fabulia and the family attorney Lucien Fernandes saw Vic on Saturday and Fabulia was allowed to spend an hour with him yesterday.

She had not brought in a copy of the Sunday edition of the Standard Times, the local newspaper. She knew it would anger him and right now Victor needed to remain calm—that way when he was allowed out of jail, he could help them all figure out how to best handle this pile of charges tendered against him. To add fuel to the fire Jazzy Coelho had been arrested Saturday morning and charged with assault on a police officer.

To top it all off, Raphael Chamorro was taken into custody yesterday for being an illegal alien. Lucien was defending both of those two men as well. He felt that Jazzy's deal would take some finagling but in the final call Jazzy'd come out alright, maybe a year's probation. Raphael Chamorro was a different deal. Customs & Immigration were a hard-nosed lot. He'd be lucky if Lucien was allowed to get the guy a taxi to the airport. Fabulia grabbed the newspaper and started reading the article for the third time.

CAPTAIN ARRESTED ON QUESTIONABLE CHARGES
BY STAFF WRITER Tom Walsh

In an incident Friday evening Victor Janes, the captain and owner of the factory trawler Gambling Lady, was arrested and charged with a number of state and federal violations that included: by-catch volume violations(one count), targeted specie volume report discrepancies(five counts), harboring an illegal alien(one count), not maintaining the appropriate permits for transferring a commercial product across dockage within city limits(one count), and maintaining an illegal gambling operation(one count). When contacted and asked for further comment Lt. Mierken Yorks of the Massachusetts State Police said that the investigation was "ongoing." An independent source said that the National Marine Fisheries Service was looking into the possibility of charging Janes with harvesting manganese nodules without a permit although it is unclear at this time how the alleged nodules could fall under the jurisdiction of the fisheries service. There were reportedly about 2000 lbs. of the nodules hidden inside of the vessel. In a related incident Joao Coelho, the cook aboard the Gambling Lady, was charged with assault on a police officer. Also expected to be charged, is crewmember Raphael Chamorro, a Nicaraugan national, for being within the borders of the United States with an expired visa.

Victor Janes first gained notoriety in New Bedford when he won the largest-ever Mega-Dollars purse in the nation at the time for a reported $286 million dollars. Captain Janes' lawyer could not be reached for comment.

Later that morning Fabulia met Lucien Fernandes at the courthouse. She almost gasped when she saw Victor being led into the court-room. He looked a mess but his face lit up when he saw Fabi. He gave her a smile and a thumbs-up. After only three minutes Victor's case was called.

Judge Haverstraw scanned some paperwork then said, "Mr. Janes, I see here that you have federal, as well as state charges filed against you. Within this court you only have to answer to the state charges which amount to one charge of not maintaining the proper unloading permit within city limits and maintaining an illegal gambling operation. How do you plead?"

Before Lucien could speak Victor said, "Guilty, your honor, on the first charge. Never even heard of that permit but I suppose my ignorance is of no relevance to the law. As for the second charge I guess I'd have to plead no contest. There was no money shown on our galley table. No foul, no harm I guess I'd haveta say."

The judge was intently peering at Victor , trying to detect a touch of sarcasm or scorn. He saw neither. After scanning his paperwork he said, "Very well Captain Janes. In that case, as this is your first offense, I hear-by order you to pay a fine of $250.00 plus court costs to the clerk for the permit offense. Regarding this gambling charge, I'm throwing it out. There is no corroborating evidence that I can see here…

…Gentlemen, please approach the bench", as he motioned Lucien and Victor forward. The prosecuting attorney made a move to come forward also but the judge waved him back. When they were within whisper range the judge said, "I do not quite understand what is going on here. In the past thirty years while sitting on this bench I have never seen anyone prosecuted for lack of this particular permit. I'll guess that ninety-five percent of the boats in our harbor do not have this permit. Mr. Fernandes, I suggest that you take care in the coming weeks. It would appear that someone has a bone to pick with Mr. Janes." Down came the gavel. "Next case," the judge barked.

Lucien Fernandes grabbed Victor by the elbow, turned him around, and started down the aisle. He wanted to get Victor out of there before he said anything else. "Victor, I'm your lawyer goddammit," he hissed, "I talk, not you. We went over this."

"Well, shit. I know, Lucien. But he was looking at me when he asked the question. 'Look 'em straight in the eye when you speak,' my mother always said. I was nervous."

Lucien sighed and shook his head.

"Aw hell," Victor muttered, "I'll do better next time. Am I going to be doing this a lot, Lucien?"

"I'll try to minimize it, Victor. You're out of jail for the time being but you most definitely are not out of the woods. The Feds are still stirring the pot and we all know they can brew up some pretty quirky shit these days."

They met Fabi at the courtroom gate and out they went. Victor inhaled a long, deep breath when they got outside.

"So what's the bottom line on all this, Lucien? I don't think I fudged my books all that bad, at least not intentionally. I guess they got me on the squid but that was only one trip. If you averaged out the by-catch volume for the last six months it would most likely be under the five percent mandate. The gambling charge was a sham; and this nodule thing is a joke. The fisheries service can't possibly think that they can make a big deal over this, can they? I mean, rocks don't have gills, huh?"

Lucien chuckled, "Never underestimate the creative zeal of the authorities, Victor. If they want you bad enough they will most likely succeed. If they can't *get* you bad enough, they sure as hell will make your general everyday life a pain in the ass until you fuck up again—then they're on top of you like piranha on chicken livers. You two go home. Let's meet tomorrow at my office. Right now I've got to get ready to meet the judge again this afternoon with Jazzy Coelho."

Off Lucien went, his large, rotund frame shuffling briskly up the street as he whistled a somewhat off-key dirge, as if he were gleaning a touch of joy from this whole affair.

^

Joe figured he'd give the site one more try before he went prospecting for a new one. It was just after Labor Day. He could dig right through October but after that it started to get too cold for his old bones. Better to keep the fire going at home, come November. Dodger stopped as they arrived at the site. Joe slid off of the saddle and grabbed his tool bag.

After an hour, to his surprise, he hit pay-dirt. It was a very nice specimen, about two inches long and one wide. Maybe too big for earrings but not too large for a pendant. Using his brush, he dusted and found another tooth right below at the same spot.

After fifteen minutes and six more teeth, Joe knew that he had a very rare find- a complete set of jaws minus the cartilage that held all of the teeth together. He set every one out just as he had found it. Many of the surface teeth had four or five more right behind, just as he'd read about and seen in photographs. Three hours later he had the full set excavated. A total of seventy-three very clean, beautiful teeth lay before him.

CHAPTER THIRTEEN

VICTOR AND FABULIA spent a low-key afternoon and evening at home with the family. Victor took two showers with an hour in between each. He couldn't seem to stop the odor of stale sweat mixed with piss, vomit and disinfectant from invading his memory. Edmund and Gramma Rose came by to drop Eddie off and got easily talked into staying for supper. It was helpful that all of his immediate family members were present. Victor only had to tell the story once more and be done with it.

After Victor went through it all, he managed to get a moment alone to speak with Edmund.

"Vic, you know and I know, you've never tried to do anything, any of this, other than straight up and honest. We all know it. Don't let this shit drag you under. We know what you're all about. Who knows? You might be able to turn these nodule things to your advantage. Are they worth anything?"

"Edmund, I've never even thought about that. Hell, I just thought I was doing O.K. by catching shrimp. I've never-ever given those damned stones a second thought. I guess it may be worth looking at, but I get the feeling that I'm going to find out before I have much to say about it. Apparently the Federales are going to take care of that for me. Lucien Fernades seems to think they might have a glimmer of a case there. We'll see."

Lucien was somewhat upbeat the next afternoon, as he reviewed the day with Victor.

"Jazzy Coelho got off pretty easy, considering the 'assault on a police officer' charge. I think Judge Haverstraw was more pissed off at Lieutenant Yorks for aggrandizing the whole affair than he was at Jazzy for slapping the fool. Of course Jazzy's genuine, heart-felt crying swayed the judge a bit. Nothing like seeing a seventy year old bulldog shed tears in public. He got a years' probation and had to promise not to even look at Yorks ever again…

…Chamorro, on the other hand, was not so fortunate. He's being deported. His two buddies were allowed in to see him this morning, but I think the feds'll put him on a plane Thursday—and oh, ya… you'll love this: Raphael told Customs he'd make his own arrangements to get home so they jokingly gave him phone access, thinking he was some stupid wetback that couldn't dial his way out of a wet paper bag. He called a friend of his who's a travel agent in Providence. Five hours later, a one-way ticket shows up via private courier at the detention center. Providence to Miami, Miami to Managua, all *first class*. The Customs boys were frosted. They thought they were throwing some spic bum outa' the country, not the fucking Aga Khan… Great theater today, just great….anyway…"

The counselor continued on with his recap of the day's events, "With regard to your stuff, the authorities are scratching their collective heads and asses. Apparently— and you didn't tell me this Victor, you silly man, you are not the legal fucking captain of your own boat. Jesus, what a break. I'm told the State Department is even involved….

…This guy Nguyen Van's whole family was granted political asylum from Vietnam some years ago. A whole slew of them. Your captain Nguyen has had a stellar record since he entered the country in the late 1970's. His daddy has become a renowned surgeon in Seattle. The Fisheries Service wants to transfer the charges over to your captain but the State Department wants it all to go away.

They're scared this flap will create some severe political repercussions if they appear to prosecute a politically sensitive immigrant that is now a naturalized citizen of the United States. I think you alone will probably get a letter of reprimand in your file with NMFS for the squid thing, but that will be it. The only fly in the ointment right now are these nodules. The Fisheries Service is still looking into them. I'm not happy to say that this all may get somewhat interesting because of those things, though I cannot quite figure out how."

So the up-shot of all this was that Victor was allowed to go fishing again. The State Department had their way, much to the chagrin of the Fisheries Service, Massachusetts Fish & Game, The State Police, and a few private citizens.

Victor was welcomed back on the dock like some kind of war-hero. All of a sudden he was back on the *positive* side of life after a brief hiatus. *"How does this happen so fast?"*, he wondered to himself.

Auntie Di was the first crewmember to welcome him back on the boat. She didn't cry but she was shaking a bit. She just kept saying, "I sorry Victor, I so sorry for teeth trouble!"

"Worry about nothing, Auntie—who gives a damn? They're only teeth."

Out the hurricane barrier they steamed; the *Gambling Lady* was in motion once again.

CHAPTER FOURTEEN

WHEN MOST MARINERS are offshore anywhere from five to five-hundred miles or more from land they are most definitely in a different mind-set. The distance volume really doesn't matter so much as the delineation medium does. They are separated from their families and brethren on land, the separation medium being the saltwater. In the back of their minds they're subconsciously wondering if their families are alright. They hope for the best but recognize that there's not much they can do from where they are located. They keep bouncing along on whatever their compass course may be, and eventually they make land-fall and then it all, most likely, falls in their laps like a big, cold, wet, exasperated codfish. "Where the hell you been? We been needin' you."

Victor was dwelling on all of this as he sat alone in the captain's chair up in the pilothouse. The day was warm for the first week in December. The wind was louder than a whisper but less than an insistent yell. Long, three foot swells accompanied the *Gambling Lady*'s slow march over the surface while the net trundled along the bottom. Good fishing weather, and really good fishing it was. He'd found a little piece of ground on Veatch Canyon that was yielding almost a ton and a half of large shrimp each tow.

There was very little detritus or by-catch and very few nodules. Auntie Di wasn't even bothering to look for the things as she worked in the factory— though it was interesting to note that all of the nodule sacks that had been hidden away in the flume tank had miraculously disappeared. Victor had to laugh with this thought. He was sure she had them all squirreled away somewhere off the boat. He flashed on a beautifully lurid picture of Auntie Di with a big old wooden mallet in her little hand maniacally smashing nodules to get at those teeth…

^

The whole crew had made up a three car caravan to escort Raphael to the airport in Providence. A fourth car took up the rear containing two gentlemen from Customs and Immigration. Their job was to insure that this illegal immigrant got on the plane. There were many cheers and tears as Raphael walked down the concourse towards his gate with his two escorts. He was met by two more gents in Miami to insure that he did not stray from his course to Managua.

Raphael was excited to be going home. Both Emilio and Octavio were jealous and somewhat low in spirit. Both men had actually considered quitting the boat and going with Raphael but, after a day-long discussion they both decided that it would be very inconsiderate of them to quit on Victor at this point in time and they certainly couldn't justify walking away from all of the money that was being made. They could go home later.

So the *Gambling Lady* fished on. Victor was on a roll with this new spot that he'd found and he was in no great hurry to head back in to town. They stayed out for eighteen days, finally heading east northeast with a very substantial volume of shrimp in the hold. Gideon came up into the pilot-house with the final tally.

"Here's a beaut for you, Cap. We're heading in with more shrimp in the hold now than we caught for the last three trips combined!" They had 147,906 pounds of finished product on board, the majority of which were large and jumbo sizes. The gross dollar figure would most likely eke out to about $828,273 and change. This meant that the crew share for this trip alone would pay out around $33,130.94 per man.

^

Joe and Carol-Jean had argued and left it unresolved. She wanted Joe to turn the whole batch of teeth into earrings and pendants. That would have given her twenty-one pendants and twenty-six sets of earrings which would have paid out over sixty-five hundred dollars. Joe said that he could re-set the whole collection into two pieces of carved, shaped piñon wood to simulate the jaw cartilage. Carol agreed that it would look quite amazing, a full set of jaws, hanging from the ceiling in her shop, but could they possibly sell the thing whole for the kind of money that the earrings and pendants were guaranteed to bring in as set pieces?

Joe was off in the canyon while Carol-Jean brooded in the store but they were both thinking a similar thought. Money could sweeten the coffee but it could also sour the stew in a heart-beat.

CHAPTER FIFTEEN

THE CONCEPT of *Freedom of the Seas* was first put into writing during the 17th century. This principal limited the sovereign control of the oceans to a narrow band extending seaward from the shore outward to three nautical miles. Beyond that delineation the oceans were considered a free-for-all zone.

This three mile figure was not arrived at inadvertently. In those days three miles was the outer limit of most of the larger cannon fire's reach. Soon after World War II many countries extended their sovereign rights to twelve nautical miles.

Oil exploration in the Gulf of Mexico started in earnest in 1947. By 1954 oil extraction in the Gulf had grown to a little less than one million tons, and by 1967 that figure had grown exponentially to 400 million tons. Technological advancements were key. This economic boon spurred many politicians and business tycoons alike towards the consideration of extending sovereign claims out much further than a paltry 12 miles.

It wouldn't be long before that boundary line was extended out to 200 nautical miles.

In the late 1960's, the zeitgeist was that the freedom-of-the-seas regulations were out-dated and in need of refinement, hence the creation of the United Nations Seabed Committee which soon evolved into the International Seabed Authority or the ISA.

In 1973 the third United Nations Conference on the Law of the Sea was convened, and nine years later the UN Convention on the Law of the Sea was adopted. This convention was ratified by over 160 nations world-wide.

It took every working day of those nine years to delve through the minutia, disputes, and intricacies created by our complex modern-day world regarding the equitable, collective rule of the oceans. Most all of the joining nations outwardly embraced this multitude of mandates, but privately some of them scoffed. Many wondered how these rules could possibly be enforced, and who would actually do the enforcing.

To facilitate nations having continental shelf areas that extended beyond the 200 mile limit, The ISA added an addendum into the mix stating that said nations could extend their domain out to 350 miles or to 100 miles past the 2500 meter depth mark—but in an effort to level the playing field and mollify those countries less fortunate in their continental shelf size, the ISA mandated that all countries exercising their right to extension must share in the proceeds from their mining efforts in the extended areas with all of the other, less fortunate club members.

Deep-sea mining was now considered a huge challenge. A struggle to find the best method of picking up stones that were from 3,000 to 15,000 feet beneath the surface of the ocean was on. To do it in multiples so that it made viable economics was the crux of the problem. Many complex ideas and schemes were bounced around and tried but none of them were relatively cost-efficient. Nobody ever considered asking a fisherman about how these goals might be achieved.

^

Victor wasn't aware of what was transpiring shore-side because he'd elected to leave the Single Side Band radio off for the last week while they concentrated on the shrimp. Fabulia tried calling him multiple times for the last three days straight, then she gave up. He'd have to deal with the surprise factor when he hit the dock.

It seemed as if someone had taken note of Victor's most recent problems with the Authorities; more specifically, somebody or some organization had taken an acute interest in those damn manganese nodules. First, Fabulia had received a strange, somewhat garbled call from a man asking for Captain Victor Janes. When Fabulia stated that he was currently offshore the man stated that his name was Dr. Guillermo Manfredi and that he was calling from the International Seabed Authority office at the

United Nations in New York. He would call again at a later date. The guy didn't even ask when he should try back before he hung up on her.

The next day she got a very curt call from Special Agent Robert Vargas with NMFS. When she stated that Victor was offshore he actually wanted to know if she had his current position in latitude and longitude figures, as if she might have been lying to him. She almost told the guy off but held it in check, instead suggesting that he was welcome to try calling the boat himself, if he knew how to use a two-way radio. She answered the same questions: Yes, Victor monitored 2182 mhz on the Single Side Band. Yes, she had been trying to reach him for five days with no luck and yes, she would give him the message that the Special Agent had called. *Click!*

The third call came from Lucien Fernades and was the most worrisome yet. "Hey, Lucien. How are ya?"

"I'm not bad but I figured I'd better touch base with you guys. I've received some very interesting calls of late on Victor's behalf as his lawyer. The first one was from a guy by the name of Manfredi from the United Nations in New friggin York. He stated that his…his mining committee was considering sanctions against the *Gambling Lady*. When I asked him 'on what grounds' he stated that the vessel in question had been harvesting manganese nodules contrary to international law and specific regulations set forth by the International Seabed Authority…

…I asked him to please forward all of the pertinent information in hard-copy to me. He said that he would. Before he hung up he said that his office wanted to give Captain Janes an opportunity to state his side of the dispute and that it would be most helpful if Victor could furnish proof of his fishing locations with the vessel for the last year. He actually called it a 'dispute.' What freakin dispute? We didn't know there was one.. where the hell is Victor at this point in time, anyway?"

Fabulia let out a sigh and said, "He's out there fishing somewhere, Lucien. I also have heard from Manfredi but I also got a call from that fisheries service guy, Vargas. He was borderline rude. I wanted to tell him to go piss up a rope but held back. What is all this about? I don't feel very good about any of it, Lucien. And Victor must have the Single Side Band turned off, the dope, I've been trying to reach him for days."

"Let me make a few calls, see what I can find out about all of this. I kind of agree with you. It's one thing to have the Fisheries Service hounding him but the United Nations? This is getting into a legal realm that I am just not versed in. I'll call you back as soon as I learn something solid."

Ten seconds after she hung up, the phone rang again. Thinking that it was Lucien, she picked up and said, "Yeah, what'd ya forget?"

A strange voice on the other end said, "Oh, I didn't forget shit, shuga. I just wanted to call and let you know that the heat is now on full...and I think that fucking husband of yours is definitely going to get his big, rich balls burned for a change. See how he likes being on the shit-end of the stick, the lucky bastard. I'll be checking in again, shuga...Tata..."

Fabulia slammed the phone down with such force that it broke in half and bruised her fingers. It appeared as if the 'shit' was most definitely beginning to hit the proverbial fan.

^

Victor did not want to trust his eyes as he neared the state pier with the *Gambling Lady*. There must have been 500 people on the wharf and in the parking lot. Some carried signs and many were chanting something that Victor just caught the jist of as he made his approach to the dock.

"...Save the Whales, Save the Snails. Save them all. Eat a Peach! Save the Whales, Save the Snails"...over and over.

"Whales, and snails, and everything in between, I'd guess," Victor said to himself, "I wonder if a person could survive on peaches...?" Dan threw the first line onto a bollard on the dock. As Vic let the boat come gently against the pilings he noted that Fabulia and Lucien Fernandes were on the pier. Standing somewhat behind them and to the side, mixed in with the crowd were Special Agent Vargas, Sgt. Harold Biggs, and Lt. Mierken Yorks. "Uh-oh, this doesn't look much like a welcome-home party," Victor muttered under his breath. The stern line went over to the dock last then Victor pushed the gear levers from astern to the neutral position, let out a sigh, and headed for the working deck to meet Fabi and Lucien.

The tide was almost at its' peak and abnormally high, this being a full moon. Victor did not have to crane his neck too far back to look up at Fabi and Lucien. "Hello my dearie. And you also, Lucien. What gives with all the hoopla on the dock? It's a trifle early for St. Paddy's Day, hey?" Before either Lucien or Fabi could respond, a barrage of eggs rained down on the deck, two of which caught Victor, one on this forehead and one just below his throat.

"Fish Killer!" was the new chant coming from a group of thirty protesters closest to the edge of the dock, as they threw more eggs down onto the boat. Fabulia'd seen Victor take his first two. Time seemed to slow down to her but, in fact, she went into hyper-drive. In a split second she stepped sideways, turned and roundhouse-slapped the closest egger so hard that it sounded like a pistol shot.

The guy's head snapped back so fast that he didn't even have time to change his facial expression from glee to surprise. Everyone along the edge of the dock went silent and still, with the exception of Fabi.

"Who do you assholes really think you are? Are you serious? If you all don't wanna eat fish that's fine but don't try and push your stuff on everyone else. Ninety percent of the human race is *still* carnivorous. What?... We shouldn't be allowed to fish at all? This's America, buddy."

The mob on the dock went nuts. The fishermen that were milling around enjoying the festival-like atmosphere turned angry in the bat of an eye and waded into the protesters. Demonstrator signs were demolished. The egg bombs tripled and went in all directions, not just towards the boat. A group on the wharf up by the bow of the *Gambling Lady* started throwing water balloons filled with pig blood down onto the bow and working deck. In a matter of seconds most of the pilothouse windows were covered.

One guy went after Fabulia but Lucien Fernandes cold-cocked him. Victor was trying to get up onto the wharf. Vargas, Biggs, and Yorks saw this and tried to move through the throng to the edge of the dock to intercept him but Lucien yelled down, *"Stay on the boat! They can't arrest you this time if you stay down there.* Hurry up, Fabi down onto the boat. Let's go."

Lucien bulldozed his way over to the ladder, got Fabi going down and then started to follow her. Mierken Yorks tried to get a foot on the first rung but Lucien put up a hand and said, "No way, Yorksie, this is a federally registered vessel and you have no legal jurisdiction onboard her and never did. You got away with it once but never again. If I ever see your ass on this boat again I swear I'll see your badge pulled. Now fuck off!" Yorks hesitated and Lucien continued down.

Once they were onboard he said, "Victor, get this boat underway and off the fucking dock, pronto."

Most of the *Gambling Lady's* crew was standing along the outboard rail of the deck trying to keep away from the flying eggs. Teddy, Jazzy, and Auntie Di were standing just inside the hatch leading into the galley. Victor spotted him and yelled, "Teddy: fire up the main engines. We're out of here. Gideon, Vinh, and Dan: throw the lines off—leave them on the dock if you have to. Van: up to the pilothouse. Get us out to the middle of the harbor. Jazzy—get into the galley and dog down that entry hatch. Don't open it until I tell you to. Now, everyone—go."

Within sixty seconds the *Gambling Lady* was slowly backing away from the dock. As Van took the boat out of gear to stop the sternway everyone onboard looked towards the state pier. A multitude of police cars descended upon it. Some people ran; most just stopped whatever they were frantically doing, as if they were glad that someone had finally intervened.

Victor turned his attention back to the boat and his crew. "OK, Jazzy Open up." One after the other, the six dogs on the water-tight hatch were released and the door slowly opened. In one quick motion Jazzy stuck his head out then jerked it back as if he expected more eggs. Everyone on deck laughed gently at the look on Jazzy's face then the surge caught them all and the laughter turned into gut wrenching hilarity.

Lucien, Victor and Fabi could barely hold each other up. Emilio, Dan, and Vinh were all on the deck holding their stomachs. Octavio and Gideon were both holding onto the starboard rail, pointing at Jazzy and just roaring. Teddy and Auntie Di were laughing but not uncontrollably. They were just taking in the scene on the deck of this boat as if it were just another day. Teddy gave her a soft nudge with his elbow and said, *"Que pensez-vous, jeune dame? Est-ce un fou ou d'asile flottant un cirque vraiment mauvais?* What do you think, young lady? Is this a floating insane asylum or just a bad circus?"

Auntie Di grinned wider as she replied, *"Qu 'importe, mon ami? Personne ne meurt et tout le monde rit. Ayons une tasse de café, oui?* It is all ok, my friend. Nobody has died. How about a cup of coffee?"

With that they both turned and went back into the galley.

Between gasps Victor finally said, "Whew. Ya. That was a definite relief. Now, please tell me. Did anyone get hurt back there?" This started them all over again. After a few minutes Victor tried again. "No, really please. I can't tell real blood from that shit they threw on us. Is anyone hurt?"

It was discovered that someone had thrown a rock instead of an egg which caught Octavio Guzman under his right eye. Vic called for some water and a cloth. After cleaning the wound he told Octavio to go into the galley and get Van to put a couple of butterflies on the cut after disinfecting it. No stitches were called for. Victor turned, focused on the boat as a whole, and became unnerved for a moment. Blood was everywhere. The boat looked like some kind of a maritime murder epic.

To nobody in particular Victor said, "Well, that whole mess didn't exactly make me feel like the home-coming queen. What got the party started, anyway?"

Fabulia chimed in, "We first got an inkling that something was up with a few phone calls early last week from various state, federal and international authorities. I tried to reach you on the side-band but I guess you had it turned off. Then Vargas called again yesterday and said that he was planning on bringing you in for questioning about those rocks. He wouldn't give me anymore information so I told him to contact Lucien if he needed anything further. But, I'll tell you, that crowd on the dock surprised both Lucien and I. It almost felt like the whole thing was contrived. We went down there to fore-warn you that the feds were working up a good boil on the pot. No way we expected the pandemonium that we all just escaped from."

"Yeah, that guy Vargas did contact me," Lucien said. "The conversation was most definitely one-sided on his part, almost as if he was probing and adding fuel to the fire at the same time by throwing names at me. 'The State Department, United Nations, International Seabed Authority,' blah, blah, blah. He said they were all going 'round and around trying to figure out whether or not you could be prosecuted for the unlawful harvest of manganese nodules. It all seems to hinge on where you actually fished up the things. These guys seem very interested in your fishing co-ordinates."

Victor snorted, "Fat chance I'm going to publicize where I've fished for the last year. The *Gambling Lady* and her crew have busted ass to get to where we are today. It'll be a cold day in hell before I give that info up. Hell— why don't I just catch the shrimp and hand them over to some of the other boats in the fleet? 'Here you go, fellas. Can I help you in any other way? Want my shirt and undies too? No problem.' I've got almost 200,000 pounds of shrimp in the hold right below us worth close to a million bucks. Caught, processed and frozen in under two friggin weeks. I will not *ever* tell anyone outside of my family where I have been soaking the net."

Lucien held up his hands and said, "Okay, Okay Victor. Let's not get all worked up over this stuff just yet. Let me deal with the powers that be and we'll go from there."

Victor took in a deep breath, but before he could start in on his diatribe again Fabulia said, "Vic, let's put all of this on the shelf for the moment. All joking aside, you really do have egg all over your face. And this boat is a bloody mess. Haven't you got a deck hose or something on this boat? You need to get this blood washed off before it dries completely and becomes permanent. And your crew's not looking so great either. Geez, what a buncha ghouls."

CHAPTER SIXTEEN

LUCIEN FERNANDES was actually getting to like 'the boating life', as he called it. Jazzy was feeding him quite well and he enjoyed the motion of the boat as it swayed gently against the dock pilings at night. He'd been living aboard the *Gambling Lady* for a couple of weeks now ever since the dockside riot. State and city officials had tried numerous times to grab Victor on a number of trumped up and fabricated charges such as inciting a riot, failure to pay state taxes in full, and inciting lewd behavior in a minor (a seventeen year-old girl was so taken up with the festivities at the demonstration that she felt certain everyone would benefit from and appreciate the sight of her ample breasts).

The only way that the counselor felt certain he could fend off the local and state constabulary was to keep Victor on the boat until this current hubbub died down. As for the third law enforcement faction, Lucien became fond of saying, "No Feds, no Dreads." It seemed to work out that way. As long as Victor refused to relinquish his fishing coordinates for the last year the federal authorities had no recourse.

The National Marine Fisheries Service had nothing to get him on. They'd already slapped his hand over the squid by-catch deal and could not try to re-enter that avenue without looking foolish and possibly face a law suit. Without those numbers, the ISA could not, immediately, make a ruling on the *Gambling Lady's* extracurricular activities. Plus, there was not enough evidence available to make a case for compelling Victor Janes to give up his latitude and longitude numbers.

The authorities only had a single nodule; not what one could call ironclad evidence that Victor was actually harvesting the rocks. At the time, none of the authorities considered the seizure of all of those bags as evidence. Nobody quite knew what they were evidence of, if anything. Vargas had gone back to the boat two days after the bust, but somehow the bags had already mysteriously disappeared.

The Special Agent tried his damnedest to get some idea from the crew as to the whereabouts of the nodules, but he couldn't make sense of the three or four foreign languages spoken between them. One crewmember would say something in Spanish, and another would answer in French. The next guy would look around, start speaking in some Asian tongue, then that infernal cook came out on deck and started babbling in Portuguese. *"How the hell did Victor Janes get anything done,"* Vargas wondered to himself?

So Lucien decided to stay on the boat to keep an eye on the captain and insure that the local, state, and federal cops didn't manage to make any underhanded mischief. Victor tried to make a case for going back offshore to get away from it all, but that idea got curtailed when Fabulia was arrested.

The man that Fabi slapped on the dock during the riot had, it was assumed, been coerced into pressing charges against her. Supposedly Fabulia'd caused some needed dental work. She spent the morning in a holding cell downtown, much to the chagrin of the officers close-by. Fabulia kept up a non-stop litany of questions. "Why were there no toilet seats on the toilets?…What was the purpose behind taking shoelaces out of all their shoes?... Did they think they were actually all going to try and run somewhere in this cell?...Why was their food stone-cold when they were given it?"...On and on.

When she received no response to these queries, she answered all of them herself which left no doubt about what she felt the police department's motives were. By the time Lucien climbed off the boat, got downtown, and arranged bail, most everyone at New Bedford Police Headquarters breathed a deep sigh of relief when bail was met and she was escorted off of the premises.

However, this tension adjustment was short-lived given the full presence of the media that greeted Lucien and Fabulia outside of the building. Fabi immediately turned as if to go back inside but Lucien stopped her and they exchanged words for a few seconds. Fabulia squared her shoulders, shook out her hair and marched forward on Lucien's arm. The barrage of questioning voices and camera flashes gave Fabulia a moment of vertigo. She leaned into Lucien as he held up his hands, asking the crowd for silence. Slowly the hub-bub died down.

"Ladies and gentlemen. At this time I will make a brief, three point statement for my client and her family. Number 1: In October of this year city and state police made an illegal search of the Janes family's fishing vessel *Gambling Lady*. At that time no arrests were made relative to illegal contraband or unlawful fisheries products onboard said vessel. The only scrap that the authorities could garnish from their 'raid' was the fact that the vessel owner, Captain Victor Janes, had neglected to apply for a city ordinance permit to off-load fish products across dockage within the city limits. He spent almost three days in a cell for this trivial infraction."

Someone in the crowd yelled, "Did they serve him shrimp while he was in the can?" This brought out a chorus of laughter but Lucien ignored it all and continued.

"Number 2: Two and a half-weeks ago an anti-fishing demonstration was orchestrated at the city pier. Once again the Janes family's fishing vessel was the target. The vessel and her crew were pelted repeatedly with eggs and balloons filled with pig blood. One crewmember was hit with a rock. My client here, Fabulia Janes, came down to the dock to welcome her husband home from a lengthy fishing trip. She witnessed all of this, particularly her husband, Captain Janes, taking multiple strikes to his body by these projectiles. Did she react? Of course she did, as any other person would who was watching harm come to one of their loved ones. She tried to stop the attacker nearest to her by open-handedly slapping that man, who, I will add, was about 6' 2" in height and weighed in at around 230 lbs." With this Lucien paused, took one step sideways, looked down at Fabulia, spread his arms in a questioning gesture and looked out at the crowd with a smile on his face. A female voice in the crowd yelled, "Way to go, girl! Next time use a friggin baseball bat!" Lucien let the noise die down then continued.

"Number 3: My client is now receiving anonymous phone threats to her family. I have repeatedly asked these good citizens to counter-sue so that we can start to get to the bottom of these events. They have, so far, declined repeatedly, stating that they only wish this malicious and unwarranted behavior towards them to cease so that they can resume their lives in some form of normalcy. But I will state, here and now, that, if it is discovered that a conspiracy on some level has been promulgated against my clients, all of the stops will be pulled out. That is the end of our statement at this time. Thank-you". The whole crowd seemed to start yelling at once.

"...Fuckin' vegeterians and Clam Cops.... Not worth a dam...give um hell, Fabulia...gotta sue, lady...make the bastids pay!"...

Lucien wrapped an arm around Fabi as they headed down the steps and started to push their way through the crowd. Lucien kept up a steady reply of 'no further comment' going. Fabulia, though disoriented once again, said, "Well thanks a lot, you jerk. Now everyone will think I'm just some kinda little house-mouse."

Out of the side of his mouth Lucien replied, "Worry about nothing, my dear. You slapped that lummox on the dock and it took a certain amount of, ah, bravado and gumption to do so. They all see that," as he waved his free arm out over the crowd. "It's all about the theater my dear, and great theater it was."

∧

Lucien drove Fabulia directly to the boat. "The kids will be fine with Edmund and Rose for another hour. But right now we three need to go over a few details," he said.

Victor was split between the joy of seeing Fabi safe and the consuming anger that it had all come to a point where his wife had been jailed. "Fabi, I'm so sorry that you had to go through that. What a bunch of bastards. I...I just..."

Fabulia stopped him and said, "Vic, it was nothing. In fact it was sort of interesting. I knew one of the hookers in the holding cell with me, went to school with her, in fact. What a deranged story she had to tell. She…"

"Hey, you two, let's save the reflections and emotive moments for later, if you please. Right now we need to talk about your current predicament.

Allow me to clue you in on a few new developments. First off, let me say that it was a stroke of beautiful luck for us when the locals decided to arrest Fabulia," Lucien stated. Victor began to protest but was abruptly cut off.

"Whoa there, captain. Let me continue. Actually there really wasn't much luck involved at all. I called your office at *Constant Vigil* to let the girls know what was going on. Martha Vanderhorn was spitting nails by the time we finished our conversation. She said she was going to call every TV network on the planet and it appears as if she may have done just that, judging by the number of cameras back at the police station. The media coverage is going to help us immensely. I wouldn't be surprised if it went national. I am almost certain the powers behind all of this crap are currently in a conference-room somewhere in the city plotting damage control. After our appearance in front of the cameras at police headquarters today you will both be able to walk around this town without fear of further harassment; for awhile anyway. The boys in blue will be told to lay off and I will be able to move back to my own home. Don't get me wrong- I love Jazzy's cooking, but I'm getting a bit tired of chorico."

Fabulia gave an exaggerated, swooning moan and said, "Such blasphemy! Do not let Jazzy or my mother hear you speak like that about the holy Char*eese*. You'll be lynched, Lucien."

"Yeah, Yeah. Strung up because of a sausage. I'll bet it's actually happened…" Lucien started to drift away with the picture. He shook his head and came back to the present.

"Anyway, before we part for the day you should be aware of two more items. It appears as if we now have a voluntary mole in the District Attorney's office. Martha already knew about your arrest by the time I called her. Apparently, said insider suggested that Martha start calling the media, even giving her names and numbers. What a connection. I wish it were mine. Also, along the same vein, yesterday I had a surreptitious phone-call from one Harold Biggs with Massachusetts Fish and Game." Lucien gave them a lopsided grin before he continued.

"Basically he stated that he was disgusted with the manner in which the local police and the Feds have handled this affair. As he said, the whole thing has been driven by jealousy, shoddy politics, and greed. Victor wins the lottery then has the absolute *temerity* to try and do something productive with the money? He went on to say that our only real threat now may be from the federal sector which is apparently being pushed along by the United Nations.

He's going to stay in touch and let me know if anymore moves on Victor or the *Gambling Lady* get brewed up. With all of this in mind, I suggest that you allow me to contact Manfredi at the UN in New York and set up an appointment to meet. Let's play ball with him. At the very least we might find out what is really behind this interest in the manganese nodules. I'll tell him we'd like to get this dispute cleared up as soon as possible so you can get back to the shrimp, Victor. If that works for you guys I'll call him today."

Victor looked at Fabulia, who said, "Yes. I mean, anything to move forward on this galling business. It would be nice if this whole pile of crap just went away."

"Absolutely. I would like nothing more than to get back to fishing. This garbage is just dragging us down," Victor stated, "see if you can resolve it by any means."

"Okay, then. I'll call him this afternoon. In the meantime please don't plan on going back offshore right away, Vic: you, most of all will need to be present for this meeting. I'll call ya later today."

With that Lucien headed for the hatchway. He stopped by the galley table and picked up a shark tooth that someone had missed. He rolled the little object around in his palm, laughed and said, "well, Victor—I certainly hope these things don't end up biting you in the ass, so to speak. Christ, this is going to be Broadway material."

As Lucien exited neither Victor nor Fabi looked overly jubilant. It appeared as if New York was going to be entering their life in the near future but it surely wasn't going to be on any Broadway setting.

∧

They resolved their little tiff with Joe acquiescing to his wife's logic. The sale of earrings and pendants was a proven moneymaker. While a big old set of fossilized teeth set in piñon would look spectacular, if it didn't sell by Christmas they'd have a tough go of it for the rest of the winter. Carol-Jean looked at Joe and said, "Besides, we really must start looking ahead a little bit. If I am going to fly to Boston to search out another source of the teeth we'll need a little extra cash this winter."

"Whoa there, my dear. Don't I get to go east with you? I mean, you'll need protection. Those eastern city people are a rough bunch. Someone might kidnap you and sell your beauty into prostitution. I'd only be able to see you if I paid at the door and entered some dimly lit room covered in red velvet."

"Joe. The only time you've ever flown is in your dreams with no plane involved. Even the thought of climbing into a plane makes you break out in a cold sweat!"

"Well, yes, that's all true but couldn't we drive?" Asked Joe.

"Ha. That old truck wouldn't make it to Flagstaff let alone Boston."

CHAPTER SEVENTEEN

VICTOR AND EDMUND threw the lines off from the dock then Van slowly backed the *Gambling Lady* out into the channel. Victor was feeling a little apprehensive, to say the least. Edmund saw this and said, "Do you recall the first time I gave you the *Sagrada Familia* for a trip? That was probably one of the hardest things I've ever done in my life. I felt something like a mother giving away her first-born baby for adoption. I actually felt sick to my stomach as you pulled away from the dock. I was feverish. Funny how a person can get so attached to a piece of steel and machinery. But that trip out you did real good. Came in with over 30,000 lbs. of nice, large yellowtail and lemon sole, if I 'member right. Van will do just fine, Victor. Let 'er go."

Lucien Fernandes and Guillermo Manfredi had arranged for them to meet in New York at Manfredi's office in the UN . The meeting was scheduled to take place in five days. Victor felt that he could not let the boat and crew lay idle any longer. Van had no problem taking the boat for a trip and the crew was very happy to get back to catching shrimp and making money. As Gideon Bloom stated, "Idle hands as well as idle machinery tend to seize up, Vic. Let's get the friggin ball rolling again here, huh?"

As the two men turned and started walking up the dock Victor said, "Ya. Van'll do just fine. I don't know about that "first-born baby" thing… I just feel, well, generally out of control over this whole ridiculous deal. It seems as if I do not hold any sway over my own life at all at the moment. I'm reduced to some sort of damned puppet, but the people holding the strings are all pulling in different directions. I feel like I'm being yanked apart and I cannot even resist because if I do I'll just make it all worse for my family, my friends, and the people that work for me. Now I've got to go off to New York to listen to this guy that I've never even met before so that he can give me the third fucking degree about rocks. I mean this is all a pitiful joke. As Lucien says, it's a tragi-comedy. These people are pissed off at me over rocks for Christ-sake. How farcical is that? I just want to know where and when it's all going to end." Victor had stopped and was looking at the *Gambling Lady's* stern as she headed for the hurricaine barrier. He abruptly turned away again and headed up the dock.

"Well to hell with it all. Eddie's got a his first little league game this afternoon. Let's take a ride over to the park. This'll take my mind offa this nodule crap if anything will. All that kid can talk about is baseball. I don't think he's starting today but I'm sure the coach'll put him in at some point just to stop the pleading. That boy's a character and a half. He could talk an Indian out of his last wooden nickel."

Both men grinned to themselves, picturing this little kid, talking to the coach man-to-man, giving him ten good reasons why he really needed to put Eddie into the game. Lucien Fernades could take lessons in debating from this seven year old.

∧

Five days later Vic, Fabi, Lucien, and Martha all drove to Providence to catch the train down to New York City. Lucien and Martha planned to stay for the night so they could take in a show, while Victor and Fabi were going to head back home right after the meeting.

The four hour ride into New York was actually fun. Neither Victor nor Fabulia had ever set foot on a train before, and New York City was going to be a first as well. Lucien and Martha paid no attention. This was all second nature to them both. They were acting awfully chummy together. Victor looked at Fabulia who raised her eye-brows for a split second. They were both thinking the same thing. "Was Lucien Fernandes that charismatic?"

Fabulia and Victor were both astonished when they arrived at Grand Central Station. It was so large, busy, and populated. Off they all went with Lucien bellowing for a cab as they pushed their way outside. They were early for the 2:00 p.m appointment with Mr. Manfredi so Lucien took them on a roundabout route passing by the Empire State building then heading south for Battery Park. The Twin Towers absolutely dazzled Victor. He had the cabbie pull over twice so that he could get out and peer up, up and up at the pair of them.

Neither Fabulia nor Victor could get over the size of just about everything in Manhattan- the buildings, the traffic, the bridges, the mega-hoards of people and the noise. The noise was gigantic.

As they sped up FDR Drive for a short jump to the First Avenue exit, Victor caught a glimpse of Governors Island, Brooklyn, and all of the various kinds of watercraft out by the entrance to the East River at the Brooklyn Bridge. He started to laugh. "Look at that water traffic!" he shouted. "Look at the size of the barge that tugboat's towing—and all the other boats buzzing around it. Good God. I bet there are a few tight sphincters out there."

The United Nations was founded in 1945. UN headquarters in New York sits on an eighteen acre parcel of land that was gifted to the organization by John D. Rockefeller Jr. Construction began in 1949 and a year and a half later delegates started moving in. Its' members include every sovereign state on the planet with the exception of the Vatican.

Lucien announced their appointment at the security desk of the side entrance that he had been instructed by Manfredi to use. Five minutes later Sophia, an aide to the ISA director, arrived and ushered them all into an express elevator that shot them up to the 39th floor. The young lady apologized, saying that *Signore* Manfredi would be a few minutes late because of a conference call with ISA's headquarters in Kingston, Jamaica.

She led them into a vacant conference room that seated thirty. Martha and Lucien immediately headed for the small wet-bar in the far corner. He poured coffee for them both while Victor grabbed a Coke for himself and water for Fabi. After he handed the water to his wife Vic ambled over to the floor-to-ceiling windows, though he did not get too close. The view was amazing. Standing stationary at this height Victor was sure that he could actually see the curvature of the earth. It was as if he was looking through a giant fish-eye lens. He scanned down until he was looking at the East River. He had to step back and grab a chair. That was a long way down.

The conference room door opened and a tall man with a mane of silvery hair entered. "Good afternoon, ladies and gentlemen. I am Manfedi. Please accept my apologies for keeping you waiting."

Lucien stepped forward and said, "Ah, Guillermo. So good to finally meet you in person." Then the two of them were off babbling in, what Victor assumed, was Italian, as if they were long lost cousins from Venice. After a few moments of this verbal dance Lucien continued on in English. "Guillermo, please allow me to introduce you to Victor and Fabulia Janes, and our associate Martha Vanderhorn."

Handshakes, hellos, and wary grins were proffered all around. Mafredi said, "Please, please. Let's sit down," as he guided Victor to a chair at the large table. Victor sat. Manfredi walked around the table-end sat down directly across from the captain, leaving everyone else to find their own seats. After a split-second pause Lucien went over and sat next to Victor, while the ladies simultaneously decided to flank either side of Guillermo Manfredi. At that moment Sophia returned and took a seat directly behind her boss, note-pad and pen in hand.

"Thank-you all for journeying to New York, my friends. Perhaps it would be best for me to give you all an overview of the ISA's function within the UN. As Mr. Fernandes has most likely told you, one of the International Seabed Authority's mandated tasks is to oversee and manage offshore mining interests throughout the world's oceans. We are—"

"Who delegated such authority and how do you actually enforce your 'mandates' over international waters?" asked Fabulia.

"Why…"

"Yes. And how do mining companies actually 'mine' out in the middle of the ocean. I thought you had to go into the side of a mountain or way down some dark shaft in order to mine." Martha had taken on the ditz persona while Fabulia had apparently opted for a lawyer façade. Lucien was suppressing a grin, while Victor was staring at Manfredi, arms crossed in front of him.

Guillermo Manfredi swivel-necked 180 degrees, looking at both women. "To address your question, Mrs. Janes, as an arm of the United Nations the ISA has the full support of all 192 delegates within the voting body which is inclusive of every sovereign nation on earth with the exception of the Vatican. I think—"

"Wow. The Church isn't behind you guys? Jeez. If you don't have God behind you what have you really got? About that dark mine shaft..."

"Yes, yes. Well, the Vatican has always tried to act in an 'impartial observer' capacity and not get involved in governance or politics on any level. Now, to get back on track here, we are actually not certain that there is, in fact, any international claim whatsoever against Mister, excuse me, I mean *Captain* Janes. In order to clarify this position we only ask that the fishing locations of his vessel, the *Gambling Lady*, be clarified. I had hoped—"

"Signor Manfredi. Please allow me to help you with your *clarity* of this situation. My family has been fishing for its livelihood for the past five generations. My husband's family in Newfoundland carries the same vocational lineage. That, sir, is a total of ten past generations that have devoted their lives to eking out a living on the water. Given this, why on earth would your *ISA* ever think that we would have any interest at all in these nodules that everyone seems so... so *enthusiastic* about? We fish. We do not mine."

"Yes, yes. I understand that, Mrs. Janes but we do have irrefutable proof that the Captain has taken manganese nodules aboard his vessel. I think that..."

Victor was having a hard time sitting still now. He felt like a little goldfish in a tiny bowl. "Come on, Manfredi," he almost shouted, "one damn nodule makes me a big mining magnate? That's not proof of anything. I believe..."

"But Mr. Janes, it is not only one nodule we are discussing here. One of your employees, a Dr. Bloom, I believe, took a number of nodules to

Wood's Hole Oceanographic Institute to have them analyzed. Also, the authorities in New Bedford swear that they saw as many as fifty sacks filled with the nodules on board your boat, although it appears as if none of these bags have been found." Guillermo Manfredi sat back, considering his next words.

Lucien beat him to it and said, "But Guillermo, one nodule or one thousand, it does not matter. What are my clients supposed to do next with these things once they supposedly have them in hand? They have no means of processing them, they would not know the first thing about selling them. As Fabulia Janes just stated, they are fishermen, not some form of aquatic, quasi-miners. Why don't we cut to the chase here. What is it that is *really* going on behind the curtains of this charade? I think you want the fishing coordinates of the *Gambling Lady* for other reasons. I think that you are being used so that some corporate entity out there can find out where the *Gambling Lady* has harvested these things. I am not versed in metallurgy but I think there is much more here than meets the naked eye. Now let's consider..."

"Is this true Mr. Manfredi?" asked Fabulia. "You are being set up and used just the same as us? How does that make you feel? Personally, I'd be ashamed if I stood in your shoes. Using us all at the behest of faceless cowards who have to get others to do their scutwork."

Martha Vanderhorn could not hold back. "What's the name of that song? Oh yeah. *Canary In A Coal Mine.*"

Signor Manfredi appeared to be gathering his thoughts. After a pause he said, "Sophie, could you please go down to my office and get me the folder on my desk marked 'Nodule Harvest Claims'? Thank-you. No need to hurry."

After Sophia departed Manfredi dove in. "Alright Lucien. As you say, 'let's cut to the chase.' This whole affair has had me sleepless for the last three nights— and I am rapidly tiring of this lady's mining analogies." He glanced briefly at Martha.

"There is a group of globally powerful people that have taken note of Victor's secondary activities. You are correct, that the *Gambling Lady's* fishing coordinates are only being used as a smoke screen, and the National Marine Fisheries Service has been sucked into this ploy also but I don't believe anyone in that agency realizes the true scope and breadth of this business. Mr. Janes, please listen to me now and take this advice. Give up your fishing locations. If you do not, I fear that these people will compel you to do so by any means possible…any means at all. I am told you are a wealthy man, but don't fool yourself into thinking that you can beat these people through the United States legal system and money. *Any* legal system. They have limitless funds and make their own rules. Please give them what they want. It is the best thing to do for your family, your friends, and anyone else that you may care about."

The room was still and silent for ten seconds but all eyes had turned to Victor. Finally he spoke.

"Mr. Manfredi, thanks for finally giving us the straight scoop on this business, and I thank you personally for your advice, but I've got to stick to my guns here. Nobody is going to force me to give up my fishing spots. The way I'm seeing it, if I do give the numbers up these corporate bastards are going to try and push fishermen, any fisherman, out of those areas just so they can get to those goddamn stones. If I don't give up the positions they'll still go after those nodules, and I'll be damned if I'm going to be a pawn for a bunch of people who think the use of toilet paper and other human beings is one and the same. No sir. I hope I don't cause you another sleepless night, but you're going to have to call whomever you have to call and tell them no latitude, no longitude, no nothing from Victor Janes."

Guillermo Manfredi sighed and said, "I understand and respect your position, Mr. Janes, but I reiterate—this will do you no good in the long term." He looked at Victor for five seconds who stared right back at him. Manfredi raised his arms, slapped his hands down on the table and stood. The meeting was now over.

Sophia re-entered the room at that moment and Guillermo asked her to escort their guests back down to the staff entrance. After halfhearted goodbyes, Sophia brought them all into an elevator and they started down.

Lucien was humming an operetta and studying the ceiling but not a word was spoken during the decent. Everyone, including Sophia, was dwelling on their own thoughts, considering the brief meeting with Manfredi.

Sophia wished them all well and saw them out. The foursome reached the sidewalk just as a service entrance door burst open and a small young man in a perfectly tailored suit came running out yelling, "Janes! Mr. Janes! Please wait. A moment of your time, please."

The man came to an abrupt halt in front of Lucien Fernandes and said, "Mr. Janes. So sorry to have missed you inside but I was…"

"Hey, Bub. I'm Victor Janes. What can I do for you?"

The man turned, looked back and forth between Lucien and Victor then said, "Oh, I'm so sorry. I was misinformed. Please allow me to introduce myself. My name is Mateus Oberegon. I work as an assistant attaché to the Brazilian Consulate here in New York. Could I possibly interest you all in joining me for an early supper? I believe we have much to discuss."

"Please excuse us, sir, but it is not every day that four strangers in New York City get invited to dinner off of the street by a representative of the Brazilian government," stated Lucien with a grin. "Perhaps you could tell us a bit more about this impending discussion?"

Mateus Oberegon gave a short laugh and said, "Oh, why of course. Yes sir. We have much to talk about regarding shrimp and manganese nodules." This last statement was said as if it were blatantly obvious.

Victor looked at the sidewalk, gave a short laugh, then glanced at Fabulia who said, "Well what the hell, Vic? I could certainly eat— and a glass of wine would hit the spot right about now. What do you guys say?" She looked at Lucien and Martha.

Martha chimed in on their behalf, "Food and wine? No problem."

"Excellent," Mateus exclaimed. "There is a wonderful bistro across the street from the main entrance to the Secretariat Building. Please—right this way. It is a perfect day for a walk. New York is beautiful in the springtime." Senhor Oberegon headed down the street. Lucien strode up beside him and started conversing in Portuguese. *"Quanto tempo você tem sido atribuido ao consulado em Nova York?"* How long have you been assigned to the consulate in New York?"

Mateus didn't miss a beat. *"Eu só tenho aqui há seis meses. Eu jovem, mas eu aprendo rapido. E você? Você foi para Brasil?* I have only been here for six months. I am young but I learn fast. And you? You have been to Brazil?"

"Ainda não. Talvez algum dia em breve, hien? Not yet .Perhaps someday soon, eh?"

"Você fala Portuguese impecável. You speak flawless Portuguese."

"As linguas são o meu 'hobby'. Languages are my hobby."

"Quantas linguas você fala? How many languages do you speak?"

"Oh, oito ou nove, se você incluir a linguagem de bullshit! Oh, eight or nine, if you include the language of 'bullshit'."

Oberegon laughed and continued on in English. "I think I am going to enjoy this meal."

The meal was enjoyable enough, though both Fabulia and Victor were feeling very subdued. Neither one of them could get the meeting with Guillermo Manfredi out of their minds. They were wondering if their family was actually in danger. They were both considering what the future really held for them.

Victor was gazing out at the street scene as he pushed around the Cod Florentine on his plate. Lucien addressed him for the third time. After he had Victor's attention he said, "I apologize for my friend, Mr. Obregon. Our meeting at the UN was unsettling for both Mr. and Mrs. Janes. Vic, I think you may want to listen up. Please continue Mr. Obregon."

"Yes, thank-you Mr. Fernandes. Capitan Janes, my country would like you to come to Brazil to help us develop a method to harvest manganese nodules off of our coast. Furthermore, if you so desire, we would be prepared to give you an open Brazilian fishing permit. In essence, this would mean that you could fish anywhere you wanted to along the coast of our country. I am told that we have a resource of shrimp out in deep water that are cousins to the species that you are harvesting here. I have, by the way, had the pleasure of dining on your shrimp in Lisbon, and I must say they were superb."

Victor's sudden grin turned into a frown. He wanted to press this man for more information on his shrimp's acceptance in Europe, but he didn't have the energy or the heart. His world was teetering and he had no clue about how he might make it stop . "That's, I'm sure, a very interesting offer, Mr. Mateus."

Fabulia kicked him under the table and rolled her eyes as if to say, "at least get his name right."

"I just don't know," Victor continued on, "well, I guess you could talk with Lucien here, sort of give him all the details and fine print, if you will. You'll have to excuse me right now Mr. Oberegon, I just don't even know which way is up at the moment. Could we possibly talk about something other than manganese and shrimp?"

Mateus would not allow them to hail a cab. He called his embassy and fifteen minutes later a shiny black limousine pulled up in front of the restaurant. Before Lucien climbed in he shook Oberegon's hand and said, "I will be calling you within the next week, sir. I cannot say if my clients could be interested in moving the whole show to Brazil but I myself believe in contingency plans. Give me a detailed proposal and I will make sure it is seriously considered."

The two parties said their goodbyes. The counselor climbed into the limo, grinned, and started humming an off-key tune that sounded somewhat like "Getting Better." He looked to Martha.

"What do you think? Perhaps we should forget about the Broadway bit and do some brainstorming on the train back to Providence?"

"Sounds about right to me, Lucien. I think it's time to start barricading the gates and loading the muskets."

As soon as they all boarded the train Victor flopped down onto a window seat and immediately went to sleep. Fabulia said, "I guess we're not going to get much help out of him," as she sat down next to her husband.

Lucien and Martha sat down facing Victor and Fabulia. Lucien closed his eyes while he thought for a minute and then said, "OK, here's what I think we've gotta do. First off, Fabi, all of this money that you guys have laying around in your various banks...."

CHAPTER EIGHTEEN

$286 MILLION DOLLARS of lottery money got taxed to the hilt long before any of the dough was dispersed to the lucky recipient. This was *CAPITAL* capital gains. Federal and state income tax administrations just adored this new lottery cash-cow. It was the ultimate bureaucratic 'mana from heaven' that fed the voracious tax monsters a tasty, fat dessert. The multi-state weekly drawings caught everyone's attention. Bored trust fund blue-bloods stood in line with anxious cabbies and tired laborers to get their tickets. All a person had to do was play their numbers and throw down a buck . Some people got a bit over-zealous and threw down large portions of their weekly paychecks thinking that their odds of winning would increase exponentially but this concept was much like standing in a rainstorm looking for that single, supernatural drop that would turn that one, single person into a Titan when the drop hit them.

Thirty-four months ago when Victor and Fabulia had gone to the Lottery Commission office to claim his winnings he was given a check for $146,192,856.13 which he immediately passed off to Fabulia, as if the paper was, in actuality, some kind of writ or summons that he did not want to deal with. Fabulia quipped, "Well thanks for that bigboy, but if yer gonna throw this paper my way I'll ask you to endorse it first."

Fabulia went to the bank the next day and tried to deposit the check into their savings account. The teller started hyperventilating. She excused herself and ran off to find the branch manager. He arrived a few moments later and politely invited Fabi into his office where he promptly but gently shut he door.

"Mrs. Janes, this is a, ah, a highly irregular deposit request. Allow me to point out that, under Federal Deposit Insurance Corporation guidelines, we cannot insure deposits of amounts in excess of $50,000 dollars into any one account. I am afraid you would have to privately insure an amount of this nature or open up multiple accounts," said the banker, who was visibly shaking.

The nameplate on the desk said 'G. Orwell'. Fabulia sighed, rolled her eyes and said, "OK, OK, Mr. Orwell. So let's see. If I do a little quick math, that would mean that I would have to open up close to, oh let's just round it off to, say, 3,000 damned accounts? Sounds like an awful lot of paperwork to me. Are you up for that, Mr. Orwell, or can possibly suggest a different route for me?"

"Mrs. Janes I am most definitely not up for it." He passed her a business card and said, "You may best be served by our institution if you call this gentleman at our 'Private Bank' in Providence. Either that or get your lawyer and accountant involved." With that said he abruptly stood up and handed her back the check as if it were a coiled African Bushmaster. And he left a greasy thumbprint right in the middle of the damned thing, to boot.

Fabi let out a breath as she slowly got to her feet. She shook the proffered sweaty, hot palm and said, "Thanks, but I hadn't planned on joining anything 'private' today. I'll call ya if I need any further assistance. Oh, but one other question I wanted to ask you, sir. How was 1984 for you, Mr. Orwell?" Gerald looked at her, trying to figure out what the trick was within this question. "Never mind," she said. "Thanks again for your help. I'll see myself out." This guy could not wait to be rid of her.

With a little help from Lucien Fernandes, Fabulia ended up depositing the bulk of their new found wealth into ten banks throughout New England with ten accounts in each bank. Later she would switch all of these accounts over to *Constant Vigil* but not before she moved $10 mil into an account for Victor to use for the birth of the *Gambling Lady*, another $10 mil into a separate account for educational and family trusts and yet another ten which she gave to a friend of Lucien's to invest in the stock market. The loose change went into their joint checking account. The bottom line here meant that, even with a modest, simple interest accrual of 2.5%, their money would gross over $300,000 a year from each bank that she had opened accounts in. Further down the road three million dollars would be the benchmark that the *Constant Vigil Foundation* would have to bequeath out into the world and hold on to its' not-for-profit status with the IRS.

∧

Presently Fabulia Janes found herself back in Gerald Orwell's office. He was just as perturbed and nerved up now as he had been three years previous when he had first met this tiring, bothersome woman. "Mrs. Janes, this is highly, I repeat, *highly* unusual. No one person in their right mind would convert all of these monies from accounts this substantial into Canadian Dollars. I mean, well, it may look really good on paper—you will have gained approximately 23% in the Canadian currency numbers- but there is no guarantee that this may not change drastically within any twenty-four hour period. This is extremely rash and risky. I implore you to please reconsider!"

Fabulia, flanked by Emily Fagundes and Rita Montrose, said, "Mr. Orwell, I understand your angst but let me reassure you once again; we know what we are doing here. Our foundation will be opening branch offices in Canada and overseas. We need to make this currency exchange in order to facilitate our international business. Also, while we are here I wish to have our corporate lawyer, Mrs. Montrose and our accountant, Mrs. Fagundes placed as signatories for all outbound wire transfer transactions. I'm hopeful that you can help us with all of this, Mr. Orwell. We need it all done in an expeditious manner." All three women were smiling at him but somehow Gerald felt far from comforted. He yanked open a draw in his desk and extracted a number of different forms.

Gerald Orwell's demeanor suddenly changed. "I'll get started on this right away, Mrs. Janes," he said, through a somewhat toothy, maniacal grin. "I will call your office as soon as I have all of the paperwork in order. Both Mrs. Montrose and Mrs. Fagundes will have to come back in to sign the wire transfer power of attorney documents in the presence of a notary." He wanted these women out of his office at once. Good God! He felt as if the earth was falling off its' axis.

^

Two days earlier all four women including Martha were sitting in Lucien Fernandes' office listening to him go over 'The Plan' one more time.

"...So ladies, we want to move this money around as quietly as is possible. We do not want to raise any eyebrows at the Treasury Department or the IRS. This whole exercise may end up being all in vain but I'm hoping, if and when the time comes, we can get the transfers done before any connection is made between *Constant Vigil* and *Gambling Lady*." Lucien paced and thought awhile then continued.

"United States banking institutions are required by law to report all U.S. dollar wire transfers going overseas in excess of $10,000. What we're going to do is convert 90% of Constant Vigil's cash into Canadian Dollars and British Pound Sterling. This way our banks will not be required to report any of our overseas transactions. Hopefully, when we do end up having to make the transfers in these currencies no red flags will go up, at least not right away. There is absolutely nothing illegal about what we are doing here but we want to keep out of the spotlight if at all possible."

Lucien pointed at Fabulia, Rita and Emily as he said, "While you three are at each bank make sure that you fill out the paperwork completely so that Emily and Rita can make the wire transfers without any fuss. Your signature will not be on any of the outbound transfer paperwork, Fabulia, because we do not know where you may be at any given time, if and when we need to make these transfers. If you're out of the country we'd be in a jam if we had to await your return in order to sign transfer paperwork. We'll keep Rita and Emily close by.

Martha spoke up and said, "So are we doing this whole thing in pairs more as a witness thing than for any other reason?"

"Well, yes, to a degree but also for the banks' sake because some of them require two signatures for business related wire transactions,"stated Lucien. "Now, after all of the money is converted to CAD and GBP Fabulia and Martha will fly to the Cayman Islands and open up accounts at each of the five banks on our list. To keep all of this on a strictly legal setting all of these new accounts will be opened in the name of the *Constant Vigil Foundation* as a non-profit entity. Martha will be listed on all of the new accounts as a co-signator along with Fabi. It's a lot of money and there's a lot of trust going on around this table right now but I think we all realize that this is pretty much the only way to keep the vultures at bay, should they start circling."

Fabulia said, "Vultures prefer carrion. We are not dead so let's get this done"

∧

Fablia Janes and Martha Vanderhorn were simultaneously intrigued by this foreign exchange or 'Forex' thing, as it was referred to in business circles. Gerald Orwell was correct when he pointed out the increase in the numbers when going from USD to CAD but Fabi received a shock when she went to the next bank and converted U.S. dollars to British pound sterling. The numbers dropped by almost half. She had to phone up Lucien for reassurance.

Lucien did not hesitate. "Don't worry about it, Fabi. The large 'loss' that you see is just a historical structure thing. The value of your money is still there. If you converted back to USD right now you'd end up with the same numbers you started with. The Pound and the Canadian Dollar are the two most stable currencies after our dollar. Fret not, my dear."

The next morning over coffee with Fabi, Martha said, "Hey, you know, I wonder if we could actually make money with this 'foreign exchange' deal? I mean, we only converted our money yesterday but I'm thinking that a person could actually turn a buck using this Forex thingy."

Fabulia nodded and said, "I've been thinking about that myself. I thought of asking Lucien about it but I think that this may not be a good time to start in with questions outside of our little deal. He's kinda frazzled at the moment. Tell you what, though. There's no harm in us looking into it on our own, huh?"

Lucien Fernandes had no idea what he had spawned when he introduced 'Forex' to Fabulia and Martha. This was all the two women could talk about the next day as they drove to Boston to catch a flight to the Cayman Islands.

∧

Carol-Jean Paya slapped the dashboard and started to cry. She was worried to within a millimeter of panic. She'd come home from the shop earlier in the night to find Joe collapsed on the floor next to the wood stove. He was breathing and awake but barely coherent. He mumbled repeatedly about the 'canyon ghosts' but she could not get him to explain which ghosts and what they meant to him. She called for an ambulance. It took the EMT's 50 minutes to find the place. An April storm was hitting the canyon hard. They'd taken him to the tribal infirmary where the doctor on duty immediately ordered that Joe be taken to Flagstaff Medical Center. Something to do with low blood pressure and an irregular heart beat.

And now this damned pick-up truck had to die on the way to the hospital. She was cold and alone, pissed off and scared. All she could do was pray that Joe was holding his own and hope that someone came along to help her with this old truck.

CHAPTER NINETEEN

EVERYONE hoped that it would not happen, that it would all just vaporize into a fine mist and blow away. But, down deep, they all realized that this was a false hope. Most everyone peripherally involved felt the on-coming surge much like a person feels the persistent presence of an impending storm. It was coming but nobody could say exactly when. The anticipation was tangible but the realization was less dramatic, much to the vexation of the few that needed a spectacle to keep their own lives meaningful.

It began at the Nguyen residence in the town of Revere outside of Boston. Ten State policemen in full riot garb raided the house at 7a.m. on a Friday morning but that in itself was of no inconvenience. All of the residents had been up for two hours already anyway. Lieutenant Mierken Yorks, being the organizer of this jaunt, got the honors and was the first one through the front door that was opened from within for him by a petite seven year old girl. The officer with the rammer had no chance to use it.

Kenny Yorks bellowed a command and his whole entourage spread out in the living room, assault weapons at the ready. All twelve of the occupants present stared back at them benignly. The police took this as a sign of bewilderment, fear and aquiescence but, in reality, it was a kind of replayed, sour boredom. All of the adult *Ngori Viet* had seen much worse from men in uniforms.No one had been killed yet, which was a good sign. But what did these soldiers want from them?

"You and you. Stay in this room and guard these people," Yorks ordered . "You three with me to search the interior and you four outside. One of you guards the front, one guards the rear and you two search the yard. You know what to look for."

After twenty minutes and his third bedroom ransacking with no luck Ken was interrupted. "Hey Lieutenant, look what I found in the shed out back." The man held out a fist that was clutching the neck of a burlap sack. Kenny Yorks snatched it, looked inside and said, "What the fuck. This one's only got ten of the rocks in it. Where's the rest?"

"There is no 'rest', sir. The only other sacks out there are all empty. There's a little pile of some kinda small, creepy teeth out on the work bench, but that's it."

Yorks pushed past the cop and headed out back. Sure enough, no more full sacks and a small pile of black shark teeth. "Well, shee-it," he muttered. "Collect these teeth into an evidence bag and put these fucking rocks into a separate one." Ken grabbed an empty burlap sack and headed back into the house. Once in the living room he brandished the bag about and said, "Alright people. I need to know where the rest of these bags are. Speak up and we'll be gone and out of your hair. Come on now. I know they've got to be around here somewhere."

This demand was met with a dozen blank stares. An elderly man sat in the back of the room smoking. "Excuse me sir, but none of my relatives here speak very good English," he stated. "I believe I may be able to help you, though. The teeth that you have seen in the garden room behind our home are all that remains of the rocks that were inside of those bags. My sister went through them all in about three months. We admired her determination. It was not an easy task for her."

Mierken Yorks scatched at his cheek while he thought, "Fifty bags of those things would have been grandiose. Ten rocks are about as useful as a half a hard-on." He let out an exasperated breath and looked around the room. He did not recognize any of the four gooks that he'd seen on the boat some months ago but that did not mean anything. They all looked the same to him anyway, either here or in that miserable country of theirs. "Alright old boy, Thanks for that, but could you please identify the people that work on the fishing boat *Gambling Lady* ?"

After five seconds of silence Yorks prompted, "Come on, mister. I need to speak with them. You want us outa here or what?"

"I am sorry sir but the family members that you ask for are not here. They are on the boat."

"God dammit all," swore Ken, as his eyes swept the room one more time. "Look at these people," he thought to himself. "Fifteen or sixteen of them living in one stinking house. What a bunch of animals…"

As soon as the last policeman was out the door the girl that had greeted Lt. Yorks asked, in perfectly good English, "Grandfather, why do those men search for the teeth? Are they all out of their own luck? Why do they need to take ours?"

"As the Americans are fond of saying, 'That is the million dollar question'. I cannot answer your query for you because I myself do not understand for certain what makes these people thrive. I used to think it was only money but these days I am not sure of anything. At this moment we should be grateful that they are all gone, for now."

^

Kenny Yorks did not make it down to New Bedford until two o'clock that afternoon. He'd taken the evidence bags back to headquarters, checked in with the desk sergeant for messages, received some halfhearted ribbing about his big raid from the other detectives in the squad room and then he grabbed an unmarked Crown Victoria from the motor pool. He was hoping that the second phase of this business would offer up a more pleasurable set of results than the first part had. Cuffing the Janes woman in front of her husband would definitely be a taste of joy.

He met Vargas and Biggs in front of NBPD precinct 6. "You guys wanna ride with me? We can always put the fucking captain in the trunk and you two can sandwich the Janes bitch in the back seat after we arrest them."

"Thanks but we'll take our own vehicle," Sargeant Biggs said, as Robert Vargas nodded in agreement. Both men could barely tolerate standing in the presence of Yorks these days, let alone being confined with him in the same car.

Fabulia got the call from Leslie MacLanahan the previous morning. "Fabulia, you most definitely did not get this from me, but they're going to serve and arrest both you and Victor tomorrow at some time in the day, probably the afternoon. Between the Feds and the State of Massachusetts they've got a host of charges lined up, all of which have a hundred holes through them."

Fabulia's heart started beating faster as she asked, "Is it the same old shit or is there any new stuff that we should know about?"

"My main worry is the Federal charge against Victor. They are going to nail him on the nodule harvesting thing. There's some heavy oil and big guns behind that one starting at the State Department. 'Operating a non-profit corporation under false pretenses' is at the top of the list for your arrest. You'd better get a hold of Lucien ASAP."

"Oh, I'll call him straight away after I get off the phone with you," replied Fabi. "At least we don't have to worry about them getting Vic. Lucien told him to head offshore last night."

There was silence on the line for a second then Leslie said, "Wow, that's a stroke of luck. I'll keep my ears peeled and call Lucien if I hear of anything interesting. I gotta run. An assistant DA on a pay phone outside of the office raises eyebrows. Bye."

When Yorks knocked on the Janes' front door it was opened immediately by Lucien Fernandes. "Well, what a happy coincidence. Mrs. Janes and I were just about to head down to the DA's office to file a phone harassment complaint. You wouldn't know anything about that, would you Lieutenant?"

Ken Yorks looked at Lucien as if he was nonplussed but Lucien noticed that the man's ears were turning crimson. "Don't know what you're talking about, Fernandes but we can help you with a trip downtown. We have arrest warrants here for both Mr. & Mrs. Janes. Please ask the captain to join us." Yorks waved the warrants in Lucien's face then produced a pair of cuffs which he started slapping into one of his palms while he stood there looking smug.

"We can't help you there, sport," said Fabulia, as she edged her way around Lucien. "He is not here and unless you plan on walking water for a good hundred miles you won't be seeing him in the near future. He's fishing."

Vargas and Biggs both grinned but neither of them uttered a word from behind Kenny Yorks' back, who was now looking down forlornly at his boots. Shit. He'd seen Janes yesterday down on the waterfront. This day was just not working out the way he'd planned it.

He took a long breath then looked at Fabulia. "Alright then, Mrs. Janes. You have the right to remain silent..."

"Fat chance, Yorks," she said as she smiled and offered her wrists. "You have not even begun to hear it from me."

∧

Once again pandemonium appeared to be the rule for the day outside of New Bedford Police headquarters. It took the two cars escorting Fabulia downtown ten minutes to go the last block. The street was jammed full with what appeared to be every person within the county, seemingly all there to protest Fabi's arrest.

Lucien double parked when the traffic first came to a halt. He half-ran the last block and was already standing in front of headquarters when Ken Yorks finally stopped the unmarked vehicle. Lucien had the rear door opened and was assisting Fabulia when the lieutenant finally made it around to the passenger side of the car. "That's my job, asshole," he said, as he tried in vain to push the counselor out of the way.

"Go ahead and try to stop me, *officer*. I may fall down and bruise my pinkie— in front of all these cameras and witnesses. I smell a sweet police brutality charge coming on..." All this time Fernandes was grinning amicably at the policeman who could do nothing but step aside while Fabulia Janes was helped out of the vehicle.

Once she was on the street Lucien smiled into the crowd that was yelling insults at Yorks. "Take the cuffs offa her, you putz..."

"...no way to treat a lady..."

"...doesn't deserve this kinda shit from nobody..."

The reporters in the fore-front started yelling all at once, also. "Mrs.

Janes, can you tell us why you've been arrested today?"...

"What have you been charged with...?"

"Mr. Fernandes, can you give us a statement, please?"

Fabulia felt as if this 'instant replay' in reverse was going to make her scream, "*Enough of this! Everyone stop. We do not need to do this anymore. Everyone go home and forget about it all.*" But she held her tongue.

Ken Yorks had taken hold of Fabi's left arm and was trying to motivate her towards the building but Lucien held fast, still smiling ear to ear and said, "Please allow me to get Mrs. Janes checked in then I will be back out to speak with you all." The crowd loved it. This guy was one of them.

"Yeah, buddy. Make sure they get her into a *suite!*"

With Harold Biggs and Bob Vargas taking up the rear, the five of them waded through the crowd, getting back-slapped, shaken and encouraged as if they were all going into some sort of gladiator tournament in the Coliseum instead of into an old, grimey police station. Everyone could not help but grin with the exception of Mierken Yorks. He was so pissed off that he could not see straight. This day was getting worse by the minute as far as he was concerned.

Once inside and standing at the sargeant's desk, Fabi was formally charged, booked and fingerprinted. As the charges were read off Lucien grinned, shook his head and muttered, "What a pile of dinosaur droppings."

"Fabulia Janes, you are hereby charged as follows: One count of money transfer overseas without notifying the Internal Revenue Service or the Treasury Department.

Two counts of failure to pay state and local taxes in accordance with profitable business mandates.

One count of money laundering and one count of operating a business with fraudulent intent."

Fabulia looked up at Lucien and said, "I think these charges are total bullshit, just a means of getting at Victor. What do we do now?"

"For now we'll have to wait until you're arraigned on Monday morning. Over the week-end I'll do a little research and be ready for the judge."

"Guess that means I'm here for a few days," said Fabi.

"Yes, that's about it. But before we part I want to speak with you alone. Yorks, give us a few moments." The lieutenant started to protest but Lucien led Fabi over to the far wall and put his lips to her ear. "How do I get a hold of Victor, Fabi? I never considered this in our plan."

"Oh, that's easy. Get in touch with my father. He can take you to his boat or to the radio at our house. He knows which frequency to use to call Vic. But look, whatever you tell him, do not let him know that I'm in the can. If you do that he'll come barreling into the harbor as fast as he can get here, no matter what the consequences are."

"Yeah, I hear you," said Lucien. "I'm just going to tell him to stay offshore and that we'll be in touch on Monday when we have a better handle on what exactly he's being charged with."

"O.K., but be careful what you say. Everybody and his brother can monitor that radio channel," Fabi said, as Yorks approached them.

"Alright you two. Enough. I got a date tonight. Let's get this done with."

"A date, huh?" Fabi smiled. "Hope I meet her someday. I think you need a 'character reference' , Kenny.

I'll give her an earful."

After Fabulia was led away by the matron, Kenny Yorks turned and started towards the doors. Lucien was still leaning against the wall and as Yorks passed, Lucien grabbed his arm and stopped him in his tracks. "Hey, Kenny-baby. Know what my new job is gonna be after I get Victor and Fabulia squared away? My new job is going to be making sure your ass gets nailed to this wall." Lucien then slapped the concrete hard enough to make people stop and stare at the two men.

"Are you threatening me, Fernandes? Oh, I know. You think you can actually nab me with that phone harassment thing? Fat chance. What's your proof that it was me? Absolutamente nada, pal," Yorks sputtered, as he yanked his arm away from Lucien.

"That's what I love about you, Yorksie. You've pretty much bungled the whole fucking day today but you still find reason to be cocky. Tsk tsk, Mierken. I was in your shoes I'd go find a nice, big rock to hide under."

Ken heard this last incantation even though he as out the door. Christ, what a day. Maybe he'd cancel on his date and just go buy a jug.

^

Victor Janes was also experiencing a somewhat interesting Friday. At 0800 hours Van knocked on the captain's stateroom door, stuck his head in and asked Vic to come up to the wheel-house. When he arrived Van pointed overhead and said, "Helicopters. They have been buzzing along, circling us since daybreak. Also, I have been monitoring two vessels on the radar that have been following us. They came out of Narragansett Bay and were making fourteen knots on an intersecting course with us. When they were both within five miles they slowed to match our speed and course. They have been tailing us for four hours now."

Victor opened the starboard hatch and stepped outside onto the stairway landing that lead down to the bow. He looked up at the helicopters just as they both turned and headed back towards the coast. "Well, they definitely are not Coast Guard." He then peered astern at the two following vessels. They were too far off to make out any of their details without binoculars. Van handed him a pair. After a minute he said, "They look like a couple of good sized, fancy-assed yachts to me. I guess we should not expect anything less from these guys. If you gotta follow someone offshore you may as well do it with champagne and caviar close at hand." He sighed and then continued. "It appears as if the wolves are out. If they want to play, let's play. Turn her due south, Van. Let's let 'em think we're working in real deep water. Take us out to 1500 fathoms then just stop, see what they do. Just before sunset we'll dump the net in the water and pretend like we're fishing. Lemme grab a bite and some coffee then I'll relieve you. This may end up being a long day."

∧

Saturday morning the *Constant Vigil* offices were raided. For some reason Lieutenant Yorks delegated that foray to a few of his co-workers but he was surprised and angry to learn afterwards that Fernandes and three women including another lawyer were there when his boys arrived with the search warrant. The women, in particular, gave the detectives such a hard, hostile time that they'd left prematurely with only two computers and no paper trail; nothing else that could have possibly been used as evidence against the foundation. The women refused to give up the passwords to the two computers. When asked, the lawyer Rita Montrose told the detectives that they could "kiss my big, white ass then I might give you a password."

"And", Yorks wondered, "why is that big bag of shit Fernandes always present these last two days, speaking of big, white asses?"

Around noon Edmund met Lucien down on the wharf. Once they were aboard the boat Eddie turned on the Single Sideband and flipped through the channels until he landed on the agreed frequency for communicating with his son-in-law. He offered the microphone to Lucien who took it and said, "How do I use this thing? It's not like a telephone, is it?"

"No it isn't. Let me get you started." Edmund took the mic back, keyed it and said, "This is the fishing vessel *Sagrada Familia*, Whiskey Yankee Tango five five one zero calling the *Gambling Lady*. How copy, over?"

After two more tries he finally got a response. "This is the fishing vessel *Gambling Lady* back to the station calling. How do you copy? Over." It was Van.

"*Sagrada Familia* back. Copy you 5 by 5, Van. Is the captain available? Over."

"He is sleeping at the moment. Do you want me to wake him? Over."

Edmund looked at Lucien and said, "Yes Van. Please get him up to the wheel-house. Over."

140

"Roger that, *Sagrada Familia*. Please stand-by."

After two minutes Victor's voice came over the air. *"Gambling Lady* back to the *Sagrada*. What's up Edmund?"

Eddie passed the mic over to Lucien who said, "Well, ah yeah, roger and over and under, Victor. It's Lucien here. Just wanted to let you know that what we have been anticipating this last month has finally happened. We'll be calling you again day after tomorrow when I have more information so keep the radio on bub, and, as your wife says, do not even think about coming into *any* port anywhere until we have more information. Well, so… roger, over and out there again, Victor. Talk to you Monday." Lucien hesitated then handed the microphone back to Edmund as Victor said, "Whoa there. Let me speak to Eddie. Over."

Edmund said, "Yeah, I'm here, Vic."

"So what gives, Eddie? I already know that the shit's flying given what's been going on out here but I'm worried about the family. Is everyone O.K.on the beach there? Over."

Edmund shrugged and said, "Yeah, yeah. Everyone's just splendid here, Victor. We'll call you Monday. *Sagrada Familia*, out."

"Roger that, Edmund. If you say so. I'll have to trust you on that one. *Gambling Lady*, out."

Lucien spoke abruptly. "What do you think he meant about what's going on 'out here'? He really didn't sound too convinced. I hope he doesn't decide to head in."

"Yeah, that wasn't good. I never could lie straight-faced, even on the damn radio. But I think he'll stay put, at least until he hears from us on Monday. I hope you can get my daughter released. If Victor doesn't speak with her then he'll know what gives and come home on the run."

"I'll get her out, don't fret Edmund. But I want to use this arrest thing and try to turn it to our advantage."

Edmund DaSilva looked down and shook his head. "That's all fine and well, Lucien but make sure your game-playing doesn't backfire and keep Fabi in jail any longer. Her mother and children do not understand what is going on here and really, neither do I. Goddamn lottery anyway…"

141

CHAPTER TWENTY

FABULIA JANES was not one to languish or pine away just because she happened to be in unpleasant surroundings for a week-end. On Saturday afternoon Martha Vanderhorn was allowed in for a brief visit. She told Fabi about the incident at their office, both women agreeing that the information on the computers could in no way help anyone frame a case against Fabulia or the *Constant Vigil Foundation*. "Besides," stated Martha, "if they try to alter anything on the hard-drives in order to make a case, I have backups for both computers which are date-stamped and now in Lucien's possession. And they didn't take any of our bank statements because those speak for themselves."

When the matron arrived to let Martha out she told Fabi to stay put in the visitation room. She had another visitor. In walked Edmund, hat in hand, looking like a bereaved giant, as he shuffled his feet. "Hi, Daddy. Why the long face?" Fabi asked, as she stood on her toes to kiss her father. He grabbed her in a bear hug and she hung on as she was lifted off of the cement floor.

Edmund gave her a scolding eye and said, "I'm not used to visiting one of my children in the hoosegow."

"Whose-gow, huh? That's a good one. That's not Portuguese, is it? Come on, Daddy. Don't look so glum. Lucien will have me out on Monday and we'll start to get through this. It's not the end of the world as we know it. At least we're no longer sitting around biting our nails wondering when the axe will fall."

"Fabi. I know you and Victor will get through this but it is not you two that I'm worried about at the moment. Your mother is in such a state that I can do nothing to calm her. I swear, her Rosary beads are going to wear out in the next hour. And Rosa is worse. All of her friends and then some are calling, asking her what's going on or just plain saying that her parents are secret criminals and that you're both going to stay in jail for a long time. The kids' gossip-mill has you labeled as everything from a cop-killing lesbian to some sort of voodoo priestess that can make huge sums of money just disappear in a cloud of green smoke."

They both had to laugh at these mental images then Edmund continued. "Loretta and Eddie are the worst. They just cannot understand why all of this is happening. They think that only the 'bad guys' go to jail and now they've seen both of their parents go behind bars inside of six months from each other. They're baffled and scared." He gently set Fabi back down and let out a breath. "And I'm so mad I just wanna punch *something*. These... these *people* piss me off to no end. I mean, just who do they suppose they are? Let 'em go find their own freakin' rocks. There's a lotta ocean out there. Leave us alone, for Christ's sake."

They both walked over to the table and sat. As Edmund threw down his hat and snorted in disgust, Fabulia tried to put it all in perspective for her father and, maybe, for herself also. "You just never know Dad. One step to the right or one to the left years ago by your father and neither you or I would be here now. I mean, if he hadn't have met Grandma that day in Horta, well, *poof.* We would, neither of us, be here now, having this conversation. Control over our own destiny is basically limited to the present but a huge portion of it is definitely written in the past. Fate and Time make interesting bedfellows. Luck is definitely born to Fate and Time, over and over again.

All we can do is try and nudge the luck so that it doesn't turn totally bad on us and that's what Victor and I will do. We're going to push our own damn luck to the hilt because we are not people who roll over and allow somebody... anybody else to control our destiny." Fabulia slapped the table softly and stood. "I feel terribly for my children also. The only saving grace is that time will change this. We all have to reassure them; let them know that we will always be present for them all. Lucky for them, there's lots of us, Daddy."

Edmund nodded and grinned at his daughter. This was why he loved her so. He started to get all mushed up then abruptly pulled himself back to the present, putting back on the 'tough old salt' exterior. "Oh yeah," he said. "We called Vic on the Sideband. We didn't tell him your whereabouts, I kinda lied, but we told him that the friggin' ball had dropped. He let on that he already knew as much, which Lucien and I couldn't quite figure out. Anyway, he's staying put until we call him on Monday.

Lucien's been rooting around this afternoon, trying to figure out Victor's odds on beating the federal charges against him. It does not sound as if they're going to let him skate this time. Lucien wants to hold off on calling Victor till Monday afternoon so that he can keep at it all day, after he gets you out." Edmund shrugged and put his cap on just as the matron opened the door and said, "Time."

Edmund was lead out and the matron escorted Fabi back to the common area where she calmly sat with the hookers, heroin addicts and scofflaws to await a new week. Monday couldn't come soon enough for her.

∧

Judge Oscar Haverstraw was in a bitterly despondent frame of mind. Earlier in the morning he'd presided over three B&E's and one rape case. All four cases were heroin related. Three of the four cases involved repeat offenders and the rape case involved a sixteen year old female who couldn't pay her dealer for her last three fixes so the guy raped and beat her as payment. It all just kept getting worse instead of better. Twenty-two years on the bench and he felt as if he had gained no ground at all, had made no difference to anyone, had not helped keep this small portion of society safe for its citizens.

And now the DA's office threw this pile of fool's droppings in front of him. "What a fucking travesty," he said to himself. He reviewed the paperwork for a full five minutes, periodically scowling at the prosecutor's table. Finally he pushed the paperwork aside and motioned for both Lucien Fernandes and Peter Schmitt, the prosecuting attorney, to approach the bench. After looking at both attorneys for a second and covering the microphone he whispered, "Mr. Schmitt, April Fools Day is long past. What is the meaning of all this waste-paper?" the judge asked as he pushed the pile aside.

Peter Schmitt took in a quick breath but Haverstraw continued. "No, no. I am not expecting you to answer me. Do not even try. Just listen. I understand that you were saddled with this pitiful mess, that you personally did not perpetuate it. But it did come from your office and I am instructing you, here and now, to bring a message back with you when you return to that hallowed, august edifice.

Tell your boss, the titular AG for the county, that I am not amused. This set of charges is pitiful. Your office is obviously grasping at straws. I want you to tell your boss that, if he must send me such bullshit, send someone in a clown suit with dogs and ponies. At the least, we'll all have a good laugh and be entertained while the crap is being flung about." The judge yanked off his glasses, vigorously rubbed his eyes and then continued.

"Here's what I am going to do. I'm going to take this set of charges back to my office and try to carefully review it all without prejudice. If, after my review, I can hold on to a shred of evidential reality, I will recall this case. If, in fact, I do not hold that shred I am going to bring this whole charade to the attention of the State Attorney General's office in Boston. Now, in the interim I will release Mrs. Janes on her own recognizance…"

Peter Schmitt blurted out, "But your honor, this woman is a flight risk! I strongly oppose…"

"Oh, please spare us of more drivel, Mr. Shmitt." The judge's hand had slipped off of the microphone. "So… tell me how that feels, Mr. Schmitt." The judge had adopted a pained, empathetic expression.

The prosecutor looked baffled for a second then said, "Well, ah, how *what* feels, your honor?"

"Oh, I was just wondering how it felt, you trying to get your foot in your mouth when your head was already up your ass!" *Bang.* Down came the gavel. "This court is adjourned for lunch." Judge Haverstraw launched himself out of the chair and headed for his chambers. A martini was definitely in order today.

∧

Lucien Fernandes was practically dancing as they walked away from the Bristol County Courthouse. Fabulia was having a hard time keeping up with him. "Hey, slow down, man." Lucien came to a quick stop and Fabi plowed into him. "Great Gods," he said. "That was absolutely blissful. And I always thought that Haverstraw was just some frumpy, melancholy, old guy in a robe. Jesus, he rocked that building today. He brought a whole new meaning to the words 'Your Honor'. I love him, I swear I do!"

"Yeah. And for once, you didn't even have to voice one word. And here I am, on the outside again. Yep, 'blissful' is a great word for it. I'm glad to be outta that place." She grinned and continued. "So, what do we do now, Lucien? We gotta call Victor on the radio this afternoon but I must see my kids as soon as school's out."

"Let's walk over to your office, meet with the girls, and order some lunch. I skipped breakfast today and I cannot think on an empty gut. I've got a lot to report to you. I didn't exactly relax this weekend," said the counselor, with a grin.

∧

Victor Janes was not feeling exactly blissful but he was far from being in a state of depression. Sunday had him more amused than anything else. This whole business was turning crazier by the minute.

Van had taken the *Gambling Lady* out really deep, to about 2,500 fathoms or 15,000 feet of international, vertical water underneath the keel of the boat. They'd dumped the net in, set out some wire, and just towed it all around for hours. They didn't catch any shrimp or nodules or anything aside from a few pieces of stray kelp. They were nowhere even remotely close to the bottom of the ocean; all the while being followed by the yachts. In the middle of the night one of them became impatient, powered up and came right alongside, within fifty feet of the *Gambling Lady*.

A powerful spotlight was shown onto the working deck of the trawler from the yacht. In the artificial glow of the deck lights Emilio Santos and Octavio Guzman were in a heated battle of ping-pong against Nguyen Vinh and Nguyen Dan. The pitching and rolling of the deck seemingly bothered none of the players though knee boots were needed to keep the players feet dry from the water cris-crossing the deck.

Victor opened up the starboard side pilothouse door as Van shined a spotlight at the yacht's bow and pilothouse. Vic chuckled as he noted that the name of the vessel was the *Shangri-La*. A man, presumably the captain, opened up a door on his port side, leaned out and saluted Victor, who immediately saluted back. What else could he do? It would have been in poor taste to flip the guy the bird out here in the middle of the Atlantic, though it did cross Victor's mind.

Just as swiftly as it arrived, the spotlight went out and the yacht peeled off to take up station once again, a mile behind the *Gambling Lady*. Victor was able to read the hailing port on the stern of the vessel as it sped away. 'London' was all that it said. Victor turned to Van and said, "Well, I guess that was Lord Nelson that just paid us a visit. Hope he doesn't figure me for a Napolean type."

Van just smiled and asked, "What do you want to do, Victor? I will assume that our escorts now know that we are playing games with them. There is no sense in leaving the gear in the water."

Victor thought for a second then said, "Yes, you're probably right about that. After the boys get done with their table tennis we may as well haul in the gear but let's not stray too far. At least let's not head north. For some reason I'm feeling a whole lot safer out here in international waters. Let's just stay out here until we hear from Fabi and Lucien tomorrow."

∧

With lunch consumed and a coffee in hand Lucien filled the girls in. "I spent most of Saturday on the phone calling in some favors, trying to find out how severely these federal charges against Victor are going to be handled. My sources in Boston and here at the AG's office both tell me that the charges are being treated most seriously. They intend to re-enter the squid by-catch charge so that they can revoke Victor's fishing permit and, also, they intend to prosecute him on the nodule harvesting thing as some sort of test case for the World Court in the Hague, Netherlands. Something to do with 'showing the world that the International Seabed Authority is taking their job seriously'. In other words, they intend on making an example of Victor and the *Gambling Lady*."

All of the women, with the exception of Fabulia, started speaking at once but Martha Vanderhorn won out. "How can they actually expect to make this work in the World Court? I mean, all they've got is a handful of those rocks, right? And nobody can prove he was even in international waters when he caught them anyway."

Rita Montrose spoke up and said, "Yes, they really don't have anything on face-value but they do have just enough on the circumstancial end of it to make a plausible case in the World Court. At the root of it all, what these people really want to do is wear Victor down so that he gives up his fishing positions. I bet they'll try to make a deal with Victor, such as, if he gives up his numbers they'll give him back his fishing permit."

Emily Fagundes jumped right in."And don't forget, they can keep this case open in the court in Europe for years. All that time Victor will be, at best, not allowed to fish, not allowed to leave the country, not allowed to do anything without a microscope on his ass..." Emily stopped just as suddenly. She usually wasn't much for speeches.

Everyone in the room was looking at Fabi. She pulled her eyes away from the floor and said. "Well...Shit. I guess we're at the friggin' crossroads. What do you think about all of this, Lucien?" Lucien hesitated, as if he was trying to find the right words, trying to soften the reality of it all.

"Come on, Lucien. Don't try to candy-coat it, for Christ sake," said Fabi.

"Yeah, yeah." Lucien began, as he stood up, started pacing and put his hands on the top of his head. "It's just that this is such a huge turning point, for us all really, but mostly for the whole Janes family. It sucks being painted into a corner by somebody else. OK. *Victor's gotta head for Brazil.* There, I've said it. Nothing else makes any sense."

Nobody in the room uttered a word in protest, all four women waited for Lucien to continue.

"Now, with that finally said, here's what I've done in anticipation of this moment. As we all know, the money is safe and out of the country, so we're all set on that score. There's a Bank of Nova Scotia branch in Bermuda so it shouldn't be a problem to get some more cash out for Victor once he arrives there. Maybe we'll have to send one of you down there to get that done in advance. Anyway, that's where he should head."

Martha Vanderhorn spoke up next. "But Lucien, I believe the United States has a consulate on that island. By the time he gets there won't there be some sort of an international APB out for Victor?"

"Yes, exactly, Martha. But I think I've pretty well got that problem covered with the help of Mateus Oberegon and the Brazilian government. You see, they *really* want Victor to come to Brazil. Victor doesn't know it but he's got certificates of registry on the boat that will transfer the *Gambling Lady*'s hailing port from New Bedford, Massachusetts to Santos, Brazil. He also has a Brazilian passport in his name with all the other paperwork. To make it legal all Vic has to do is sign the passport and registry paperwork. Presto-chango, Brazilian registry and citizenship. Oh, and we have to open up a Brazilian bank account in the name of Victor Janes for a quarter of a million dollars; no strings attached, it's just a legal matter so that Victor's complete, immediate family can also become instant Brazilian citizens."

There were four sets of dazzled, amazed eyes staring at the counselor.

"Hey, come on, now," he said. "Don't look at me like that. I did it as a fail-safe. If we ended up not needing it I could have just snuck back onto the boat and removed all of the paperwork from the hiding place that I, alone, put it in. I was just trying to look ahead a little." Lucien flinched as Fabulia jumped up and took two, quick steps over to him.

She jumped up once more, wrapping her arms around his neck. "Oh hell, Lucien. We are definitely *not* mad at you. I just cannot believe that none of us thought the deal this far through." She then planted a big, wet kiss right on his lips. "Thanks Lucien. I think you just saved my husband from a life of legal drudgery. Now, I gotta run and pick the kids up at school. How's about I meet you down on the wharf around four-thirty? We'd better give Victor a call on the sideband. I don't want to call him from the house radio if the kids are around. Bye girls. I'll check in tomorrow morning."

^

Victor was swearing profusely as he paced the wheelhouse, port to starboard, starboard to port. Back and forth for the hundredth time today. Van could barely make out the curses above the roar of helicopter blades beating a very loud, invasive, staccato that permeated the whole boat. There were actually two helos but currently the biggest one owned by the United States Coast Guard was directly overhead and harassing Victor periodically over the VHF radio. "Fishing vessel *Gambling Lady, Gambling Lady*. This is United States Coast Guard helo 11549 calling the *Gambling Lady*. How copy? Over."

"Yeah, yeah, 11549. Read you fine. Over," was Victor's impatient reply. He'd already been through this whole drill with the helo pilot three times.

"11549 back to the *Gambling Lady*. Request you alter course and make way for a U.S. port, captain. Your fishing permits have been revoked as of 0900 hours this morning. How copy on my last, *Gambling Lady*? Over."

150

Before Victor could respond, the Single Sideband radio started warbling. "*Gambling Lady, Gambling Lady*. This is Whiskey Yankee Tango 5510, fishing vessel *Sagrada Familia* calling the *Gambling Lady*. Pickin' me up, Victor?"

"*Gambling La…*"

Victor turned off the VHF radio with a flourish then he reached for the Sideband microphone. "*Gambling Lady* back to the *Sagrada*. Pickin' you up fine, Edmund. What's up? Over."

As Victor heard her voice he let out a deep breath that he felt like he'd been holding in for three days.

"Hey there, honey-bunch!" shouted Fabi over the air-waves. "How's it going out there, my dear? Catching lots of shrimp? Over." She didn't quite know how to break the news to Vic over a very public radio frequency but he solved the problem for her.

"All we're catching out here, at the moment, is a lot of flack, Fabi. I've got two helicopters and two big-assed yachts tailing me like shoo-flys on a cow's back. The Coast Guard helo keeps asking me to head home, telling me I no longer own fishing rights in United States waters. Funny thing is, in my current position, I'm 53 nautical miles outside of U.S. waters anyhow. Either way, I get the distinct impression that the guillotine has definitely started to drop. How's things on your end? How come you didn't talk to me Saturday? Over."

"Yeah, Vic. Well, I was kinda preoccupied with this whole business on Saturday. Then it got late… But here's the thing, Victor. Yes, your fishing permit is revoked and what's more, they are going to take you to court, to the World Court, over those rocks. It does not bode well for you on the beach. Over."

"Well, well. Isn't that all just peachy…I guess that leaves me with just the two options that we discussed last week. Stay and fight or cut and run. Don't look like much of a fair fight. What's Lucien think about all this? Over."

Lucien took the offered mic, keyed it and said, "Ah, Roger Wilco there Victor. Yes, it is not good here in town. I think this whole mess will only get worse if you return. You will be in court for years and, honestly, we'll have to find more lawyers that will be able to deal with this World Court business. We are all in agreement here, Vic. You gotta head for Brazil. Over."

Victor leaned his brow against the bulkhead, closed his eyes and sighed. The airwaves were silent for a ten-count then Fabulia came back on. "Victor. Are you there, Vic? Over, please."

"Yeah. Yes, I'm here, Fabi. Just trying to think. So what's next. I guess now I've got to learn that Brazilian version of Portuguese, huh?"

Lucien came back on and said, "Yeah, Victor but that'll be no problem. Now listen up, please. Your first stop is going to be Bermuda to take on fuel, potable water and grub. Then you can keep heading south. I'll arrange another stop for you, in Trinidad, maybe.

You are going to have to make some changes to the boat before you get to Bermuda. Go into your quarters and take out the middle drawer under your bunk. Take all of the stuff out and find the manila folder with all the documentation papers. Sign on all the places where you see the little smiley-face yellow tabs that I attached. The rest, you'll know what to do but make sure you get it all done before you even come in sight of Bermuda. Over."

"Yeah, yeah. I copied all of that Lucien but, you know, I've gotta talk to my crew about this. I can't just say 'We're going to Bermuda, guys.' What if one of them doesn't want to go? You guys stand by for ten minutes. I'm going to ask them all, now..." Victor shifted his attention over to Van. "Take her out of gear, will ya, Van and get the whole crew into the galley, please. We gotta have a little meeting."

Van had everyone assembled in two minutes and Victor wasted no time. "All right, here it is guys. My fishing permit has been yanked out from under me. We cannot legally fish in U.S. waters anymore and the friggin' *authorities* are going to go after me for catching those damned nodules. In some world court, no less. Now, we can either head back into New Bedford and I'll fight it all or we can head for Brazil where the authorities there will let this boat fish as long as I help them figure out how to pick up a lot of those goddam rocks. But I'm not going anywhere unless you all, right down to the last man, agree to go. So I'm looking for a vote. What about you, Gideon?"

"Brazil? Are you kidding me? Rum punches on Ipanema? Take me away!"

"And how's about you guys?" He was looking at Octavio and Emilio.

"Hey, no problema, Cap. We go with you. Maybe we get Rafael to come to Brazil, eh?" said Emilio as Octavio nodded in agreement.

"And what do you four think of all this?"

Auntie Di spoke up with no hesitation. "We stay with you and *Gambling Lady*, Victor. You treat us all good." Van just smiled.

Victor turned to Teddy Thibodaux who laughed and said, "*Cette partie est mise en route. Je vais aller au Brésil.*"

Finally Victor looked at Jazzy Coelho and said, "So, what do you think of all this, my *chef extraordinária?*"

Jazzy was looking quite forlorn and sad. After a brief hesitation he asked, "Will I ever be able to go home, Victor? I mean, are we all going to be banned from the United States? If we are, that sucks. I'm definitely gonna have to write my congressman on that one."

The laughter was short-lived as Victor said, "Whoa. That's a really good question that I'll have to ask Lucien Fernandes about. And don't worry about it, Jazzy. Our first stop will be Bermuda. If anybody has second thoughts they can get off there. And I'll be paying the airfare when anybody wants to go home; no matter where we end up." Victor started to leave then turned back to his crew and said, "Thanks. Thank you all."

Victor hailed the *Sagrada Familia* on the Sideband and Fabi came back at him immediately. "Yeah, Vic. Read you fine. So, what's the verdict?"

"Well, I guess we're gonna turn her south, Fabi. It was pretty much unanimous. They all want to stick it out, God bless 'em all. Over."

"Okay, Victor. That's great. I'll see you in Bermuda. Keep this radio on. We'll try you every day around five in the afternoon. And Lucien says to go slow. He doesn't want you there for at least a week. Okay. *Sagrada*

Familia clear with the *Gambling Lady*. Out."

"*Gambling Lady*, over and out." Victor hung up the microphone and headed into his quarters. After pulling the drawer all of the way out of the slot he felt around inside and immediately located a box. Once he had it out on top of his bunk, he slit the tape and found one manila envelope that contained a pile of papers and a Brazilian passport in his name. "Where the hell did they get that picture from?" he wondered.

The next item was a set of ten inch high stencils that spelled out 'SANTOS, BRASIL'. Next in line was a neatly folded Brazilian flag. Victor liked the color scheme but the flag meant little else to him. Another heavier manila envelope appeared. Victor opened in up and started to laugh. There was, by his quick count, $20,000, all in new hundred dollar bills. The last item in the care package set Victor off into a full fledged belly laugh. It was a set of eight cassette tapes, a Berlitz language course for Brazilian Portuguese. "That freakin' Lucien has thought it all right through," he said to himself, as he headed back to the wheelhouse, grinning the whole way.

Once there Victor noticed that the helicopter beat was still with them. He switched on the VHF and keyed the mic. "U.S. Coast Guard helo 11549. This is the *Gambling Lady* calling, channel One Six. Over."

"*Gambling Lady*, helo 11549. Over"

"Roger, helo 11549. Please be advised- we're all set here. You can terminate your, ah, escort duties at this time. Over."

"Helo 11549 back to the *Gambling Lady*. Ah, Roger that on your last. Can you please advise us your intentions? Over."

"*Gambling Lady* back to 11549. Sure, Cap. I hear Brazil's very nice this time of year. I think we'll give it a whirl. *Gambling Lady*, Over and Out." Victor switched off the VHF and headed out to the bow. Both helicopters had taken up positions on either side of the *Gambling Lady*, almost at eye level with Victor who turned to the Coast Guard helo, waved and saluted. He then pivoted 180 degrees, waved at the other helicopter and gave it a big, middle-finger salute. Both helos turned and headed north towards land. One of the yachts turned also but the *Shangri-La* brought her power up and passed the *Gambling Lady*, heading south. Victor went back to his quarters and grabbed the Brazilian flag. He then went out the aft second level hatch and started to un-cleat the lanyard that held the American Flag flying high overhead in the rigging. After a long, agonizing pause he finally did it. Down came the flag that he had come admire and respect. And down with it also came Victor's own, personal version of the American Dream. They were on their way to Brazil. "Head her south, Van, a hundred and ninety three degrees on the compass, please. We're outta here."

∧

Tribal policeman Thomas Walathoma came upon Carol-Jean and her truck on Route 66 at 2:30 in the morning. She was deathly cold, shivering convulsively. Thomas got her into his car and cranked up the heat. After five minutes Carol-Jean said, "Thomas, can you please run me into Flagstaff to the Medical Center?" She explained about Joe. Thomas called in to headquarters on the radio then hit the overhead lights and started down the road towards the city as the snow swirled around them.

Three hours later he came to a sliding halt in front of the ER. When they got through the automatic doors the receptionist looked at Thomas and asked what the problem was. Carol-Jean said, "It's not me. My husband was brought in around nine last night. His name is Joe Watamohigie. Can you please tell me where I can find him?"

The woman consulted her computer and said, "He is in ER number eleven. I'll buzz you in through those doors."

Carol-Jean, followed by Thomas, hurried to the double doors and yanked one open as it buzzed. She hesitated and asked a passing nurse where eleven was. They hurried down the corridor and stopped in front of the room marked "11". She heard someone murmuring inside and slowly pulled back the curtain. There lay Joe, covered head to foot in a white shroud as a priest recited the Last Rites over him. Carol-Jean collapsed and Thomas Walathoma caught her before she hit the floor.

CHAPTER TWENTY-ONE

THE SARGASSO SEA is the only named body of water on the planet that is not bordered by landmass. It is a sea within an ocean. Its' amazingly clear, cobalt blue waters comprise an area that is roughly 2000 miles long, east to west, and 700 miles wide, north to south. The island of Bermuda lies within the northwest corner of this sea that is surrounded by four ocean currents forming the North Atlantic Sub-tropical Gyre. It was first named by Portuguese sailors in the 15ᵗʰ century that encountered large sections of the sea covered in Sargassum weed that fouled many a sailing ship's rudders and spawned many more imagined sea monsters. Part of the famed 'Bermuda Triangle' also lies within its' boundries.

Victor Janes gazed out over the flat, calm sea from the starboard side wheelhouse wing as the *Gambling Lady* slowly pushed south. He could barely discern the horizon. The color of the water and the sky were closely matched at this time of day. For a moment he empathized with the ancient sailors that first discovered this sea. The unknown had always been and would always be a frightful place, giving birth to lurid perceptions. Did they fall over the edge of the sea or float up into the sky when they reached the terminus? The imagination of men was outdone only by the imagination of women.

Their stop on the island of Bermuda had been just another fiasco, at best. They'd made all the required changes to the vessel while they were at sea. Victor, Teddy and Gideon were awed at how easy this legal process was. Change a flag, paint over some letters and, presto. Instant nationality change. They all felt that, somehow, it should be more difficult than this. But, when they arrived in Hamilton it became abundantly clear that there were differing agendas behind the curtains in the mix of, what Lucien Fernandes was now calling, '*The Gambling Lady Saga*'.

At the sea buoy Victor slowed down to a speed of three knots so that a boat could get alongside and transfer the harbor pilot over to them. Victor's antenna went up when an armed policeman followed the pilot onboard. "Good morning sir. Good day for it, what?" Victor shook hands with the pilot, Harry Barrington, but peered nervously at the ebony black, impeccably uniformed, large policeman. "Oh, please don't worry yourself about Officer Weatherly. Jacob is here for your protection and nothing more. I dare say you have quite the welcoming party awaiting you all shore-side," said Senior Pilot Barrington, as he took over the helm from Van. "The Brazilians and Yanks are about to come to blows over you boys. I dare say, our lads may end up having to throw a few 'diplomats' into gaol to remind them of their manners. Nothing like a touch of political mischief to get the blood boiling, eh?"

Victor looked over at Teddy and said, "Let's just hope that there's no blood and eggs involved in this welcoming party." Harry Barrington gave a puzzled look between the two men but said nothing. Teddy just shook his head and laughed at the memory as he adjusted the toothpick in his mouth.

As Harry made the final approach to Penno's Wharf in St. George's Harbor, Victor gave Teddy an elbow nudge and pointed. Teddy said, "Well hell, man. Ain dat a big piece a serendipity. Or is not, which means we gonna have ta watch our ass double sure 'round dis place."

Up ahead on the far end of Penno's sat the *Shangri-La*. Apparently the *Gambling Lady* was going to tie up just astern of the yacht.

"Tabarnac. I d'own feel too good 'bout all dis right about now," declared Teddy.

Victor just shrugged and said, "Not much we're gonna do about it. Look," he said, as he pointed again. There on the dock was Lucien and Fabulia, standing separately from a group of five men and one woman. "My guess is, if Lucien thought this stop was going to be that big a problem he would not have given us the green light to come on in."

Teddy peered at the group on the dock and said, "Hey. Isn dat da cop wha's his name…?"

Before Teddy could finish Vic said, "Yeah, yeah. That's that damned

SOB Yorks. Why is *he* here? I guess we can be certain that this meeting will most likely get interesting with that sweetheart around." He grimaced as he wondered why Vargas and Biggs were not also present then he had to smile as he recognized Mateus Oberegon also standing in the group.

Harry guided the *Gambling Lady* up against the dock and came to a stop. Lines went over and within three minutes they were snugged up and moored in Bermuda. A gang plank with hand rails was pushed over the side and secured on the wharf. The group decended onto the *Gambling Lady* with Lucien and Fabi taking up the rear of the procession. Van met them all and ushered everyone up to the wheelhouse where Victor and Teddy awaited them. There was barely room to contain this menagerie of bureaucrats, mariners and one newspaper guy.

Fabi gave her husband a big smile and a wave from the outside starboard wing, as she stood on her tip-toes. She could not get further inside. The man next to her was Francois Riendeau, a reporter from *Le Monde* magazine in Paris. It was a slow day in paradise. He immediately started taking photographs of Victor across the wheelhouse, who started to become annoyed.

Lucien signaled Vic with an index finger to his lips as he pushed his way through the crowd and stood next to his friend and client. One of the visitors whispered to Harry who then pointed at Victor.

As he extended his right hand towards Victor the man said, "Captain Janes, my name is Trevor Watson. I am your assigned agent from His Majesty's Department of Immigration, Customs and Health here on the island. I will need to see your registry paperwork as well as a list of all crewmembers on board and all crewmember's passports, if any are available." The man gave a slight sniff. He was much more used to dealing with pristine yachts and colossal cruise ships as opposed to odious fishing vessels. "I will also need to be apprised of any health issues you may have on board, what? Any flu present or any, ah, other communicable diseases?" Another sniff.

Victor, being aptly prepped beforehand over the radio by Lucien, immediately handed Watson his Brazilian Registry, crew list, all of the collected passports and one State of Massachusetts driver's license. The only crewmember without a passport was Jazzy, though he, by the time they'd arrived in Bermuda, could not have cared less. He'd let his Portuguese passport lapse some fifty-three years ago and had never applied for the United States version after he gained citizenship. "To hell with it," was his response when asked by Victor if he wanted to apply for one at the U.S. Consulate on the island. "I don't care if I can come and go. I'm alive and doin' it just fine right here on this boat. Besides, we won't be here long anyway, right Cap?"

"I hope not, Jazzy. I hope not. But that remains to be seen."

Roger Hornsby, Secretary to the Bermuda Premier said, "Please have a quick look at the paperwork, Trevor, and let me know if you find any abnormalities. In the interim let's get to the meat of it, shall we? Mr. Janes, we're at a bit of an impasse; a conundrum, if you will. Mrs. Cloe Hadley here is the U.S. Consulate attaché on our island." Hornsby indicated Hadley with a deferential nod.

"She has in her possession a United States federal warrant for your arrest." Hadley started to speak but Roger Hornsby held up a finger and continued. "Our difficulty lies in the fact that said warrant is for a citizen of the United States and it is not clear at present if you fall within that category." With this Hornsby raised his eyebrows and Cloe Hadley leapt in.

"That is correct, Mr. Secretary. And I do not give a good, goddamn where this, this modern-day pirate is now calling home. When he departed Massachusetts over a month ago he was flying a U.S. flag and carried a U.S. passport. It only stands to reason…"

"Am I to assume, given this last statement of yours, Mrs. Hadley, that the United States has now, by your power alone, elected to disavow Brazil's existence as a sovereign state that, up until this very moment, has had nothing but cordial relations with the United States?" Mateus Oberegon finished and held out his hands, palms upward, waiting for Hadley's reply.

Lucien spoke up and said, "My client has been negotiating a business deal with the Brazilian government for the past twelve weeks. That this business finally came to fruition in the last week while Captain Janes was at sea is purely coincidental. A section of the agreement stipulates Brazilian registry for this vessel and Brazilian citizenship for Captain Janes and his family, if they so desire. All vessel registry and nationality transfers have been done legally, legally I might add, within both U.S. and Brazilian parameters."

"I do not give a fig about your 'parameters' Mr. Fernandes," barked Hadley. "I have a copy of Janes' *United States Bureau of Shipping* registry right here." She waved the papers around ominously and continued. "In order for any new registry to be taken as a bonafide document the vessel owner must first sign off and nullify the old registry. Captain Janes has not done so, therefore this vessel and the Captain still fall within United States domain."

"That is all fine and well, Mrs. Hadley," said Roger Hornsby, "but let us not forget that you are, in fact, on British soil…"

"And as you say in America, 'hogwash'. Brazilian law is in no way bound by the U.S. legal system. We have our own laws and, as of the date on the Brazilian Registry documents and on his passport, both have become subjects of Brazil, no *ifs*, no *ands* and absolutely no *buts*." Everyone in the wheelhouse was staring at Oberegon. How could such a seeming youngster command such presence? Even the very jaded Cloe Hadley was dumbstruck for a moment. She knew the game was about up so she tried her last-ditch game card, which, as it turned out, was a painful bet at best. "Oh, this is just political hyperbole and bullshit," she said. "Officer Yorks, handcuff this man and let's be out of here." She pointed disdainfully at Victor. "I've already missed two late morning appointments because of this foolishness."

Kenny Yorks started to joyfully push his way forward to get to Victor. Before he got within a yard of the captain he found himself lifted off of his feet by his neck and immobilized. Jacob Weatherly turned Yorks slightly, looked him in the eye and said, "You sah, have no aut'ority to be 'cuffin no one a'tall. If anyone is to do the restrainin' twill be me, sah.

Now mind your manners and do not make me angry." With that he abruptly set Yorks down, turned him around and sent him back to his place on the opposite side of the wheelhouse.

Trevor Watson looked up from the chart table where he had been studying the paperwork. "Ah, sir?" He addressed Roger Hornsby. "All of the paperwork is in perfect order."

Hornsby let out a breath and said, "Thank you Trevor. Captain Janes, I see no need to detain you. I will, however, ask that you and your full crew complement remain onboard this vessel while you are taking on stores, potable water and fuel-oil. This request comes directly from the Premier's desk. We feel that it would be in everyone's best interest if you were back out to sea as soon as is possible. Please have a pleasant but short stay in our harbor." With that, Hornsby, Watson and Harry Barrington, who gave Vic a silent grin and thumbs up, departed the wheelhouse heading down to the galley and the main deck. Cloe Hadley followed, after giving Captain Janes a venomous glare.

Fabulia took advantage of the sudden vacancy and ran over to her husband whom she embraced in her own version of a bear hug with both arms and legs. She hadn't seen him in almost five weeks. Kenny Yorks hung back under the still watchful eye of Officer Weatherly.

"Whew," said Victor. "Another set of bullets dodged. When do you think the shooting'll stop, Fabi?"

"Damned if I know, Victor." Said Fabulia. "I can't even remember when or where all of this nonsense started. I sure as hell won't make a prediction on when it'll all cease."

"All right folks. Let's clear the wheelhouse and give the Janes's here some privacy," said Lucien. "Come on, Yorks. Out. You're like a case of herpes. Ya never quite go away."

Kenny wanted to respond but thought better of it with Jacob Weatherby bird-dogging him. Down the companionway they went followed by Mateus Oberegon and the reporter, Riendeau, who stopped briefly by Vic and asked, "Pardon me, Miseu, may I have an interview before you depart the island? *Est il possible?*"

Victor glanced over to Teddy and said, "Why don't you take this one, mon frère. I've got boat business to attend to if we're going to be outa here in a timely fashion."

They were finally alone then Victor remembered that he hadn't said a word to Mateus. "Come on, Fabi. I never said a word of thanks to Mr. Oberegon." They both went down to the galley and headed out to the deck. Kenny Yorks was standing against the outside bulkhead and Victor missed seeing him as he stepped over the water-tight combing with Fabulia at his heels.

Kenny snatched her arm as she passed and whispered in her ear. "See you back in New Bedford, bitch. We'll catch up…" Before he could say more Victor had turned, took two steps back, grabbed the man by his face and snapped the back of his head into the bulkhead while bringing a knee up into his groin at the same time. And that was it for Yorks. He wasn't crippled but he hurt. Bad.

Victor leaned over the crumpled form at his feet and whispered, "Yorks, that is the final… that was the last time you will ever lay your stink on my wife. Hopefully, for you, we will never see each other again because, if we do ever meet, I will put you in a box." Victor straightened up and turned. Fabi was frozen in place as were people on the deck, the gangway and the dock. It happened so fast that no one had any time to react before it was over and done. Fabi said, "Holy shit, Vic. That was a bit much, huh? I hope he'll be alright." Officer Weatherly stepped next to Victor and said, "Well Captain, I think it would be best if you painted that hatch combing bright yellow, sir. You cannot have people tripping over those things and hurting themselves. 'Safety First' we always say." That being said, the policeman bent over, helped the moaning figure half stand, then he effortlessly hoisted Kenny over his shoulder like a sack of mashed potatoes.

^

By three p.m. Victor had everyone ashore that could go ashore with the exception of Fabi who wasn't due to fly out until the following afternoon with Lucien. Grub and hard-goods would arrive in the morning along with fuel. The counselor showed up again earlier in the afternoon to report that all was well at the moment and to reiterate that it would be in their collective best interests to leave the island before someone decided to start stirring the damned pot again. He also told them that Mierken Yorks, although up and about, was moving at a reduced rate of speed due to swollen testicles and a good sized egg on his figuratively deflated head. He would live to antagonize humanity once again. After giving this abbreviated report Lucien hurried off the boat mumbling something about a date with a baccarat table at the casino in his hotel.

By four o'clock Victor gently left Fabi sleeping in his quarters. The onboard bunks were not made for two people and definitely not for two people that had no intention of sleeping right away. He walked up to the wheelhouse and noticed that a man was just walking off of the *Shangri-La*. Victor immediately recognized him as the same guy that saluted Victor out in 2000 fathoms of water. Feeling curious, Vic walked out to the wharfside wing as the man strode down the dock. The man stopped as Victor smiled down at him and saluted again.

"Well. Captain Janes. It is a pleasure to meet you though I'll freely admit I am glad that it is not face-to-face. We saw your brief encounter on the working deck earlier today."

Victor shook his head and looked down at the water for a moment. "That guy has been begging for a beating for quite some time. I finally had to oblige him. I don't go off like that often and I certainly don't go off on strangers. Come on aboard. I won't bite."

"Thank-you for the offer but I have some business in Hamilton that I've got to take care of. Tell you what though. I would be honored if you would join us for dinner aboard the *Shangri-La* tonight. Say around six?"

"Thanks for the offer but we're all kinda under house arrest. The authorities don't want us on dry land for some reason."

"Well, to hell with all those in authority everywhere. But if I send the inflatable over we'll ferry you between boats and you will not be upsetting anyone. What do you say to that?"

"That sounds like an offer that I can't refuse. I'd like to see your yacht and I'll bring you a box of our shrimp. Can I bring my wife?"

"Of course. Well then, I'm late. See you at six. Oh, by the way, Anthony Favazza at your service, sir," he said as he once again, saluted Victor.

∧

Teddy insisted that he come with them saying that he'd always wanted to see the engineroom of a yacht. They'd all dressed up as best they could with Teddy even coming down to the galley in a natty blue blazer. Fabulia whistled and Auntie Di walked up to Teddy and smiled. "L 'homme est très élégant, n'est-il pas?"

Their water taxi for the 200 foot ride arrived. While Van held the bow line Fabi, Victor and Teddy decended into the skiff then Van passed down a box of Royal Reds. The ride took all of twenty seconds; long enough for Teddy to check out the driver, who did not offer his name, his position on the *Shangri-La* or any amicable charm whatsoever. The man was a hefty one and a single gold earring seemed to accentuate his size.

Captain Favazza appeared on the aft deck as they bumped against the swimming platform that jutted out from the stern of the yacht, saying "Welcome, welcome." He held out a hand as if to assist Fabi but she ignored it and jumped nimbly up onto the small stage. Victor followed, grasped the still extended hand, smiled and said, "Pleased to meet you, Cap. This is my wife Fabulia and this is my friend and engineer Teddy Thibodaux. Please meet Anthony Favazza. He and this fine boat were our escorts for about a week a few weeks ago." Fabulia'd heard the story about the yachts but she laughed in feigned surprise and said, "Well, isn't that nice! I'm so glad to hear that somebody's watching over my boys." She ruffled Victor's hair and poked Teddy in the ribs.

As Anthony led them into the main salon Vic said, "Maybe we'd better get this shrimp into the galley before the box leaks onto this beautiful carpet."

Favazza spoke into an intercom and before he turned back to his guests a woman in a chef's jacket and pants materialized. Victor handed her the box as Anthony asked, "How would you suggest these shrimp be prepared?"

"Oh, hell. We'll leave that to your, ah, cook's choice." The woman smiled at Victor and left without a word.

"Now, please, everyone. Have a seat and I'll take drink orders. How about you Mrs. Janes. What can I get you?"

Oh, heck. I guess I'd have a drop of scotch if you have any?"

"Why certainly, my dear. Will Talisker do?"

"Talisker will be just fine, dearie. Over ice, thank-you."

"And you, Mr. Thibodaux?"

"Well I suppose a glass a dat 'whiskers' would do me 'bout right, about now. I'll take it neat, please"

Anthony looked at Victor who said, "A beer would be good for me; any old kind would be fine."

As their host stepped behind the bar he said, "It's shameful that they will not allow you on shore, Captain Janes. I would think that, with a boat named '*Gambling Lady*' you would look forward to a few hours in the casinos. They have many here, you know."

"Yeah, I've heard as much but I'm really not too big on gambling. All that noise and flash just gives me a headache. How about you, Anthony? You like to gamble?"

As he delivered the drinks Favazza said, "Yes, I prefer the craps table but I always cut myself off after I've lost a hundred or so, which is the only constant in my gaming record." He took a seat across from Victor and started in on a new tack. "My employers have quite a folder on you, Victor. Though they take this business very seriously, I am more amused and then also, well, more respectful. You and your wife have actually tried to make all of that lottery money work for you and your community. But tell me, please. For my own curiosity, did you just stumble on those manganese nodules or were you after them all along?"

Anthony Favazza caught the astonished glance that passed between Fabi and Victor but Teddy put the collective thought into words as he grinned and said, "Say what? Y'all tink we done all dis on purpose? Hell man, we smart, good lookin' and maybe lucky …but we ain dat smart. Hell man! Y'all couldn't *write* dis shit…I mean- *all we ever really wanted was to catch s'rimp.* Dem rocks was a surprise. Auntie Di liked 'em cause a the teeth inside but past dat, we never cared a damn about 'em."

Now it was Anthony Favazza's turn to look bewildered as his guests smiled at him. "What…who's Auntie Di and what about *teeth*?"

Fabulia started to laugh loudly then said, "Yeah, it's so bizarre sometimes I don't believe that any of this could have actually happened. Where's that bottle of scotch, Cappy? I've been dying to tell this whole story to *somebody* and I guess you're it."

The story carried through into dinner and two bottles of wine. By the time coffee was offered Anthony's sides hurt him. "It's absolutely true," he said out loud, though he hadn't meant to, "reality is way stranger than fiction." This brought on more halfhearted laughter but it didn't last. They were, all of them, tired. Teddy had been monitoring the movements of their taxi-driver all evening. At present the man was behind the bulkhead that separated the dining room from the salon.

And Captain Favazza had one more surprise for them. "I've got to tell you all that my instructions from on high were to get Captain Janes over here for dinner then I was to kidnap and deliver him to the Federal authorities in New York. You've pissed off some very powerful people, Victor. When they do not get what they want the hissy-fits can turn very ugly. But after that story how can I possibly do this?..." Fabulia had, almost imperseptively, moved to the edge of her seat. "…In fact, I will not do it. I enjoy your company and wish you all nothing but the best. I am afraid my employers have made a mistake, have had a lapse in judgement.

For God's sake,Otto. Quit lurking around out there. There will be no skullduggery this evening. The big man came into the dining room with a set of nunchuks in hand. "But Anthony, we have our orders. We cannot just let this asshole walk away."

"Oh, but we can and will, Otto. Now put those damned sticks away somewhere."

"I don't think so. This one stays with us," as he pointed a chin at Victor. Otto then noticed that Teddy had slowly arose from the table. In his hand was what looked like a 9mm Glock.

"Victor was staring open mouthed at his engineer. "Where the fuck did you get that, Teddy?"

"D'own matter. Only ting does is dat Otto here realize dat a drunk Cajun wit a gun is not a good combination. Otto, you move, I gonna turn you into a human sieve. Fabi an' Victor. We be goin' now. You boys stay put. We jus borrow you's little dingy an go home wit nobody hurt. You getchyo boat back in da morning."

Fabulia and Victor were making their way through the salon to the aft deck with Teddy backing along with them. Fabi opened the door and stepped out. Vic followed and said. "Well, I guess we're screwed. The inflatable's not here." Teddy came out after them and looked around for the little boat just as a large crash erupted from inside the *Shangri-La*.

"Well boys and girls. Only one ting left to do. Y'all can swim, right?" Teddy didn't wait for a reply. He pushed Victor and Fabi in and jumped after them. As the trio started breast stroking towards the *Gambling Lady* Victor felt something gently bump his face as it floated into him. He grabbed it, took one look and started to choke on water as he tried to laugh. "Fabi, look at this, will you? It's a fake. Teddy Thibodaux's packing a toy gun!"

Fabulia started choking also and said, "No.No.No more laughter, please. I'm already weak. I'll drown."

While he was treading water next to them Teddy said, "Whatch y'all tinkin? I hate doze fuckin' tings. I would never have a real one, me. Somebody might get hurt."

Just then a life-ring with a rope attached to it splashed into the water in front of the swimmers. Van had been watching the whole show from the wheelhouse of the *Gambling Lady*. He towed them over to the side of the boat where he'd already attached a ladder. They all climbed over the rail and flopped down on the deck, breathing hard.

In between gasps Fabi said, "Damn, that was good scotch."

CHAPTER TWENTY-TWO

DURING THOSE EARLY DAYS of euro-human exploration around the globe, chance was always the predominant factor in any discovery, and so it was with the Portuguese when they stumbled upon what would later become known as Brazil. In the year 1500 the lucky guy was one novice explorer named Pedro Alvares Cabral. In 1501 the veteran explorer Amerigo Vespuci was sent to check out Pedro's claims and Vespuci had to agree that yes, aside from Yellow Fever and the Dengue, a whole slew of poisonous critters and some rather ravenous fish, the place had potential. And the fact that the French showed interest in the real estate definitely spurred the Portuguese Powers that prevailed at the time to lay a claim down. The Crown strengthened this claim with the colony settlement of Sao Vincente in 1530.

Sugar Cane was introduced into the colony in the latter part of the 16th century and before long cane plantations flourished with the help of the African slave industry. The French and then the Dutch tried repeatedly to establish foot-holds in the region but were repulsed and sent packing each time. In 1695 gold was discovered in the fledgling country and, to this day, is still a much sought after mineral throughout many states in Brazil. Other products still an integral part of the country's economy are coffee, rubber, and cotton.

For a brief time Rio de Janciro became the Capitol of the Portuguese Empire after Napolean invaded Portugal in 1807 and forced Queen Dona Maria into exile. After Boney was finally put down and the Queen could return to Lisbon Dom Pedro of Braganza stayed on and proclaimed himself Emperor of Brazil in 1822. He lasted nine years but in 1831 he was forced to abdicate his crown in favor of his five year-old son who was then allowed to grow a bit to a more mature fourteen before he was crowned Dom Pedro II. The kid did a fair job but in 1889 the monarchy was finally overthrown in favor of a republic.

In the early 20th century the pandemic economic depression also gripped Brazil sparking violence and revolution. Getulio Vargas stepped in as president and then dictator of this economically ravaged country. A couple of World Wars didn't help matters and the Brazilian economy did not fully rebound until the late 1970s.

^

Some five weeks after leaving Bermuda behind Victor Janes and company floated into a Brazil that was enjoying a buoyant, thriving, economy. The *Gambling Lady* had limped into the port of Santos with a blown reduction gear on the port engine. Yet, to Victor's mind, this was no big deal. The boat needed to go into a shipyard for a total re-fit anyway, plus, this would buy him some time to figure out what in hell he was going to do about this nodule business. Victor was starting to feel like a caged lab rat. A whole passel of Brazilian Big-Wigs started poking and prodding him as if he were some form of a human cash register soon after they'd tied the boat to the wharf in Santos.

Every one of the *Gambling Lady's* crew flew to their respective homes for some well deserved R&R. Victor even managed to get a U.S. passport for Jazzy with the help of Mateus Oberegon and his associates who had pointed out to the U.S. Embassy that Jazzy Coelho was just a hired hand on the *Gambling Lady* and was in no way part of any 'conspiracy' by Victor Janes.

Mateus had become Victor's liaison between industry and government on the manganese nodule project and was able to deflect some of the poking and prodding aimed at Victor. Anyway, they could not start in earnest until the *Gambling Lady* was out of the shipyard.

And Victor really did not have a clue as to how he was actually going to produce the manganese nodules in workable numbers. The concept of trying to *fish* for *rocks* seemed totally anathema and alien to him.

Victor rode the taxi with Teddy to the airport when it came time for

Teddy to head home. "D'one worry 'bout da boat, Vic. Doze boys in dat yard know what dey about. An dey know dat, if dey fuck up, Mateus will pile a worlda shit on dem. Not to worry, man."

"Yeah. I get that fine Teddy but the boat's not what I'm worried about. These guys are expecting me to come up with some sort of crazy adaptation for catching rocks, mon ami. What in God's Name am I gonna do?"

Teddy gave his friend a bemused look and said, "For Christ sake Victor. You caught da damn tings witout even tryin', alla deese las' eighteen munts an look at da trouble ya'll got us into. Imagine wha you might do if'n you set yo mind to it! God sakes man, ya'lls sweatin' da small shit, Vic. Lighten it up. I'm only goin' to da bayou fo' a munt. I get back we'll figure it all out, an dats a fact."

That was three weeks ago and Victor was beginning to wonder if Teddy was going to make it back down here before Fabulia and the kids finally arrived. The last time Vic had talked with his wife she'd sounded a bit pinched; as if there was something she was not about to relate to Victor over the phone though she'd sworn that everything was just fine. He knew that she had a lot of loose ends to tie up before finally going to the airport but something in the back of his head was ever-present but unidentifiable none the less. Finally Fabulia called Victor and said, "OK. We're booked for a flight out of Newark non-stop to Sao Paulo for October 8th. Pan Am flight number 3126. We'll arrive on the 9th at 10:50 a.m. your time." Before he could reply or ask any questions Fabi hurried ahead. "You got that, Vic? I gotta run. Goodwill's here for the furniture. I'll call before we get on the plane."

On the given day Victor found himself in the VIP lounge at Guarulhos International Airport waiting for his family to clear Brazilian Customs and Immigration. Mateus Oberegon had paved the way, alerting Customs of their imminent arrival. Victor had to wait only ten minutes before the smoked glass doors opened. The first ones out, Lorrie and Fabulia followed Eddie through the doors. Just as fast as his smile bloomed, it wilted away as the realization overcame him. Rose was not with them. That had been it all along. The three of them ran up and latched onto Victor before he could even speak. Fabulia gave him a sad, lop-sided smile as Lorrie said, "We're sorry, Daddy. We tried so hard to make her come. We really did. But she wouldn't do it, Daddy. She says that she loves you but doesn't trust you right now. Maybe later but not now."

"Yeah, it's really alright, Dad." Eddie said, in his squeeky voice as Vic ruffled his son's head... "Rosey said she couldn't leave Grammy and Grampa alone. Maybe we can get them all to visit for Christmas, huh?"

Lorrie and Fabulia moved in closer and hugged this man who was as sad as he'd ever remembered feeling. His oldest child had not died on him but Victor now felt as if he'd somehow lost a daughter through his own negligence. "Well... uh... I guess it's a good thing... that somebody will be keeping an eye on Edmund and Gramma but... yeah, well, maybe we can all get together for Christmas somewhere." Victor gave them a lame smile and they all played along with it.

Fabulia kissed Vic as she silently cried with him. "I'm so sorry, Victor. I guess I'd hoped to change her mind right up to the last moment, but then it was obvious that I wasn't going to and I just couldn't bring myself to tell you over the damned phone. I chickened out, Vic. I'm so sorry."

"Not your fault, Fabi. I guess it's really nobody's fault. It's just the damn cards, is all..." Victor took in a deep breath, getting a grip on his emotions. "Alright then. Let's get this rodeo underway," Victor said, as they headed for the doors, "Lorrie, how's your Brazilian Portuguese coming along? And tell me, Eddie. How are your soccer skills...oops... I mean 'futebol' skills these days? Maybe you can introduce baseball to your new classmates. It's always warm down here, you know."

Eddie said, "Yeah, I brought my glove but I think I wanna work on the futebol. Pelé was from Santos, you know," he said enthusiastically, as they stepped out into the hot, humid air.

It didn't take long for the Janes family to meld into their new life. Santos was a spectacular microcosm of a spectacular country. Though this city was well below the equator it still maintained a tropical rainforest climate. It rained every day for a while but the rain was warm and seldom interfered with outdoor activities with the exception of January through March which was considered the rainy season. Then it poured.

Mateus Oberegon got them started in an apartment overlooking Praia de Santos beach that had them all awed. Across the boulevard there was a beachfront garden that stretched for almost two kilometers running parallel to the beach. The smells alone made Fabulia heady. Both Lorrie and Eddie brought their cherished skateboards with them all the way from New Bedford and in less than a week they were known as "O Rolo Crianças" or The Roller Kids.

They all voraciously explored the city from the wonderful open-air markets to the fringe of the decrepit favela in the north-west portion of the city though Victor warned his children that this was no place to go alone, day or night. "We're all marked people in there," he told them. "None of us would make it a block before we were beaten, robbed and maybe worse. You gotta keep well away from this place, guys."

"But why, Daddy?" asked Lorrie. "It doesn't look that bad from here. And look. Those kids are smiling at us."

"Yeah, sweetie," continued Victor. "They're smiling alright. But they aren't smiling to be friendly. One, just one of those kids would beat you close to death just to get that skateboard from you, and that's no lie. Then they'd take your clothes. It's a different world down here, kids. It's not like home where there's the 'middle class'. Down here you are either rich or in-the-gutter, dirt poor. The magnificence of this country is incredible but the poverty at the low end is one of the things that makes the beauty at the high end so pronounced and larger than life itself. We've got to constantly remember this all the time in this country. This is the real world. New Bedford and the United States is great but it ain't what goes on in the rest of the world." Victor took Lorrie's hand and started to walk away but, after a few steps they stopped and turned back. Fabi had Eddie's hand but neither of them was moving. They were both still staring at the children that were gazing hungrily back at them from the edge of the slum.

^

Teddy stayed an extra month in Louisiana. By the time he got back to Santos the *Gambling Lady* was almost ready to go back in the water and Victor had already begun to build a net that could catch nodules, if they were as prevalent as Mateus had assured him. "It will not be your problem to *find* them, Victor. They are there. Getting them up to the surface from three kilometers below and then onto the deck of a boat in viable numbers will be your greatest task," he'd said with an iridescent grin.

^

Joe had died almost four months ago and Carol-Jean still found herself in a puddle of tears every so often. But she was tired of stumbling around the trailer like a lost soul and the shop was deathly quiet this time of year so she just closed up for two weeks. Then she got on the plane to Boston.

They'd had a bitter winter in the canyon with bone-freezing winds and one snow storm after the other. Boston, much to Carol-Jean's joy, was experiencing an early spring thaw. She even spied some Crocus poking up through the fast melting snow. This was all good. Somehow, she felt a revitalization. She was looking forward to the 'Shark Show' as she was calling it. She let out a deep sigh and said out loud, "Forgive me Joe, but I guess I may as well make the most of it while I'm still kicking. And don't fret about me. No mini skirts and go-go boots for this old girl." She had to giggle at this image then she got ready for the next day.

CHAPTER TWENTY-THREE

AUNTIE DI was enjoying herself immensely. This shark gathering was so very entertaining. She had an oversized handbag with her that had about three pounds of teeth in it; a small sample of her stash that she had hidden away in Revere. She wasn't quite positive why she brought it; it just seemed like the thing to do, going to a shark party and all. She thought she could possibly sell a few, though she really didn't need the money. Maybe she'd just show a few to people that understood about *may-man*.

She was standing at a booth ogling a Megalodon tooth that had to be all of eight inches long and almost the same in width. It was so beautiful, almost the same grayish hue as some of the much smaller teeth in her collection. She could just imagine the size of the beast that had once owned this tooth so many eons ago. It was a thought that was at once frightening and exhilarating. Such incredible beauty and power and here was a piece of it right in front of her all these millions of years later. Time travel most certainly did exist; a person just had to fill in some of the pieces with imagination.

The man behind the showcase said, "Please don't touch, ma'am. Human oils tend to corrode the patina." Auntie Di looked up. She hadn't even thought about touching it. Then a person next to her said, "Oh, I'm so sorry but the beauty and size of this tooth makes it almost impossible to *not* touch it."

Auntie Di and the woman next to her both turned and looked at each other almost simultaneously. The other woman spoke first and said, "I never imagined that such sharks ever existed. This is truly amazing. If Joe had ever dug something like this up I think he would have left me sooner," she said with a sigh.

Auntie Di replied, "Yes, is most surprising. I also have not realized that such fish existed. This one could swallow us both at once, eh?" This produced a smile and a laugh from the other woman who flipped one of her gray braids out of way. Auntie Di noticed with a start that a small shark tooth made into an earring was hanging inside of the woman's braid. On an impulse Auntie Di said, "My old bones are telling me to sit. Would you join me for a cup of tea? There is a small café in the next isle."

After they were seated and content both women watched the parade of people. Apparently sharks were big, popular business. Everyone seemed to be in a rush, hurrying about, jabbering away.

After some time the woman across from Auntie Di said, "Oh, I am so sorry. My manners have escaped me. My name is Carol-Jean Paya."

Auntie Di smiled as she leaned forward and grasped the extended hand. "Very pleased," she said, "my name is Nguyen Thi Bian but please call me Auntie Di. I am most used to it."

Carol-Jean said, "My, what a wonderful sounding name that is. You make it sound like water running over pebbles. It is definitely not of English origin. Would I be rude if I asked where you are from?"

"I take no offense, Carol. I am *Nguoi Viet* or, as you say in English, I am Vietnamese. And, please tell me. I hope I am not seeming, ah, rude in return but you do not appear to be akin to most Americans. Is that so?"

"Why yes, Auntie Di. I suppose that is very much so. But please believe me," Carol-Jean leaned forward and put a conspiratorial tone to here whisper, "we were here long before any of these new-comers even thought about getting on the boat to come over to this continent." Both women had a good laugh at this. They understood each other perfectly and Carol-Jean continued. "I am of the *Havasupai*. We have inhabited what is called the 'Grand Canyon' west of here for many thousands of years. We were erroneously called "Indians" not so long ago. Where that ever came from I haven't a clue because, as far as I know, none of my past descendants ever went to India. Now the word-makers have at least had the courtesy to refer to us as 'Native Americans' these days. It's not much but a little dignity goes a long way since it was all taken away from us not so long ago."

The two women talked about the weather between Boston and

Flagsataff, finished their tea and decided to browse the show together. Carol-Jean noted that Auntie Di had a hand-bag that obviously contained some weight to it, which Carol found curious.

Both women were most interested in the price of the different types and varied sizes of shark teeth that they saw. At one booth Carol-Jean said offhandedly, "Good gracious, if I have to pay these prices for the teeth I'd have to raise my own prices on the earrings alone to over 100% of what they are now. I just do not know about this. It worked so much better when Joe found the teeth and set them in silver wire for me." Auntie Di listened but asked no questions. She knew that all answers came with time and she felt that she'd have them sooner rather than later from this interesting woman who was obviously still grieving a loss.

As the afternoon wore on it became clear that Auntie Di's bag was becoming a burden for her. Carol-Jean said, "Auntie Di, may I carry that bag for you for a while? I really would not mind."

Auntie Di hesitated for only a split second then she handed the bag over to Carol-Jean saying, "Yes, thank-you Carol. I don't know what made me bring so many. Very foolish of me."

Carol-Jean said, without missing a beat, "Sometimes foolishness is just a sign of youthfulness, and at our age we have to take all we can get." as she put the strap on her shoulder.

At 4:50 the loudspeakers announced that the show would be closing for the day in ten minutes. Both women were happy for this. The constant walking and getting jostled about by the crowds had tired both of them. Carol-Jean said, "You know, I have a hotel room in this building. If you would care to use the bathroom we can freshen up, relax for a moment, then I would like to buy you dinner."

Auntie Di smiled and said, "Yes. That is a good idea. But please. Allow me to take you to dinner. I have a nephew who owns a restaurant not far from here. We will eat for little money and therefore the food will taste *much* sweeter."

After they'd made use of Carol-Jean's room Auntie Di insisted that they take a cab to the restaurant. It was only three blocks away but neither woman wanted to do anymore hoofing today. As they arrived all Carol-Jean saw was a small neon sign that said '*Vietnamese Cuisine*'. As they entered the front door Carol-Jean was taken aback. It was like entering Alladin's tent; very understated on the outside, huge and dazzling on the inside.

It was obvious that Auntie Di was considered the Belle of the Ball. Five youngsters ran up to her, all chattering away, as they took her bag, coat, and scarf. She said something indicating Carol-Jean and all five immediately shifted over to her and gave this exotic, old woman the same treatment. Just then a elegantly dressed gentleman came over and took Auntie Di's hand. They conversed for a minute then the man turned to Carol-Jean and said, "Mrs. Paya. My name is Nguyen Lo Quan. Auntie Di is, in fact, my most revered aunt. It is my pleasure to make your acquaintance. We have never had a Native American grace us at our establishment. I hope you will find our food to your liking." With that he turned, clapped his hands together twice and rattled off orders in rapid-fire Vietnamese.

Two beautiful young women materialized and escorted Carol-Jean and Auntie Di to a round table in an alcove that had a 'reserved' sign on it. Both women were seated side-by-side so that they could look out over the restaurant. The place was jam-packed. Carol-Jean saw many Asians but there were smatterings of different ethnic groups throughout the large, elaborately decorated room. And she could not make out one word of English. Auntie Di broke into her thoughts and said, "Would you care for a glass of wine? I usually have a touch of Bristol Crème Sherry. They keep a bottle hidden here just for me."

"I'm not much of a drinker but, as that saying goes about Rome, sure, I'll try a glass of sherry with you."

A menu was brought and placed in front of Carol-Jean along with their drinks. Auntie Di started explaining about the choices. "The little pepper drawings next to the offerings tell you how hot or spicy each dish is. Do you like hot food?"

"Yes, I like it but I think it is all a matter of, so to speak, degrees?

What I call spicy you may call ho-hum."

"Yes, yes. That is so true. Why don't you allow me to order for us. I will not get anything that will burn you but I will get a little bit of many different items. This will be fun for us and make this experience much more memorable for you."

Carol-Jean was astonished by the smells, tastes and textures that assailed her. It was all so good and so different. She only had one melancholy moment wishing Joe were with her then something new was brought to the table and she forgot her sadness. In between all of this a small man came in, bowed and addressed Auntie Di who turned to Carol-Jean and said, "This is my nephew Nguyen Van. He is second-in-command of the fishing vessel that we both work on."

Van bowed again and said, "Mrs. Paya, it is my pleasure to meet you."

"Oh, the pleasure is all mine. You have an incredible family. I have not enjoyed myself so much in quite some time but please tell me," she asked as she looked between aunt and nephew, "—did you say that you both work on a *fishing boat*? That you actually work on the ocean?" The Nguyens could only smile and nod. Carol-Jean continued. "Oh, that is so wonderful. Do you know, I've never seen the ocean? I've dreamed of it often enough but I've yet to see one."

Van said, "This is not a problem. We are, from here, only about five miles from the Atlantic Ocean. Perhaps tomorrow we could take a boat-ride? I know my aunt never passes up a voyage, even a brief one."

"That sounds like a wonderful offer but I'm afraid that I have to go back to the Shark Show in the morning. You see, I've come here to buy shark teeth to make into jewelery for my store at the canyon. I would like to take a boat-ride but I'd better tend to business tomorrow."

Van gave his aunt a quizzical look who just said, "Carol, I think your search for teeth is finished. I am feeling very thankful this evening. Let's have one more glass of sherry to celebrate, shall we?"

^

The summer months south of the equator took up December through March. Victor and Fabulia had been warned that life would get a little crowded in Santos during these months due to the influx of tourists. For that reason they decided to look for a place to buy outside of the city.

Santos shares the island of Sao Vincente with the smaller city of the same name. To the southwest and inland of Santos lies the industrial city of Cubatão where the large petroleum and chemical plants are located. Just to the northeast lies the city of Guarujá which is separated from Santos by the Estuario de Santos. This dredged estuary is where all commercial shipping is conducted and where the *Gambling Lady* was currently moored. Though Guarujá was not much tamer during 'the season' it did have a few neighborhoods that were more sedate and there was easy access to schools right from the house that they'd decided to buy. The whole Janes family was quite happy with their choice. There was a pool out back as well as a little dock that accessed a small estuary river. Victor perked up when he was told that it led all the way to Santos.

He bought the Brazilian version of a skiff with a sixty horse outboard on the stern. He found that he could take the meandering stream from their new home to the Estuario de Santos and be at the wharf where the *Gambling Lady* was tied up in thirty minutes less time than if he'd driven to the ferry dock in Guarujá, then taken a bus up to the wharf once on the Santos side. Anyway, it was more relaxing to take the skiff though he did go aground a number of times while he was learning where the deeper water lay in the waterway.

Fabulia set up the computer they'd bought for the house. She was itching to start communicating with Martha back in New Bedford. They'd both agreed to start working the foreign exchange as soon as everyone was settled and Fabi felt she could start in on it without being interrupted every five minutes. Fabi rubbed her hands together rapidly and said, "OK, then. Let's see if we can make some money with this Foreign Exchange thing." She typed in Martha's address and then hit 'Send.'

∧

Victor and Teddy bounced ideas around for almost two weeks then decided that, rather than yammering in idle speculation, they may as well go out and see what happened when they put Victor's new net in the water and actually tried to *catch* the damned things. Of course, Victor built a net that took into consideration all of the parameters of what they were trying to do and *not* do. He knew that these nodules, if they were as prevalent as Mateus promised, were going to be rough on the netting so he had a company in the U.S. make him some out of this new material called 'Kevlar'. It was supposed to be tough as nails but it should have been called Golden Kevlar for what it cost, though nobody seemed to choke when Vic mentioned the price to the Brazilians.

First of all, Victor knew from Gideon Bloom's pilot-house lectures that these nodules took a long time to grow and didn't get that big.

"Vic. These amazing *turds with teeth*, as you so callously refer to them, take ages and ages to form. A nodule a measly inch in diameter was probably started when we were still single-celled, freakin' amoebas!"

Victor reasoned that, if they were going to harvest these things in any volume they'd have to have a pretty tight mesh on the bottom section of the trawl so he ordered one inch webbing which, when stretched tight would leave openings of no more than a half an inch.

His next consideration was for what he was *not* trying to catch. He knew that there were shrimp and other aquatic species down here that were desirable catches on one level but definitely not on this one. Any live creature that they caught would presumably get mangled by the rocks if they also were forced to swim or get pushed into the 'Cod-End' of the trawl. With that in consideration Vic built the top part of the net out of twelve inch mesh reasoning that the swimmers would stay above the rocks as they entered the net and then be able to escape through the larger mesh as they were funneled back. Victor doubled the diameter of all the ropes and wire that were built into the Nodule Net, realizing that he may have

181

some dead weight to deal with.

Victor flew Van down from Boston and Gideon took the bus to Santos from Rio where he'd rented himself a nice little cabana on the beach. Then, with Mateus Oberegon and some Brazilian deckhands aboard, they went 'fishing'. Teddy, Gideon and Van all grinned as Teddy said, "Oh yeah. Now da fun begins!"

Mateus stood next to Victor at the wheel, who snorted at Teddy's last quip.

"Fortuna favorese aqueles que poderá experimentar," said Oberegon, as he also smiled. *Luck favors those who try.*

They all watched the sonar screens as the net decended to the bottom. Victor slowed the trawl wire speed a little at one point but the four underwater currents that the net passed through were surprisingly weak. "As you get closer to the equator these currents tend to weaken," croaked Gideon, who was starting to feel a little bit better. His two months in Rio de Janeiro had started to wear off as soon as he'd gotten on the boat. There was a reason that Mardi Gras lasted only one week per year but the fact that he'd missed the official version did not deter Dr. Bloom. He had his own version that had turned it into an eight week burlesque show.

Gideon slept for twenty-four hours after they'd thrown the lines off and headed east from Santos. Victor woke him when they reached the coordinates that Mateus had supplied. The net settled to the bottom without any mishaps and started 'fishing' as Victor increased the RPMs on both engines.

Vic had built this net with very little vertical rise. From the footrope to the headrope the opening of the trawl was only four feet high. For this reason the headrope transducer had very little side-to-side angle viewing but every so often a dark, purplish spot would show up on the screen. He knew what those were. Victor was wishing he had a 'fish-eye lens' or some such thing because the width of the trawl opening from wing to wing was about sixty feet and he knew that he was only seeing about 5% of that.

After about half an hour Victor noticed that the strain gauges on the winch monitors were rising. "After a half-hour?," he asked himself. "OK boys. I'm hauling her back in. I'm not liking these winch readings."

In came the trawl wires, at a normal speed at first then it seemed like the winches were slowing. And, Victor noticed, the boat was being dragged backwards to the trawl, not the other way around. Teddy leaned over Victor's shoulder and said, "Whoa bub. Look at dat hydraulic oil temperature. Better stop it now, give da motor a rest." Before Victor could comply the stern of the boat started to settle deeper in the water then the winch just stopped. Victor threw the pneumatic brake on, took the winch out of gear and looked around. Each one of them had an "Oh, shit" look on their faces.

Van spoke up and said, "Victor I think you should ease off on the brake. I am not comfortable with our stern sitting so low in the water."

Victor slowly released the brake but it gave way immediately and the stern bounced about five feet out of the water. "Phew. I think we either got a friggin' boulder in there or a lotta little ones. Any suggestions?"

Van didn't hesitate. "We will not be able to retrieve any portion of our net or rigging at this depth given the apparent weight involved. I suggest that we must tow the trawl around on the bottom, as is, and hope that we chafe a hole in the cod-end that allows everything in it to escape."

Gideon summed up everyone else's thought. "The only other option is to cut the trawl wires. Let's try Van's way first."

Victor put the boat in gear and slowly brought the RPMs up to the max. They were moving forward but only making about a knot and a half. After about twenty minutes he had to take both engines out of gear to let them cool down. Half an hour later they started the whole process over again. Victor was just about ready to take the boat out of gear once more when he noticed that their speed had risen to three knots. Then four. Half an hour later they had the whole rig on the boat. Luckily they'd worn a hole right through the rings on the cod-end.

On their second try Victor let the repaired trawl 'fish' for only seven minutes. They'd retrieved it all but still had a hell of a time getting it onto the deck of the *Gambling Lady*. These rocks had no fish slime to help the bag slide up the stern ramp. This was *totally dead* weight. After they managed to dump out the contents of the cod-end, Gideon said, "Okeedoke Cap. What do we do with 'em now?"

"Well hell, Gid. We didn't think that far ahead. I guess we'd better have these guys push it all into the pen in the factory. It'll all be harder to unload at the dock but we can't just leave it on the deck to roll around while we're steaming for Santos. There's gotta be 10,000 lbs. of the things here." Victor picked up a handful of nodules and started throwing them on the deck then he started to laugh. Every fifth one had a shark-tooth inside. "Uh Oh. Better not tell Auntie Di about this," he said. "She'll be raisin' a rukus with the Brazilians, tryin' to divert every rock for her own inspection before they get 'em."

"Oh hell. She already know, Victor. She got betta smell dan any ole' shark dead or 'live," deadpanned Teddy.

CHAPTER TWENTY-FOUR

NINE MONTHS AFTER they had arrived both Lorrie and Eddie had adapted as if they'd actually been born to the country of *Brasil*. At first there was so much to do, to learn and assimilate, that they had not recognised their parent's increasingly erratic movements and actions, but in the past week both of them took note of their parent's acute preoccupation with two very different forms of *busy-ness*.

Fabulia was always there to get them up and off to school but both kids noticed the fact that, lately, their mother was absent from the house until late into the evening and more often than not, their father slept on his new ship which was tied up in Santos while the hydraulics and deck machinery were being installed.

Fabulia had hired a maid three months ago. This kind-hearted woman would welcome Lorrie and Eddie home from school, get their supper for them and try her best to fill in but she was not their mother and she was certainly not Fabulia Janes, whom the kids were currently discussing. They sat at the dining room table toying with their food, conversing in English, thinking that Luana could not.

"Lori. Do you know where Mom goes all day?" asked Eddie as he forked a piece of plantain into his mouth.

"Well, she says that they're going to start up the *Constant Vigil* business down here, she and Martha. But where Martha is, and where they're planning on doing it, I don't know. Did you see the way Mom was dressed when she came home two nights ago? She took those clothes right out into the trash before she took a shower."

"Yeah. And that scarf-thing she was wearing over her head smelled like a mouse nest. She scared me when she came into the house. I didn't know it was her at first. Does Dad know that Mom's dressing up like a gypsy?"

"Yes, I think he does. And he's not too happy about it either," said Lorrie. "I heard them talking the other night when they were both home. I heard him say that Mom was being reckless. She told him to be quiet and not wake up 'the kids'. After that I couldn't hear them."

"Where do you think she goes?"

"I'm not real sure. But it can't be good, dressed up the way she is."

"I think she goes into that slum in Santos," Eddie said. "She's not dressed up to go anyplace else. They wouldn't even let her into a movie theater down here, dressed like that, or, if she drank, even into one of those *tabernas*."

"Yeah, yeah," sighed Lorrie. "Let's just watch and see what they do next. It's not like you and me got a lot of different options here. We can't exactly go running over to Grampa and Gramma's."

Luana smiled inwardly. She liked these two children. They not only watched after each-other but they watched after their parents also. She'd forgotten about her own parents by the time she was nine.

Victor and Fabulia did have many a whispered but insistent conversation lately but now it was Vic that held the floor most of the time. "For Christ sake, Fabi. What in God's name are you thinking? We've been here less than a damned year and you think you know the lay of the land well enough, to feel comfortable enough, to go traipsing through the slums of Santos? I've warned you about that place. Fabi—It's not safe on any level. I don't care if you have a friggin' army of women surrounding you even if they are all 'girls from the neighborhood'. You're putting yourself and your family in jeopardy by going in there repeatedly. It's bad enough that I've sold my soul to the Brazilians for these nodules. You do not have to be sticking *your* neck out. I'm begging you please. Cool it with the forays into the favela."

"Come on, Victor. I think you're the one needs to cool it. I'm fine, really. Martha will be down soon. We'll open up a nice, respectable office in downtown Santos for the Foundation and everything will be hunky-dory."

It was Lucien Fernandes who turned Victor's head around and got him to view his current position in a positive light rather than dwelling on the 'soul selling' thing. Lucien kept promising to come down for a visit but as yet, he was unable to get out of New Bedford. For one thing, he was still trying to get Victor Janes' name cleared with the U.S. State Department, but so far he wasn't having any luck. It appeared as if Captain Janes was the new Fidel Castro in Washington, D.C. People there were still plenty pissed at Victor. Lucien, in reality, saw no end in sight because he figured that it would only get worse if Victor started to produce the nodules in volume down in Brazil.

In one of their weekly phone conversations Lucien said, "Victor, stop worrying about your *Brazilian Handlers*. You've brought them their cash-cow. Who's handling who here? You've proven that the manganese is accessible. So the *Gambling Lady* is too small for the task. So what? Give her to Van and let him fish her. You told me once that the same shrimp are there also. Build another vessel that is up to the task of fishing for the nodules. Build a ship if need be. You've got the dough. Tell them you want a partnership."

So Victor did just that and Lucien, through Mateus Oberegon, negotiated a 40% equity position for Vic in a Brazilian corporation that became simply but, after a time, very well known as *Mineraçao Alto-Mar*. And the deal only cost Victor a paltry $15 mil. He promptly signed thirty percent of his shares over to Teddy Thibodaux. Victor knew that this was only fair. He had been thinking about cutting his friend in on the *Gambling Lady* shrimp business but he'd gotten a little side-tracked after their trip to visit Manfredi in New York City.

Rather than start new they bought a well used offshore oil support vessel and put her into the shipyard in Santos for conversion. Teddy smiled at Victor and asked, "How often we gonna be doin' dis, Bubba?"

Victor didn't hesitate for a second and replied as if he was being asked a serious question. "I don't know, Teddy. My crystal ball's been in the shop for the last twenty years. And I gave up calling about it a long, long time ago."

She was about 250 feet in length and the deck area comprised about

180 feet of that. She wasn't, by any stretch, a graceful looking vessel but she'd do for what Victor and Teddy had in mind. The *Mineiro do Atlantico* was launched back into the water four months later.

^

It had been a wonderful summer season in the Canyon. Not too hot, breezy but not windy. The tourists were plentiful and they were spending their money freely. And Carol-Jean was repeatedly counting her lucky stars. Meeting up with Auntie Di had been a God-send. Every month now Carol-Jean received a package in the mail with about a hundred nice, uniform teeth inside. Auntie Di was obviously hand-picking them for Carol-Jean who had hired a young man in town to set the teeth in silver just the way Joe had done it. Business was, indeed, very good—money was being made. She was planning another trip back east this coming winter to visit her friend and, to top it all off, she was now able to keep her horses.

Carol-Jean's day-dreaming was interrupted when one of the browsers in her shop said, "Did you actually find these shark teeth in the canyon?"

CHAPTER TWENTY-FIVE

THE FOREIGN EXCHANGE (Forex) market is ultimately never mentioned in any depth by the media except within the business pages of most major newspaper publications. The daily trading of the various national currencies is a very viscous, subfusc, and unappealing money tool in the eyes of the majority of the general public around the world but, to a few, it is the most vibrant, energetic monetary contrivance that ever was created. There are, unless in times of great catastrophe, usually no huge, abrupt leaps and falls in this market as there are in the much more volatile and therefore news-worthy stock and bond markets. But it must be noted that, on a daily basis, an average equivalent of $2 trillion US dollars is traded between all the national currencies in the world. That equates to an equivalent of about US$200.00 per day for *every human being* on the planet. Martha Vanderhorn read this fact in her foreign exchange tutorial, laughed and said, "Yeah, baby. I'll take my $200 back every day without a problem."

So they started trading on the Forex and felt their way along. Both women began with a bankroll of $1000.00 each. Being small-time beginner spot market speculators, they both had to have a dealer involved who made the actual trade of the 'pairs', they being the two currencies involved in any given transaction.

In Fabulia's first trade she bought $500 worth of Brazilian Reals(BRL) for about $250 USD. The next day she checked in with her dealer in Rio de Janiero and was informed that the BRL had devalued overnight by about 1.5% while the US dollar had made a modest, comparative gain in value by 0.7%. She should have bought USD with BRL instead of the other way around. The bottom line was that Fabulia had lost about US$12.00 for her first dabble into the *Forex*.

Martha, back in New Bedford, did much better in her first trade. Her dealer suggested that she start conservatively but she opted to buy $1000.00 of Canadian dollars or CAD, with US funds. That was her idea of *conservative*. The next day she was pleasantly surprised to be told by her dealer in New York that the Canadian currency had taken a 3% jump in value while the US dough had devalued comparatively by about 0.9%. Martha had made about $30.00 with this trade but, thinking that there may be some kind of a trend going on here, she went and bought another $1000 of CAD. Sure enough, next day she was informed that the CAD had taken a 2% jump against the USD. She'd made a little better than $50 bucks on her first two trades and it felt pretty good.

Fabulia and Martha conversed over the week-end and came up with a strategy where they'd combine their funds and start trading between USD, CAD and BRL. They found out later that what they'd done when they combined their money was to start their own little 'Hedge Fund'. The light bulbs just kept popping off in these two women's collective heads. *And* they were having fun.

Λ

The other side of the coin was Victor and Teddy who were not having near as easy a time of it. In fact, they were having no fun at all. Victor proved that the nodules could be harvested and getting them close to the surface was no big deal; it was just a matter of brute force. To say that the hydraulic winch system that they'd installed on the *Mineiro do Atlantico* was substantial would have been a polite understatement. The system was just plain massive all around. The trawl wire drums were each thirty-two feet tall and just as wide. They were designed to hold up to three miles each of four inch diameter steel cable. Used in unison these massive cables guaranteed that up to 100,000 pounds of nodules could be lifted straight up from the ocean floor to the surface, but, that in itself got only 50% of the work done.

Victor and Teddy were both experiencing many sleepless nights because they could not figure out how to get even a minimal 20,000 pounds of the manganese nodules in the cod-end from a vertical position hanging just below the ship into a horizontal position so that it could be dragged up the stern ramp. They'd been lucky with the 10,000 pounds that they'd managed to get up the ramp on the *Gambling Lady* but they figured that they'd have to target, at the least, 30,000 lbs. per tow to make this whole fiasco a viable exercise from an economic viewpoint. Both men seemed to be suffering from a joint case of brain-freeze, then Victor remembered something that immediately started to thaw his head.

Most fish have, to one degree or another, what are known as air bladders which assist the fish in controlling their buoyancy. Once, when Victor was still green, he'd witnessed a redfish trawl with a full cod-end come to the surface. Redfish have somewhat larger air bladders than most other species of fish and are commonly found in the deeper water off of Newfoundland. While the fish are on the bottom the air bladder stays compressed due to the extreme, deep water pressure but if the fish is taken off of the bottom and the pressure is eased, the air bladder expands as all of the oxygen in the fish's body is transferred to the bladder.

Victor was barely fifteen when he stood on the deck of a trawler as they hauled back the gear. An old deckhand said, "Now, look out thar, ba'ay and ye'll see somthin' ta make ye laff." Within five seconds and about 200 feet astern, the cod-end exploded out of the water as if it were actually a submarine surfacing in an emergency. Though they'd had 8,000 lbs. of Redfish in that net, after the ascending trawl had reached a certain depth the physics changed and the expanded air bladders of the fish gave the whole cod-end bag a 'positive floatation' factor instead of a negative one and all of a sudden, up she came, fast.

Victor had totally forgotten about his first trip on that trawler those many years ago, until he was, once again, wide awake at three in the morning, in bed, laying next to Fabi at their house in Guarujá. Suddenly he sat up with a start. "Holy shit," he yelped.

Fabi jack-knifed up out of bed with a panicked look in her eyes. "The children...the kids...are they alright? Please don't let it be the kids..."

Victor hugged his wife and said, "Sorry, Fabi, sorry. But I think I just figured out the last part of the puzzle. Go back to sleep. I gotta tell Teddy." It was so simple! Why hadn't he thought of this sooner?

Victor knew that Teddy was staying on board the *Mineiro do Atlantico* which had a landline phone while tied to the wharf but the phone was in the galley. Teddy would never hear it ringing. Vic threw some clothes on and headed out back to his skiff. Hell, he'd rather tell him in person anyway.

^

Martha arrived in Santos about three weeks after Victor had taken his hurried, joyful early morning skiff ride to find Teddy. Fabulia put her up in a four-star hotel right on the beach. Both women were sipping piña coladas on the expansive veranda.

"...So, to answer your question, I really do not think that we can do the *Constant Vigil* business down here the same way that we did it back in New Bedford," stated Fabulia. "The basic problem is that there is no 'social support' mechanism down here at all for us to work off of. Not within the government and definately not privately. The Church does as much as they can but the Vatican says they're stretched pretty thin these days."

"Yeah, right. That's a laugh. Talk about 'More money than God.' Sounds like we're going to be starting from scratch," said Martha. "And that will most likely take the kind of resources that are above and beyond even your bank accounts."

Yeah, that's about the crux of it all," replied Fabulia. "But I think I may have an idea that could help us cover our goals and then some." Fabi smiled at Martha and continued. "Feel like taking a stroll into the favela this evening? I keep a small apartment a block from the slum. We'd have to stop there and alter our attire a bit so that we fit in."

"Oh hell. What's one more big old black woman in a slum anywhere on this planet? I don't think anyone'll bother with me, but you? How do you do it? I would think that the slum-dogs would be all over you like flies on doggie-doo."

"Let's just say that I have some pretty good protection while I'm in there. Come on. It'll be dark in a couple of hours. Let's go to the apartment and change up. Then we can meet some of my newfound friends."

"Boa noite, senhores," said Fabulia. *"Gostaria que todos os meus amigo do Boston. Esta e Martha Vanderhorn.* Good evening, ladies. Please meet my friend from Boston. This is Martha Vanderhorn."

They were deep in the favela. Fabulia and Martha were seated at a small table inside of a dirt-floored, tin roof shack that was illuminated by a single bare bulb. Four other women were seated with them at the table and there were eleven other women standing around the perimeter of the small room. It was close and crowded. Fabulia knew most of them by name but there were four new, skeptical faces here now. Fabulia took notice and smiled inwardly. Word was getting out. Without saying anymore Fabi reached into her bag and pulled out three bundles of 100 Real banknotes. There was only one way to gain attention in the favela. Hard cash opened doors *and* ears.

The skeptics all smiled. Their full attention was on Fabulia now. "What sort of a *Cabeça Louca* would dare bring all of that cash into the favela," they all wondered.

Martha looked around in bewilderment. "What was going on here?," she was asking herself.

Fabi wouldn't tell her anything while they were preparing for this little junket. She just said, "You'll get it all soon enough. Better for you to see for yourself rather than be told." Martha had long since noted that all of these women were dressed like warm weather street walkers. What the hell did Fabi have up her sleeve?

One of the women seated with them ceremoniously picked up the money in front of her, put it in her own bag and said, *"Cinquenta mulheres foram agora pago por uma semana do seu tempo. Considere o que nosso amigo Fabulia tem a dizer.* Fifty women have now been paid for *one week* of our services. Please listen to what my friend Fabulia has to say."

Fabulia said, *"Obrigado, Gisela,"* and continued speaking in Portuguese. "And thank-you all for giving me the time to speak to you this evening. Before I go further please understand, this plan of mine could possibly show short-term benefits to each of you and your families within three months but the long-term effects on this society could possibly be far-reaching. Patience and commitment will be the key to success. My organization, the *Constant Vigil Foundation*, is willing to commit the monies needed if you all agree that this plan could be of benefit to you, your families and, quite possibly, to future generations of Brazilians, especially the women. So. This is what I propose to you all..."

^

The air thing was an easy detail for Victor and Teddy. They had two 40 foot, two inch thick rubber air bladders custom made for them in Sao Paulo. Attaching them to either side of the cod-end had been a cinch. Knit one, pearl two. The air delivery method had been somewhat more complex but they solved this minor conundrum with a 200 foot long umbilical hose made out of a collapsible rubber and plastic composite. The theory was that, as the net with a full cod-end neared the surface, the umbilical, with the help of a small set of buoys would surface first, hopefully close to the ship, be snagged with a thrown grapnel hook from the deck and then get attached to another hose that was connected to multiple 500 psi capacity compressors on board.

And...viola...up she came. Victor had to make sure that they had headway on the ship before they started to inflate the bladders. He didn't want to bring the whole rig up into the ship's propellers.

It all worked dandy until they tried to tow all of the dead-weight up the stern ramp. The air bladders were of no help once they tried to get the net onboard the *Minereçao Atlantico*. Even the massive hydraulics strained with a mere 20,000 pound cod-end. Friction was the enemy of all movement at this point in the exercise. So back to the drawing board they went once again. Teddy said, "Ain no big deal, Vic. We just gonna have ta build one big-assed conveya-belt, hep move all dem rocks onto da deck."

Victor and Teddy ended up installing not one but two heavy duty conveyors on the *Mineiro do Atlantico*. The primary ran the full length of the stern ramp at a 45 degree angle and a secondary ran horizontally for a 60 foot stretch running forward on the deck centerline. Each conveyor was geared way down; they simultaneously only moved at about a mile per hour but speed was not the issue here. The conveyors, coupled with the assistance of a large wire block and tackle, brought the first 30,000 pound bag of nodules onto the deck like a giant worm with kidney-stones on a slip-and-slide.

CHAPTER TWENTY-SIX

THE GIRLS INTENDED to start out small but they found a huge office space on Rua Padre Visconti that was so inexpensive that they could not pass it up. They'd be able to expand freely and not have to worry about moving as the company grew.

Fabi and Martha picked four very willing girls to train but first Fabi gave them all some cash and had them go shopping. Her girls were bound to attract attention if they walked into the office building dressed in their night-time garb and neither Fabi nor Martha wanted to draw any attention to their new venture.

Shop was set up and in no time all of the new women had the mechanics down but it soon became apparent between Fabi and Martha that more was needed here. If they were going to seriously turn a profit with this business they were going to need someone who had a track-record in the *Forex*. They needed a Forex Guru. Martha said, "You know, my dealer in New York sounded envious when I told him that I was coming down here for a visit. I found out, in a round about way, that he was going through a kind of messy divorce. Maybe I could get him to come down here."

Fabulia thought for a half-minute then said, "Well, maybe but I'm not sure it would be a good idea to have a man thrown into the mix with our girls, given their previous form of employment."

Martha said, "Well yeah, under regular circumstances but not necessarily here. You see, Balthazar is getting divorced because he's discovered that he's gay. The girls will adore him."

Fabulia didn't know whether to laugh or start weeping when she first caught sight of Balthazar Metaxas at their new, cavernous offices. He had arrived that afternoon from New York and Martha brought him straight to the office. The man was just plain huge, even bigger than Edmund

DaSilva. And he was extremely hairy but when Fabulia looked through his jet-black beard and big head of curly hair at is eyes, she was immediately fearful that the man may start crying at any moment. Her first impulse was to run and hug him, to assure him that everything was going to be fine, just fine. And it was plain that all five of the other women in the conference room felt much the same. They all wanted to cuddle and coddle this giant that looked as if he'd lost his mother the day before.

"I… don't speak much Portuguese…but I'll learn, I guess," he said, as he stared down at the floor. It was obvious that this man was frightfully shy also.

Liliana, one of the new-hires, could not hold back any longer. She stepped forward, took one of Balthazar's hands in both of hers and said, "Eees OK, Balt-A-sar, we take care of you. You weel learn to espeek joos fine."

Fabi and Martha set him up in a corner office that had a great view of Santo Antonio Cathedral and beyond to the southern Atlantic Ocean. The local girls had a hard time with his name so they knicknamed him 'Bebê Urso' which got shortened in time down to 'Urso'. The Bear had arrived and 'school' was now in session five days a week with three new teachers that Fabi had found through the newspapers.

And a very interesting school it turned out to be because many of the girls that decided to give it a try in *'O Reta Vida'* or the straight life, could not read or write. As a result of this, *Constant Vigil's* very first endowment in Brazil went into three class-rooms that were set up on the same floor as their new offices. And, in usual fashion, Fabulia went a step further. One of these classrooms was used to teach English to the girls that could already read and write Portuguese and had a desire to become bilingual. As Urso had lectured them all, it was of the utmost importance that everyone in their office be able to read because, ultimately, that was how they were all going to prosper in this business. Information was the key in this money game and, still, the best way to gain information was to read the newspapers.

"These women have got to be able to read the Brazilian rags, at the least," Urso explained. "We'll keep an eye on the English language papers for the time being but these girls are going to have to learn how to spot business trends that will directly or even indirectly affect the Brazilian Real and the *Forex*."

Fabulia's promise to the girls that night in the favela was met. After three months *Constante Vigilia do Brasil* did in fact show a modest profit but of more interest was the fact that they'd brought ten more girls into the office. One afternoon Martha Vanderhorn said offhandedly to Fabulia, "Well, it seems as if the girls are adapting pretty well though a few of them seem to be having difficulty getting to the office at ten a.m. Do you think they're ah, double-dipping, so to speak?"

Urso didn't, for the time being, have the time or inclination to get into the more complex facets of the *Forex* such as interest trading, currency swaps or options trades. He stayed with the spot market. And they all stuck to the BRL, CAD and USD primarily, but skirmishes into the British Pound, the Swiss Franc and a few other of the more stable currencies were becoming less and less uncommon. Urso smiled. This whole thing had vast potential; potential that he wasn't sure his two bosses yet realized. Hookers doubling as Traders doubling as Hookers? He was amazed that none of his former collegues in New York had ever thought of this. He mused further, wondering how much, if any, pillow-talk was going to make its' way back into this office. Wow. Talk about insider trading. This could be epic.

Six months into the business they had a total of fifty women working computers, trading currency with dealers in Rio de Janiero, London, New York, Basel, Hong Kong and Tokyo. Each woman was forwarded an amount of currency which went into her personal *Constante Vigilia* account at the beginning of the week that a) suited her level of expertise and b) best suited a currency match for that particular woman. Granted, most of the girls started out with BRL but it soon became known that some of these women actually came from Hong Kong, Tokyo or Paris and that they were fluent in the languages spoken there. Urso had these women paired up with dealers in those respective cities.

Some of the girls lost and learned, some won and laughed but, at the end of each week the company showed a profit; small at first but a profit none the less. Fabi and Martha didn't take any time to gloat, they just kept running girls through the classrooms and filling the still-vacant cubicles in their vast office space.

Balthazar Metaxas came out of his shell after a time and he proved to be as sharp and quick witted as Martha had promised. "You know ladies, we could increase our monthly bottom-line substantially if we started a hedge fund and listed all of our fellow office workers as investors."

Fabi and Martha looked at each other and Fabulia `said, "Yeah, Urso. We've thought of that also. We just were not sure that we should jump into it this soon. It's kind of hectic around here. We've only got twenty seats left in the place. But tell me what you had in mind for numbers."

Balthazar smiled and replied, "Oh, I wasn't thinking of anything too large to start with. Maybe a $20 mil fund. We could always bump it up after we got it rolling." He was definitely testing the waters and he knew that they knew it.

Fabi smiled and said, "Let me talk it over with Martha. Off the top of my head, that dollar amount seems a little small for a hedge fund. I'll talk with you more about it over the next couple of weeks."

Back in Fabulia's office Martha asked, "Do you trust him that far? Obviously, he'd have to be the one that controlled any hedge fund."

"Yes, I'll be dwelling on that for a while. My first impulse is to trust him but I think the only way to really cover our collective asses here is to have someone looking over his shoulder. I think we need to hire a CPA anyway. This whole thing is starting to explode on us. Do you think you could make some quiet inquiries? I'll ask Gisela, see if she knows any female CPA's in Santos or Sao Paulo that may be interested in coming onboard full-time. I think we're gonna need some help here."

A 'hedge fund' is quite simply a group fund where a number of wealthy individuals pool their money, strengthen their trading power on the *Forex*, and thus reap larger profits. The dealers who control these funds either have to have cast-iron constitutions or lots of stock in antiacid production companies. $100 million dollar funds are not uncommon. It takes a lot of dough to make bread in this market. Often times a dealer will only make a half a point on the money he or she controls but that person has thirty days in a month with which to do this in a market that does not stop working. This means that, on paper, a dealer in control of a hedge fund could possibly make up to 15%, more or oft-times less, on their respective fund in any given month. That works out to a $15,000,000 gross profit. If there are 100 investors in the fund that then works out to a $150,000 profit on any million dollar investment into the fund. For a single month that is a pretty good turnover on a million USD.

Banks do not pay that kind of *daily* interest. In fact, banks and most governments do not much care for private trading in this *Forex* thing. They'd just as soon have it all to themselves but as yet they had not been able to find a bonafide reason to shut down the general public from participating in this remarkably lucrative game. Granted, the dealer could also lose money in any given month but if that person couldn't make even a smidgen of a profit in that time, well then, it was most likely his/her's last month in the *Forex* business. Back to tending bar in SoHo.

^

The kids were in the pool. A heat-wave had stalled right over Santos keeping the city in 100+ degree temperatures and ninety percent humidity. Eddie came up for air and continued their conversation. "At least Martha's finally here," he said. "She'll keep an eye on Mom."

"Oh great. Who's keeping an eye on Martha? Those two are like kids in the candy store, and the whole world's the store." Lorrie shook her head. "At least she's not coming home at two in the morning dressed in rags anymore."

"Yeah, and talk about playing dress-up, how about the way those women were dressed that Mom and Martha introduced us to last week in town? What's that word? *Gauzy,* or something like it. They shoulda been on the beach. What's Martha and Mom doing with them, anyway?" Eddie dove under again.

When he surfaced Lorrie asked him, "Do you miss being home? I mean do you miss New Bedford?"

Eddie thought for a moment. "I guess what I miss is Grampy and Gramma. And Rose. But I guess I like it down here. I don't miss the cold weather at all and I like the kids we go to school with. Futebol's fun. I like it down here," he said again. Eddie hesitated then continued. "I just don't get what's going on with Mom and Dad. Why are they doing all this *stuff*? I mean, everybody knows that they've got buckets of money. Why are they working like they do if they don't have to? It seems sort of like, well, sort of like *un*logical, you know?" Eddie started to dive under again then stopped and looked at his sister, wanting to hear a reply to his question.

After a few seconds Lorrie finally spoke. "Grown-ups are weird. Since all of that lawyer stuff went on back home it's almost like they've got to prove something to someone. Who and what that that is, I can't figure out yet but I think it has to do with being stubborn, you know? It's kinda like two kids pushing each other in the playground. Back and forth, back and forth and nothing ever really gets done."

"So you mean that being stubborn and stupid is the same thing?"

"Yeah, I guess I do, sort of. But I'm still trying to figure it out. I just wish it would change back to the way it was. When we were a family and together, not all willy-nilly. I don't miss New Bedford either. I just miss the way it was for us all when we were still back there."

^

Van could barely make out the super-structure of the *Mineiro do Atlantico* through his binoculars from the wheel-house of the *Gambling Lady.* Victor's new ship lay some twelve miles away to the south-east of Van's position where he was currently fishing for the Brazilian Royal Reds. He had just gotten off the VHF radio with Victor, who seemed somewhat subdued, to say the least. Perhaps he was tired but Van did not believe that this was the case. Even after Van reported their catch rates to his boss,

Victor showed no happy response. If anything his voice grew softer.

He then reported that the *Mineiro do Atlantico* was doing very well on the nodule harvest; their last trip in to Santos they off-loaded close to 2,700 metric tonnes of the things. He went on to explain that the metals market was kind of shakey at the moment but they were still getting substantial returns from the smelting foundry that had been converted in Cubitão, specifically to separate all of the semi-precious metals in the nodules. Victor'd glumly signed off but before he did he said, "Well Van, keep the net on the bottom and give my regards to everyone onboard. I truly wish I was over there with you all. This rock fishing ain't my cuppa tea."

Van smiled at Vic's final statement. So that was the problem. And Van could not blame him. 'Rock Fishing' was not fishing at all and Victor was, at the heart of it, a fisherman, pure and simple. Auntie Di came up into the wheelhouse while her nephew was looking through the binoculars. She looked out in the same direction and said, "You see Victa? I think of him often. Like he is here but not, yes? We have not seen him in many months, even at the dock. We are never in at the same time."

"Yes Auntie," replied Van. "I think that Victor is thinking of us all at this time also. I am wondering when he will finally decide to come back and go fishing with us for a while. I think his heart is here."

Victor and Teddy were, actually, doing considerably better than 'very well'. True, the metals market definitely was a rocky roller coaster ride lately but all of the semi-precious stuff that was being extracted called for big money, even on a bad day. Bottom line was that, over the past six months the *Mineiro do Atlantico* grossed well over $11 million USD. Teddy was quite happy but Victor, at face value, couldn't have cared less. He wanted to get back onboard his *Gambling Lady*. He was just doing the time until both he and Teddy felt that the Brazilian guy that was sailing with them as mate could take over the Captain's chair.

^

Presently the *Atlantico* was tied up for a week while some repairs to the stern ramp conveyor were taken care of. This gave Victor a chance to spend some much needed time with his family. He'd spent the afternoon horsing around with the kids in the pool then, when Fabi got home they all sat down to a supper of Feijoada(beef stew) prepared with great care by Luana. After Lorrie and Eddie went off the do homework Vic grabbed two beers and they went out to sit on the porch by the pool and watch the sun vanish in a flash of tropical color.

"So tell me how your *Constant Vigil* stuff is going now," asked Victor.

Stuff? Fabi did a five count before she responded. "It's actually going really well. We've now got 97 girls working in the office and we are about to launch a hedge fund that should increase our profits substantially. Of course, getting the girls off the streets has been our first goal but now we're going to move on to the second phase which is to set up free food pantries in the favela so that all of the inhabitants that don't get fed regularly, particularly the children, have a shot at getting at least one good meal a day. After that, phase three will be medical clinics next to the pantries. Then, much later, we're thinking about schools."

"Jeez, Fabi. You've been busy. I understand you and Martha wanting to get those girls off of the street and away from that life but I guess I don't understand this foreign exchange business. Is it really that lucrative? If it's like the stock market can't you lose money too?" Victor was trying his damnedest but he'd forgotten that Fabulia had already given him a synopsis on this subject a few months ago. She didn't want to ruin their precious evening together so she just gave him a quick rundown again and held back her ire.

"So. Enough of my *stuff*. How's it going with you? Last time we talked on the radio you said that you were catching the hell out of the nodules. Is it going to pay off for you and all of your Brazilian partners?"

"Well, yeah. It's already paying off. I mean the *Atlantico* has been making damned decent money but the real story will be written next week after *Mineraçao Alto-Mar* dumps about two hundred tons of nickel onto the world market. Mateus Oberegon and the others are concerned about the effect this will have on the Brazilian economy but they've got to get rid of the stuff. For one thing, the foundry is cash poor and for another, if they keep stock-piling the nickel it's sure to lose value even more. I would have thought it would have been better to put it into the market in small amounts. I don't know, Fabi. It's all just a big crap shoot."

Fabi let that hang for a minute then asked Victor, "So when did you say they were going to dump all that nickel?"

∧

Carol-Jean's latest carton came from Brazil, of all places. She did not realize that Auntie Di's fishing boat went all over the world. In the past gift boxes from her friend there was never any note inside, no indication of how Auntie Di was or what she was doing. Carol-Jean assumed that Auntie Di did not read or write English. However, in this box there was a letter in neatly written script.

"Dear Carol-Jean Paya,

I am including a note for you with these teeth because I am sure you will be a little confused by this box's origin. It is a long story that I would prefer to tell you in person. Would you care to come to Brazil this winter for a visit? The plane trip is really not as bad as some say. I mostly slept. If you can join me in January I will be sure to take a few weeks off of the boat so that we can talk and explore this most interesting country. And do not worry about the cost. I am making much money and I would be grateful if you would visit me.

Please respond to the return address on this package.

Your Friend,
Nguyen Thi Bian

PS- Isn't the color of these Brazilian teeth quite different?"

CHAPTER TWENTY-SEVEN

THE GENTLEMAN in the impeccable suit hurried along Rua Padre Visconti, he being late for a business appointment. As he passed the glass doors of an office building he bumped into a small woman that was exiting onto the sidewalk. "Perdão," he said. As the woman turned to acknowledge the man's pardon they instantly recognized each other. "Liliana," the man gasped. "Where have you been and what in God's name are you doing in there?" He nodded at the immaculate, glass fronted building. "And those clothes you are wearing. *Silk?* I have looked everywhere for you. I called Gisela for months asking about you. Finally I just gave up and took another girl that she offered me. Where have you been? Please tell me." This last request came out as a moaning lament.

"*Meu Senhor*," said Liliana, "please calm yourself." She noticed that passersby were starting to stare at them. "I have been working in this building for the last eleven months. I no longer work for Senhora Gisela."

"But how is this possible? You need to be able to read and write to work in an office. You once told me that you could do neither."

"Yes, Senhor. That is all true. But people *can* change you know. I am not dumb and stupid simply because I was once a prostitute."

"Well, what is it that you do in this office, Liliana? Are you a secretary or a clerk of some kind?"

"No, Senhor Julio. I work in the foreign exchange. We trade money. I have my own desk."

"Ah," the man said, slyly. "So you work as a money counter. Are you *laundering* this money? Do you work for one of the drug cartels? Maybe this is for the *Máfia* ? Oh, I hope this is not so, Liliana. They are a dangerous lot."

Liliana scowled at the sidewalk as she realized that she had said too much. She had to get away from this man. She looked back up and said,

"No, no and no, Senhor. This is a respectable business. Now I really must be going. Please take care of yourself. *Boa tarde*, Senhor Julio." She made to walk away in the opposite direction she had intended but he grabbed her arm.

"Do not think that you can just walk away from me, you little slut," he grunted angrily. "Once a whore, always a whore. I will find out who you really work for and do my best to put an end to it. Then we will see who is calling who when you are back out on the street where you belong." With a predatory grin he released her arm and gave her a little shove before he, once again, started walking towards his business meeting.

Supply and Demand was, first and foremost, a concept couched in economics though in this instance it could have been refered to in terms of *socio-economics*. A large portion of the male population of Santos was infuriated. First of all, most of their favored 'short-term' girls had seemingly disappeared from circulation off of the streets in their city. This was, in itself, a small catastrophy but, secondly, to make matters much worse, the girls that were still working were charging the proverbial arm *and* leg for their services. $2,000 Reals for a lousy twenty minutes. *Mãe de Deus!* Even lawyers couldn't get away with charging those prices.

It was criminal, plain and simple. Who did these girls think they were? First of all, most of them abandon ship then the ones that remain on the job take all of your money with no remorse at all? It was totally unconscionable. This social relationship had gone from symbiotic to parasitic in less than half a year. Something had to be done, but how? And what caused all of these girls to just stop working? Many of the men involved in this imbroglio were pillars of the community and quite far up both the corporate and bureaucratic ladders yet not a one of them cared to stick their necks out too far on this touchy issue. God forbid, if their wives, girlfriends or mistresses ever caught wind of this there would be hell to pay. It would be a debacle of grand proportions after all of the women had a chance to talk. And the men had already *paid* way too much anyway.

^

Victor was one of fifty-eight men seated within the huge board-room inside the *Mineraçao Alto-Mar* offices. He was feeling somewhat uncomfortable for two reasons. First off, he hated this suit and tie that Fabulia had bought him specifically for this occasion. Secondly, he was feeling somewhat unwelcome here. The other shareholders that did greet him did so perfunctorily, as if they did not want anyone to notice them in the presence of *Capitão* Janes. Most of the board members did not even bother to greet him but sneered openly at Victor from across the expansive table. Teddy, seated on Vic's right, said, "Hmm. Funny ting' Bub but I'm gettin' da *dee*-stinct impression dat soma deese boys ain' so happy wit ya'll. Wha gives?"

Mateus Oberegon, seated on Victor's left, leaned in and said, "You are correct in your observation, Mr. Thibodaux. I know the reason for this animosity but we will have to save further discussion until this meeting is over. I believe we are about to begin."

Teddy smiled to himself. He'd wondered if and when this was all going to come to the surface. Actually he was surprised that it had taken as long as it did.

The secretary to the CEO called this first annual meeting to order. An eight foot square screen at the far end of the table came alive with a graph showing production figures against net profit margins. The secretary droned on in a tinny, high pitched voice. Apparently *Mineraçao Alto-Mar* was showing some startling profits for such a fledgling company. The graph indicated that lithium alone had jumped in value to almost one hundred percent of what it was valued at half a year ago on the world market. Other minerals such as titanium, cobalt and platinum also listed large jumps in value. The lesser elements such as nickel, copper and iron were all lumped together at the bottom of the graph, Victor noted.

The young woman brought up a new graph onto the screen and started in on the projections shown for the next two years. Apparently the computer boom was feeding this new demand for these odd metals. Victor tuned all of this out for a moment and thought about what Mateus had said a few moments ago.

He had a sinking feeling that this animosity shown by some of these men was tied to Fabulia's business in some way, though he was not sure how money trading could effect *Mineraçao Alto-Mar's* business. And besides, he reasoned, Fabi was just trying to help a few people. What was the harm in that? Victor brought his attention back and scanned the graph on the screen. Yes, they were doing gang-busters with this nodule business that he had helped create. How could they possibly be be mad at he and Fabulia? Hopefully this meeting would not last much longer. He wanted to take this damned tie off and hear what Mateus had to say.

After an hour the meeting thankfully came to a close with most everyone present in fine humor. The future was indeed looking rosey for the shareholders in this infant corporation. Victor Janes was afforded many greetings and smiles now as the men exited the conference hall but there were three that were outwardly unhappy as they approached him before he could also exit. One of these men was Julio Tavares, the man that had bumped into Liliana a week previous on Rua Padre Visconti. It was blatantly obvious that the hostility that Vic encountered an hour ago had not so easily vanished from these men. Senhor Tavares spoke first. "*Capitao*," he said scornfully, "I do not yet understand exactly what your wife's agenda really is but, please make no mistake. We intend to find out and put an end to this foolishness of hers. Whores belong on the street. Your wife's intervention in the natural order of life in this city will do you and yours no good. None of you are born to this country. How is it that your wife feels she can manipulate our society? Perhaps she was *putana* before you all came here, eh?"

Before the man could say any more Victor shot an arm out, grabbed the man's tie and brought their faces together, stopping so that a half-inch separated them. "I do not know where the rock is that you live under but I suggest that you go there and hide. Nobody talks about my wife like that without consequences. You have underestimated me sir but, as you have pointed out, this is not my country of birth so I must show some restraint now. However, the next time you and I have occasion to meet, you will either apologize for this behavior and rudness you just spouted or I will bitch-slap you until you weep. Now get away from me, you little pimple." Victor released him but stood his ground, making sure that the Tavares man and his mute friends moved off.

Teddy and Mateus watched the whole encounter from the opposite wall. Teddy immediately moved to go to Victor's aid but Mateus held him back. "No Mr. Thibodeaux. Let Victor handle this for now. I know those three men well. I get much pleasure out of watching that TV show of yours in New York of the three fools in America. Moe, Larry and Curly, I believe. That is what Victor is dealing with over there," he said, as he pointed with his chin. "Leave him to it. We would only insult Victor if we intervened."

Afterward Mateus took them to a small café on a side street off of the beach boulevard. When the three men had beers in front of them Mateus raised his and said, "Here is to our good fortune gentlemen. *Saudé.*" They clinked glasses as he laughed and continued. "I must say, I was not totally sure that I was doing the right thing when I, myself, invested all of my small savings in *Mineraçao Alto-Mar*. But now, as we all learned today, I did the right thing, thanks to you both." Victor put on a smile but he was still mad as hell about that guy Tavares. Teddy grinned and shrugged as if to say, "It's all fate's fault. No need to thank me."

Mateus continued. "Victor. I can see that you are still angry about your encounter at the end of the board meeting. Please do not give that fool Tavares another thought. He will not bother you again; I promise you that. Now, to help you understand what caused that bit of unpleasantry, allow me to explain a few facts that you may or may not already know. A small but powerful portion of the male population of Santos is in an uproar due in full to this business that Fabulia has started here. Do you realize that your wife now has, as of last week, over one hundred and eight women working for her and that sixty-three of those women were once prostitutes?"

Victor looked at Teddy and shrugged. This was no news. "Yes, Mateus, of course I know this. But I can't see how this would have all these guys tied up in knots. What gives here? Fabi's running a legitimate business. In fact, she's doing better than that. She's taking women and girls off of the streets, out of a life of prostitution and giving them something better. What's bad about that?"

Teddy didn't even try to hold it back. He burst out in a bray of laughter and Mateus joined him. Vic looked back and forth between the two men. Why was that so hilarious?

After Teddy calmed down a bit he said, "Well, come on, Vic. Is right in frona ya'll, dude. Fabi's been takin' da crème de la crème offa da streets hea. Da boys is pissed because dey havin' to pay big bucks fo da girls jumpin' in to take da vacated spots. Problem is, deese girls ain' as, well, dey ain' as *seasoned* as da ole girls an' dey inflatin' da whole business. I been watchin dis shit fo munts, man. Yo girl Fabi causin' a ruckus by takin' deese girls outa circulation, is what it's all about, man. Hell, it'll all calm down sometime but until den, ya'lls name's mud. And ain' no way Fabi's gonna stop dis business even if she hire each and every female in dis city. Is da oldest *pro*-fession in da world, man, sellin' tail. Ain' gonna stop for nobody."

Victor was staring at Teddy. He was speechless. Yes, it was right in front of him but he never connected the dots. Again. He'd missed seeing the whole thing in front of him, again. Oh, hell. How was he going to relate all of this to Fabulia? He couldn't ask her to stop, could he? He knew full-well where that conversation would go. Ouch. No, he wouldn't ask her to stop under any circumstances anyway. Fabi never had done any of the *Constant Vigil* business with an ulterior motive in mind. It was always a straight shot with Fabi.

Mateus pulled him from his quandary by saying, "And to add injury to insult, Victor, your wife has been making some huge profits with this 'Forex' business she's into. Many of these men are agast that a group of whores could actually make money without lying down. These same men feel that your wife is making a mockery out the capitalist system as a whole. There is talk that what Fabi and Martha Vanderhorn have been doing is illegal in the sense that there has been *insider trading* in progress here. Some of your wife's employees have, in fact, been working their old jobs as well. They are bringing after-sex small talk back into the office with them and actually *trading* on that information *and making money with it.* The only saving grace will be if these men that are making the most noise behind closed doors decide to drop the idea of a lawsuit because of the exposure. That is, none of these men want to expose themselves in public and that is just what will happen if they carry this whole thing into the legal system."

Teddy let out a snort and said, "Jesus, what a buncha pussies. I tink ya'll got nuttin' to worry on, Vic. Dem boys'll neva allow dat crap to be seen in court. Dem boys may loose more dan they's hoes, dey not careful. You boys gonna have somthin to eat, or what?"

Victor eyed his friend and said, "Oh sure,Ted. I'm real hungry. Tell you what. You have a sandwich and I'll just have a bottle of anything stronger than this friggin' Brazilian ale." Vic pushed the warm beer away and looked around for the waitress.

˄

Later that night Victor and Teddy made their way unsteadily towards Teddy's apartment located about a half mile north on Rua Pindorama. As they entered the Praca da Independencia a lovely young woman stepped in front of them and said, "Oh. Hi Teddy. You boys looking for a party?"

Both men immediately started laughing hysterically. Victor went down on one knee. "What in God's name is this all about," the woman wondered aloud?

After he caught his breath Victor said, "Ah, you wouldn't, by any chance, know my wife Fabulia, would you?"

CHAPTER TWENTY-EIGHT

"SO, WHAT DO YOU WANT me to do, Victor?" Fabi was feeling a little vexed this morning ever since her husband had waltzed into the house at eight-thirty looking like shit and smelling about the same with a heavy hint of cheap cachaça as his morning cologne. Thankfully, the kids had already left for school. He immediately asked Fabi to sit down so they could talk. He then related the whole previous day to Fabulia including the street walker's advances. This brought a smile to Fabi's lips. "That sounds like Isobel. What did she look like? What was she wearing?"

It was Victor's turn to be exasperated. "That's not the point, Fabi. It wasn't exactly a social call. I'm filling you in on all of this because it is directly affecting our lives now. These guys are angry because you have effectively taken most of their noon-time rendezvous girls out of circulation. And all of this is now coming back at me because some of those 'guys' also happen to sit on the board of *Mineraçao Alto-Mar.*"

"Oh, tsk, tsk. The poor boys can't have their noon-time spasm? Tell 'em that's what hands are for. Are you seriously trying to tell me that I should stop taking girls off of the streets of this city because a group of men are missing their daily punches? I'm surprised at you, Vic."

"God-dammit all, Fabi. I am not trying to tell you to do any such thing. I *know better than to try and tell you what to do.* It was my most ferverent hope that we might be able to talk about this whole thing that we're doing down here and come to some sort of an agreement about how we're going to continue our lives. That's all. For the past year all you and I have been doing is shooting from the hip in two different directions. You've got your stuff and I've got mine and never the 'twain shall meet. Christ, our own kids are looking at us as if we've got aliens bumping around in both our heads. And you getting all defensive when I mention 'your girls' is kinda telling. What the fuck, Fabi? All I want to do is come

213

back down to earth and have my family. I honestly do not give a rat's ass about this fucking nodule business. 'Yesterday' I was standing on Water Street in New Bedford when I first laid eyes on you. Now we're in Brazil and I do not know whether to shit-or-go-blind. How did all of this happen? I mean, really. *Where the hell are we?* We've got more money than all the gods put together but we're loosing ourselves. We have no base-line. Rose was the smart one. She saw the goddamn handwriting…"

Fabi grabbed one of Victor's hands. Both just sat there for a short time thinking. Finally Fabi spoke. "Shit, Vic. I can't argue with any of that. I'm past that now. It's time for us to move on. Thanks for voicing it all." She let out a breath that she'd been holding for months. "OK. So what do you suggest. How are we going to turn it all around for us. We can't very well cut and run at this point, can we? And where would we go, anyway? I mean, we set all of this in motion and there are a lot of people that are depending on us. We can't ditch 'em, right?"

Victor stood up, stretched, and went over to the coffee-maker. As he started filling the pot with water he said, "Yeah, you're right but we do not have to do all of this in the same old way that most other businesses are run. I mean, hell. Why don't we join forces? Why don't we start a new company that sort of combines all of our business stuff including the *Gambling Lady?* Let's put it all under one roof, hey? I mean, I don't quite know where all of this will take us, but we never knew that before anyway. Fishing, mining and money trading with a side of prostitution? Sounds like one hell of a 'conglomerate' to me."

"Yeah, but I think I'm going to have to do something about the girls that are working two jobs. This will only hurt everyone if we allow it to continue. *Constant Vigil* cannot be seen as a cover for a call-girl business. Prostitution is legal here in Brazil but running a brothel or an organized service is not. Martha and I have been chewing on this for some time now."

Victor smiled and looked at his wife. "Oh. So I really didn't tell you anything you didn't already know about, huh?"

Fabi smiled back at him and said, "Well, actually you did. I didn't realize that all the boys were in such a dither over these girls changing occupations. Interesting, huh? I guess it ain't love, after all, that makes the world go 'round."

"Oh yeah? Don't count on it, toots. If that were true we most likely wouldn't even be talking right now."

∧

Five days later Lori and Eddie were walking home from school. It had stopped raining for a moment and the temperature was relatively cool for twenty-four degrees of southern latitude in the month of March. The weather had started to change a week ago. It was no longer steamy, just hot. Brother and sister were in no rush. Rushing was considered a sin right after gluttony in this city.

"What do you suppose is going on with Mom and Dad now," asked Eddie. "It's kind of scaring me. I mean, aren't we the ones that are supposed to be running around the house giggling? Last night I think they were in the pool till one in the morning. And they're being so darn nice to us. It's almost like they're feeling guilty about something and trying to make up for it. Neither one of them has gone to work for three days. I heard Dad say that 'the friggin boat could stay tied up for a damn week for all I care.'" Both kids laughed. Eddie was the best at mimicking their parents.

Lori nodded as she pulled a pack of cigarettes out of her school bag. Eddie said, "You know, twelve's way too young to be smoking those things. When'd you start that stuff, anyway?"

"Most of the kids in my class smoke and besides, my teacher says I'm ahead of my time and teacher's always right, you know." She nodded again as she took a drag then continued the discussion. "I've watched it all too. You're not the only one with eagle eyes and ears, kid. But jeez, it's almost embarrassing. If it was just you and me it would be one thing but with Luana in the spare bedroom… well, it's weird. I mean, sure parents have sex; we're living proof, but they don't have to *broadcast* it, for God's sake. I mean, that's a picture that I do not want coming around in my head all the time, you know? Yuck."

"Oh yeah. Yuck is right. And how about that talk at the dinner table last night? We're not going to let them forget about that, are we? Taking us to Florianopolis for two weeks in April to learn how to surf? I'm all in. They can scream and shout and stay in the pool for days for all I care as long as we get that trip." Eddie took a deep breath. No use getting too worked up. He wasn't on that surfboard yet.

Lori crushed out the half-smoked butt then picked up a fallen palm frond and started swishing it through the air as they continued walking. "It's all good, I guess. They're happier and that's what matters. They did kind of forget about us for a while there but I guess they forgot about themselves too. Maybe we'll all be OK. I suppose that's about all we can wish for."

^

Victor wasn't able to roll his stock holdings in *Mineraçao Alto-Mar* over to their new company due to Brazilian legal minutia but he did transfer the *Gambling Lady* into the fold. *Janes Explorações* or 'Janes Holdings' became a registered Brazilian corporation with it's own small office space within the *Constant Vigil* maze of offices on Rua Padre Visconti. Victor now had full access to the pair of CPA's working there as well as in-house legal counsel.

Victor showed up at the office whenever he was in port. Fabulia and Martha had a great time watching Vic and Urso interact. Niether one of them quite knew what to make of the other. For Victor's part, he often wondered to himself how such a giant of a man could actually be gay. For Balthazar Metaxas, he was just as stymied, wondering how such a muscle-bound little oaf could lay claim to Fabulia's full attentions. Urso was actually in love with Fabulia in some kind of quasi-protective, brother/sister way. Martha got a kick out of watching *that* dance go on also. She often caught herself thinking, "I've got to get Lucien down here soon. He'd write a play about all of this stilted human interaction."

Teddy was now overseeing the nodule operation on board the *Mineiro do Atlantico.* Victor had jumped back aboard the *Gambling Lady* and was happier than he'd been in months. Everything and everybody was moving along smoothly. And the money they were all making was simply unspeakable. Even Auntie Di, at Teddy's urging, had bought a few shares of *Mineraçao Alto-Mar* from him.

Victor and Teddy were sitting in the office with Martha and Urso one morning waiting for Fabi to show up so they could go over the numbers from *Gambling Lady's* latest trip and then talk about scheduling some shipyard time for the boat. Fabi was now about an hour late and Victor was thinking about calling the house again when the phone on Martha's desk jangled. She let it ring once more then picked it up and said, "Janes Holdings." After a few seconds a quizzical, frightened look came over her face. She tentatively held the receiver out towards Victor and said, "It's for you."

Vic took in the expression on Martha's face and the hairs on the back of his neck stood up. He grabbed the offered phone and said, "Hello?" A synthesized, androgynous voice came back at him and said, without any preamble, "We have your wife. Go to your home in Guarujá and stay there until we contact you this afternoon with our demands. Do not contact the police or talk to anyone about this. You, and all of your associates are being watched closely. If you do as you are told your wife will not be harmed. If not, your wife will become ugly, scarred and disfigured in a matter of seconds." *Click.* Nothing more. The line went dead.

Victor limply handed the phone back to Martha, blinked his eyes a number of times and said, "Shit."

Everyone in the room started throwing questions at him at the same time. Victor just stared out the window, hearing none of it. Finally he said, "I gotta go."

Teddy stood up and said, "What gives, man? I'm goin' witch ya'll."

Vic shook his head and said, "No. Nobody goes with me. You all have to stay put. Please do not talk to anyone, anyone at all. I think we're all being watched. On second thought, Teddy, go back to the dock and go about your business. I'll call you all when I can but right now, I gotta go." He swiped up his keys and about ran out of the door heading for the elevators. Fabulia had been kidnapped.

∧

There was a muffled gun-shot then all was quiet again. Fabulia relaxed back onto the mattress but sat back up when she heard the sound of a key rattling around a lock in a door which creaked open and then closed just as abruptly. She felt hands loosen the sack that covered her head then it was gently lifted off. Out of her one good eye she blinked at the unaccustomed light then she focused on a person, a woman, standing in front of her with the same kind of sack over her head but this woman's sack had eye and mouth holes cut into it. "I am truly sorry for this *contusão ocular.* This was not supposed to happen."

Fabulia grimaced as the woman dabbed at the black eye with a tepid cloth. "What was that gun shot?" Fabi asked.

"The man that hit you when you fought has been dealt with."

"You shot him because he hit me?"

"Joao killed himself when he struck you. I do not tolerate disrespect or insubordination of any kind."

"So, I'm guessing it's money you want, yes?"

"Of course."

"And how much money would you be asking for me?"

"You are asking too many questions. Please be silent while I clean this wound. I'm afraid your beauty will be marred for a few weeks to come."

Fabulia let out a snort but complied with her captor's request. No sense in upsetting this applecart, not yet anyway.

"I will have some food brought to you shortly. Later today we will contact your husband again and make our demands. I will allow you to speak with him for one minute so he can know that you are alive.

Hopefully for you, this will all be over within one day's time." With that the woman knocked on the door and exited without any further words. Fabi wondered if the woman had intentionally left the sack off or if she could have possibly forgotten about it.

Five hours later the door opened again and the woman with her hood in place came in and removed both the handcuffs and ankle manacles that bound Fabulia. She was allowed to stand, shake her hands and legs to get the blood flowing before she was ushered out the door past a young man holding a carbine of some sort. Fabulia was led through a maze of windowless rooms and corridors then turned into a room that had three chairs and a table that contained a phone and some form of electronic equipment. In one corner of the room lay a large Doberman that barely opened its' eyes when they entered. The woman pointed to one of the chairs and Fabi sat as the receiver was placed into the machine and a number was dialed into the phone.

After two rings Fabi heard Victor say, "This is Victor Janes."

The woman held a button down on the machine and said, "Mister Janes, your wife is here with us. I will allow you to speak with her for one minute after I am done giving you instructions. Now listen carefully. You will, with the help of your good friend Mateus Oberegon, withdraw one million dollars cash in U.S. funds out of your account with Banco Bamerindus here in Santos. These will all be used bills, non-sequential and of no denomination greater than twenty dollars per bill. Insure that no dye pressure pack is included within the plain canvas bag that you will personally place the money in. We have a dog that can sniff out the dye packs. Tomorrow morning, after you have the money in hand go back to your home to await further instructions. That is all for now. Here is your wife." With that the woman released the button and signaled that Fabulia could now speak.

Fabulia didn't hesitate. "Hey there, sweetie. How ya doin'?"

"Well I'm just pisser, as I'm sure you can imagine. Did they hurt you, Fabi?"

"Oh, hell no Vic. They've actually been quite, ah, quite gracious. I've been eating well and the handcuffs are not too tight, really."

"Godammit all, I wanna call in the cops in the worst way, Fabi. I think the Brazilian paramilitary types'd make mince-meat of these assholes, whoever they are."

"Oh yeah. That'd be just splendid, Vic. You'd never see me again, ya dope. Just do what they want. It's only a mil. Don't you think I'm worth it?" This brought a small laugh from the other woman in the sack.

She said, "That is enough." She depressed the button again and continued. "You have your instructions. We will contact you tomorrow afternoon, Mister Janes. Until then, *boa-tarde*." She broke the connection then looked at Fabi. "I will bring you back to your room now." She waited for her prisoner to stand.

Instead, Fabulia said, "Please. Can we sit for a while. I know that I ask too many questions but I am truly interested in your reasons for going to the trouble of kidnapping a person for money. What is your organization called, anyway?"

The woman straddled one of the chairs and said, "We are a group of students from all over Central and South America. In English our name would translate to the *Liberty Student Council of the Americas*. Or just LASCA, as we call ourselves."

"Oh, okay," said Fabi. "So your group LASCA believes that you need to go to this extreme in order to correct all of the wrongs suffered upon society by those that are in the ultimate positions of power? Is that about right? And what exactly do you intend to do with this money?"

"You think this is *extreme*? As you say in the U.S., I consider this to be *Ho-Hum*. I consider it to be extreme that this government in Brasília is more concerned with profits than with its' immense rain forest that produces a large percentage of this globe's oxygen. The gold mining that goes on in this country and within the Amazon Basin is criminal. Just for starters, the human beings that mine that gold are paid about one dollar per ounce and at this moment the ore is worth three hundred times that on the open market! And then those same people that do the dirty-work have to buy their food at hugely inflated prices from government run cantinas.

Who says slavery is a thing of the past? These are just a small, few of the things that I call *extreme*."

Fabulia thought for a moment then asked again, "And what exactly do you intend to do with this money? How do you expect to start changing all of these points that you consider harmful to humanity? Don't get me wrong. I am not disagreeing with you—yet. I'm curious about your means to an end. What will you do?"

"Why, we will buy guns, of course. This and most other governments in the Americas have no interest in listening to us or anyone else that sees what is really going on. We believe that the only way to fight these plutocrats is through force."

Fabulia started to laugh but stopped quickly when she realized that she was making this woman very angry. "No, please. I apologize. I am not laughing at your ideals, I am laughing at your monetary naiveté. I mean, come on, girl. A measly million bucks? What'll that buy you? I'll tell you. That'll most likely buy you about two thousand used Kalashnikovs, not including the bullets. What in hell's name will you do with that? Hell, you couldn't even whack Somoza with two thousand of those things."

The hooded woman stood up and kicked the chair away. Before she could get around the table Fabi said, "No. No. Wait a minute. You have got to hear me out." The other woman stopped but remained standing while she glowered as best she could at Fabulia and tried to control her breathing. Fabulia continued.

"You've obviously done your homework so you know who I am and what I do. I think that, in one respect, you and I are of the same mind…"

"Taking whores off of the street and getting them to make money for you is not the same."

"Oh but it is very much the same, my friend. My intentions are not just to have 'the whores make money for me'. *Our* objectives have always been to help create a better society for the little person, for the people that have no edge with which to 'get ahead' while they're stuck on this rock. Sorry to tell you, but my objectives are just as noble as yours and I do not need to go out and buy a buncha guns to carry mine out. *I'm doing it behind their fucking backs, girl."* Fabulia stood. She was now ready to leave.

Later that night after Fabi had eaten the stew that was brought in for her, she once more heard the key in the lock. The woman walked in holding the same chair that she had kicked earlier in the day. She set it down right in front of Fabi. After seating herself she pulled the burlap sack off of her head. Fabulia gasped. It was as if she were looking in the mirror fifteen years ago. This woman, no, this girl, looked like Fabi's younger twin sister right down to the color of her eyes. "Don't look so surprised," she said. "My family's roots also go back to Portugal. Now it is my turn. Please indulge me with a few answers to a few questions."

The two women talked long into the night and before either one of them realized the time, the guard knocked on the door and said, *"Perdão, Gerente. São seis horas da manhã.* Pardon me, madam. It is six o'clock in the morning."

The woman stood up and stretched then said, "I must go but first, please listen. I will accept your offer but I cannot just run out on my people here or at LASCA in Rio. Therefore, I suggest that, when we call your husband this afternoon, you must instruct him to only bring half of the money with him. I will make my excuses to my collaborators. This amount will not be enough to make the purchase of guns viable but will be sufficient enough to passively help in the favelas. The money will be overseen by me personally to be distributed for food, clothing and medical assistance in Rio de Janeiro. There is obviously no need to use any of the money here; you have Santos covered.

When the time is right and it is obvious that I am not being searched for in connection with your kidnapping I will contact you so we can meet again and make a plan of how I will be able to 'sneak in the back door', as you put it, into Brazilian politics. Now, please go to sleep Mrs. Janes. I will come for you when it is time to make the call."

That afternoon Fabulia was led, once again, into the phone room. The woman placed the receiver in the voice scrambler and dialed up the Janes residence. Vic answered on the first ring. "Yeah, it's Victor Janes."

"Mister Janes. I will now put your wife on for a moment then I will give you instructions for the money drop. You have the money? Is that correct?"

"Yeah. Yes. I've got all of the money. Put my wife on."

The woman gestured to Fabi. "Hiya Vic. Now listen up. I've re-negotiated this deal a little bit. Take half of the money out of the bag and stash it in the house someplace where the kids can't get at it."

There was silence on the line for two seconds then Vic said, "Fabi. What the fuck is going on here? You want me to take half the dough out? Isn't this the part where the kidnappers demand *more* money? Fabulia, I…"

"Come on, Vic. Work with me here. Today's the *'50 Percent Off Sale On All Fabulias'* day. Just do it, huh?"

"Well, okeedokee, Fabi but…"

"No buts, Vic. Just do as I ask now and I'll see ya soon."

The woman depressed the button on the scrambler and said. "At two o'clock tomorrow morning take the money with you in your skiff and drive it towards Santos. The moon is almost full. You should have no difficulty. You will be stopped somewhere along the river. Hand over the money then go back to your home. At four o'clock you may go into Santos by any means you wish. There will be written instructions for you on the front door of your wife's office building. Follow all of these instructions and you will see your wife soon." The woman cut off the connection and looked at Fabi. "Let's have some food now," she said. "It will be a long night tonight. Perhaps while we eat you could tell me more about your ideas for infiltrating this government."

∧

At five a.m. Victor and Teddy pulled open the side-door into the sacristy of the Santo Antonio Cathedral across from the *Janes Holdings* offices. The two men walked slowly towards the light in the inner church. A single bulb illuminated a figure in the front pew. Victor half-yelled, "Fabi.

Fabulia! Are you there?"

"Yeah, Vic. Right here," came her muffled reply. "The keys to these cuffs are on the pew behind me. And please be careful when you take off this damned hood."

With trembling hands Victor fumbled with the hood while Teddy got the keys. "Shit! Godammit, Fabi, they *did* hurt you. Oh shit... I'm so sorry Fabi, I'm so sorry!"

"Oh, don't you dare start that 'guilty-blame-yourself' shit', Vic. It's only a black eye, for God's sake."

Teddy finally got the cuffs freed up. Victor and Fabulia hugged for a while then Fabi sat up straight and said, "Hey. Either of you guys got any idea what a damn *plutocrat* is?"

POSTLUDE

The two old women were now well known figures along the Santos beachfront gardens and palms that stretched for a full mile along the praia. *From a distance the man mistook them for just another pair of homeless people but as he got closer he realized that they were both much too well dressed. And the cart that they both slowly pushed was not for their meager belongings at all but was an elaborately made mobile display stand for their wares, whatever they could be. As their paths slowly closed the man was further stymied. The smaller of the two was wearing a black head-scarf and appeared to be of some Asian decent while her partner looked to be of Indio blood but definitely not of Brazilian origin. This was curious. He increased his step. Both women were grinning right at him. He was now close enough to see that they both wore identical pairs of some kind of dangling earrings. He stepped closer and peered at the set that the Indio wore. Just as quickly he stepped back and said, "Mãe de Deus!" He recognized these. They were teeth, for God's sake. Shark teeth.*

The Indio then spoke and said, in broken Portuguese, "These teeth were dug out of the Grand Canyon in the United States. They are very ancient"

And then, as if on que, the smaller woman said, "The pair I wear came from the deep ocean right off of your coast here in Brazil. Why not buy one pair of each? They are very good luck, you know! One for your wife and one for your mistress, eh?" said the woman, with a sparkle in her eye.

© Black Rose Writing

CPSIA information can be obtained at www.ICGtesting.com
Printed in the USA
LVOW042203241012

304235LV00002B/135/P